All the characters in this publication are fictitious and any resemblance to real persons, living or dead, is purely coincidental.

White Lobster

For Suzanne

White Lobster

To Jane,
Thanks for reading my 1st book.
PG Raven

The devil's finest trick is to persuade you that he does not exist.

Charles Baudelaire

White Lobster

-------- Part One --------

White Lobster

CHAPTER 1

Café del Mar, Cartagena, Colombia

The Café del Mar was embedded into the lilac bougainvillea-covered walls of Old Cartagena. The scent of hibiscus and fragrant jasmine perfumed the air. The panoramic views across the sea were spectacular, each evening you could watch the sun melting into the indigo-blue Caribbean Sea.

It was an extraordinary place to be viewing a severed head.

El Jefe had the disembodied head concealed in a sports holdall. He shifted to ensured that Cristiano and Danny could both view the contents of the unzipped holdall. Danny peered at the human head. It was tightly shrink-wrapped in polythene. The hair was matted and pressed against the transparent plastic. The eyes, nose and lips were smeared and lifeless.

El Jefe zipped up the holdall.

"Cristiano tells me you're Nicaraguan," said El Jefe, who was a Mestizo, a combination of Spanish and Amerindian ancestry.

Danny was still in shock having seen the disembodied head, he mumbled, "I was born in Pearl Lagoon, just north of Bluefields."

"Speak up will you, do you know the Caribbean coast?"

Danny started to regain his senses, "Yeah, I've been sailing the Caribbean my whole life."

El Jefe smiled, displaying to Danny and Cristiano his neglected and tobacco-stained teeth. He lowered his voice and said, "I'm looking for someone trustworthy and capable."

"That's Danny," said Cristiano.

"Shut up, you idiot," said El Jefe.

Cristiano looked down at his shoes.

El Jefe said, "The person would discreetly move bales of product across the Caribbean, from Cartagena, across to Nicaragua."

Danny was having second thoughts, human heads in holdalls? "I understand," he said.

"You'd better understand," said El Jefe, "Because the guy in the holdall wasn't trustworthy, capable or discreet."

CHAPTER 2

Manchester, England UK

Black bowtie, dinner jacket and patent leather shoes. Paul concluded that he resembled a young James Bond.

He had lucrative business with Lowry Airport in Manchester, so he felt obliged to attend their annual dinner. The client had decided to host a formal black-tie dinner, in aid of a children's cancer charity. Paul considered it a worthy cause. Unfortunately, it had potential to be a boring evening.

He thought that it was okay to fake-smile your way through the day as you win business, but when it continues throughout the evening, and into the early hours of the morning, it became an irritant.

There was also the risk of drinking too much alcohol and your client mask slipping. It wasn't a good sales technique to inform your client that they're talking rubbish or that you're not interested in their children's school, brother-in-law, or house extension.

Paul's attention was attracted to the charity auction. It seemed organised. There were iPads on each table, and you typed in a bid for the item you craved. It was a modern technology-enhanced silent auction. As it was an airport event, there were numerous travel-related items for auction, such as flights gifted to the charity by specific airlines, quality luggage and designer handbags, usually seen in duty free. There were also the obligatory signed Manchester City and Manchester United football shirts, as they were local teams.

Football wasn't a sport in Manchester, it was a quasi-religion. Paul often utilised *football talk* to encourage clients to relax and engage. Talking football was great for relationship building, unless the client preferred rugby or cricket. In that case Paul would have to nod politely and try to recall anything relevant he had seen on TV. Only heaven could help you if the potential client had no sporting interest at all.

Entertainment, music, and travel could be manageable. Politics, immigration, and current affairs were a minefield. One step in the wrong direction, and you were *persona non grata*.

Paul identified a holiday auction item:

Pelican Island: Seven nights on a secluded island in the Caribbean, exclusive location, 5-star luxury, only three guest suites, infinity pool, swim-up bar, spa, all meals and drinks included.

To Paul, it sounded fantastic. It was worth bidding for and would keep the evening boredom at bay. Paul entered his full name, and the company he represented to participate in the auction. You could use either a nickname or be anonymous to the other bidders. Paul selected anonymous.

He started to formulate his strategy for securing the holiday. The website showed the highest current bid for each item. Paul noticed that the CEO of a local demolition company had already submitted an offer for the holiday at £3,500. Paul presented a counterbid of £3,600 and waited.

Paul observed the bids for the assorted items steadily increasing in value on the iPad. He noticed that it had took around ten seconds for his counterbid, under the tag *anonymous*, to register on the website. That was interesting and would become crucial to his strategy.

Another guest, *Frankie,* posted a bid for £4,000. The CEO retaliated in ten seconds with £4,500. Paul watched and waited.

The iPad had a countdown timer in the top left-hand side of the page. It illustrated that the auction would end at 11:00pm and that there would be no further bids accepted after that time. The current time was 10.25pm, Paul submitted a counterbid of £4,600. The ten second delay was still present.

The CEO responded with £4,900. Paul thought that there must be a great deal of money in demolition.

It was 10.55pm, He checked the iPad. The CEO's bid for £4,900 was still in place. Paul suspected that the CEO had concluded that his competitors had been seen off by his formidable personal purchasing power.

At 10.59pm, Paul tapped in the counterbid for £5,000. He didn't send it immediately but watched the seconds tick away on the countdown timer. With fifteen seconds to go, Paul pressed submit. The auction closed automatically at 11pm.

At a table near the stage somebody shouted, "Jesus Christ, that's not right." The Caribbean holiday had been secured by anonymous for £5,000.

Paul concluded that some people just aren't comfortable with losing. He was relieved he had used the anonymous approach.

. . . .

Paul threaded his way through the crowd of people. They were all supplying their credit card details for designer handbags and silk scarves. He spotted a guy who was juggling a pile of paperwork and a portable card machine in his hands.

"Hey, I'm anonymous, I've just secured the Caribbean holiday," said Paul.

"Congratulations," said the auction guy "You've really helped our charity, it's a very worthy cause."

"Yeah, yeah, I like to give back whenever I can," said Paul.

"I'll need to check the final bid status and your personal details. You need to provide your credit card."

"No problem let's do this. Do you have any specific information on the resort and the flights?"

The guy looked through his paperwork, "It's Pelican Island in Nicaragua and the flights are with AeroMexico. I just need your credit card."

Paul began to have a serious case of buyer's remorse. What was he going to tell Charlotte?

CHAPTER 3

Mexico City

The flight from Managua banked to the left and headed towards Benito Juarez International Airport. Augusto could see thousands of crudely built houses on the hills around Mexico City. Many of the roofs were orange or red and were reflecting the noon day sun. As the plane banked to the right, the sheer immensity of Mexico City could be seen out of his window. This was once the richest city in the Americas, when New York City was just a backwater.

Augusto was a Lieutenant Commander in the Nicaraguan Navy, responsible for the Caribbean Coast Region. He was pleased to have been instructed by his bosses in Managua to attend a meeting in Mexico City. The other meeting participants would be representatives from the Consulate General of Nicaragua in Mexico City, the U.S. Drug Enforcement Administration (DEA), the U.S. Coast Guard and the meeting's host, the Mexican Government. This would be a meeting on neutral ground. It was obvious what the subject of the meeting would be.

After exiting the airport, Augusto jumped into the backseat of a taxi, throwing his overnight bag onto the passenger seat to his side.

"Nicaraguan Consulate, 136 Fernando Alencastre," said Augusto.

"Si Senor, no problem, I know exactly where it is," said the taxi driver, "Are you from Nicaragua?"

"Yes, I am. What's wrong with your airport, it took me two hours to get through immigration and customs?"

"It's too small. A new airport should have been built years ago, but you know, Mexican politics."

"Politics is a problem in every country."

"Customs can be quite tough because of the narco stuff that people keep trying to smuggle into Mexico. Being from Nicaragua, I suppose you know all about that?"

"We don't have a major issue with drugs in Nicaragua. We have no narco gangs in our country. The Nicaraguan people do not want to be involved in that terrible business."

The taxi driver looked at him through his rear-view mirror, Augusto caught his eye and looked away. No point discussing this. The taxi driver didn't believe him for one second. Augusto also didn't believe what he had said. The narco business was a curse, but it was also a reality, for all the countries in the Americas.

. . . .

Augusto wondered why he had been selected to attend this meeting. His heritage had ensured that he was a trusted member of the Nicaraguan ruling party, the FSLN. Augusto's father had been with the FSLN when they fought against the Somoza government. They ousted Somoza in July 1979 and took power. His father had only been twenty-two years of age.

The issue for the FSLN leadership was that Augusto was not a Mestizo. His late mother was a descendant of the Miskito and Garifuna Indigenous people. She was once voted *India Bonita, beautiful Indian*. Augusto's mother was embarrassed by that title later in her life.

Augusto understood that his knowledge of the Nicaraguan Caribbean coast, his local contacts and language skills were invaluable to his FSLN bosses in Managua. However, he often felt he was deemed an outsider because of his race and background.

CHAPTER 4

The taxi driver deposited Augusto outside the Nicaraguan Consulate. It was a rundown building. The tattered blue and white Nicaraguan flag hung limply on the flagpole. Nevertheless, the consulate was in a prestigious location, next to Chapultepec Park, one of the largest public parks in the Americas.

    Augusto pressed the button on the door and informed the consulate staff who he was. He was permitted to enter. After presenting his credentials, the staff ushered him into a side office. He politely refused coffee or water from the secretary and waited. He looked around the office. He noted the mandatory portraits of President Daniel Ortega,

Comandante Daniel to his supporters, and Vice President Rosario Murillo, his wife.

Admiral Antonio Espinoza entered the office, and he gave Augusto a robust handshake.

"Lieutenant Commander Romero, I was pleased to be notified that you were being sent here by Managua," said Espinoza.

Espinoza was formerly a senior member of the *Naval Forces of the Army of Nicaragua*. Augusto knew him from his occasional visits to Bluefields and the Caribbean coast. Espinoza didn't have time for the Indigenous or Creole people of the region, especially the diverse cultures and languages. Espinoza hated the fact that Creole English was prevalent along the Caribbean coast of Nicaragua, due to the influence of both African and English heritage in the region. He once announced on a visit to Bluefields,

"The official language of Nicaragua is Spanish, I will not have conversations in English and will not have signs translated into Miskito, or any of these prehistoric languages." Espinoza was certainly not multicultural, tolerant or woke.

However, he was acknowledged as a FSLN loyalist. He had taken a career sidestep and became a diplomat in the Nicaraguan government. Augusto gathered, from his boastful explanation, that Espinoza had been promoted to Mexico City and was enjoying himself in the big city. Espinoza was the grandly titled *Minister Plenipotentiary, First Class*, whatever that meant, thought Augusto. He informed Augusto of his many important duties in Mexico City, on behalf of the Republic of Nicaragua. Eventually he turned his attention to the meeting.

"It will take place in the Four Seasons hotel, it's just on the edge of Chapultepec Park. As it is a pleasant day in Mexico City, pollution excluded, let's walk over there and I can brief you as we stroll through the park," said Espinoza.

As they walked through the park, Augusto agreed that it was a nice day, he observed tourists wandering around and Mexicans sauntering to work. Espinoza didn't waste any time.

"I am fully aware that the DEA has meetings with representatives from many of the countries in the region. The strange aspect about this meeting is that it is vague: no agenda and no named participants," said Espinoza.

"Is that unusual, Admiral?"

"Yes, I'm certain the CIA is behind this."

CHAPTER 5

The Four Seasons hotel in Mexico City was impressive, thought Augusto. It was an upmarket designer shopping centre within a luxury hotel. The smartest hotel in Managua was the Intercontinental, but the Four Seasons was in another league, premier league, mused Augusto.

The Concierge directed Espinoza to the San Juan meeting room. There were four people already in the meeting room. There were two men, whom Augusto guessed were the Mexicans. The other two, a man and a woman, he assumed were the Americans.

"Greetings my friends, my name is Juan Reyes, I am the representative of the Federal Government of Mexico," said the smaller Mexican guy. Augusto thought that he seemed pleased with himself.

Indicating towards his larger colleague, Reyes said, "this is my compatriot from the National Guard, Chief Inspector Eduardo Franco, Directorate General of Drug Intelligence Operations." The larger Mexican guy forced a smile. Augusto thought Franco didn't want to be here.

Espinoza and Augusto introduced themselves but didn't give too much away. The two Americans stepped forward.

"Hi, I'm Captain Craig Weber, U.S. Coastguard." He was a huge Linebacker, all-American guy, with perfect teeth, noted Augusto.

The American woman held her hand out.

"Hello, a pleasure to meet you, I'm Madison Walker, Manager of Intelligence U.S. Drug Enforcement Administration." Madison invited everyone to make themselves comfortable. Augusto was struck by her southern U.S. accent and her natural beauty.

Reyes said, "I would like to welcome you all to Mexico City. You are our guests here. Please take advantage of all the hotel facilities, I can assure you they are excellent. Please have a cocktail, or two, in the Fifty Mils bar, my favourites are the *White Rabbit* and the *Ant Man* cocktail. Please enjoy the restaurants, I recommend the Zanaya, it serves excellent food from the Pacific coast. If you want to try something specifically Mexican, I recommend Chapulines, crispy crickets and guacamole."

"Thank you, Senor Reyes, for your hospitality, and for hosting this meeting," said Madison, Augusto observed his beaming smile.

Madison said, "It is important that I am immediately clear and concise."

"It would be appreciated," said Espinoza.

Madison said, "Unfortunately, there is a certain residual animosity between the United States and the Republic of Nicaragua governments. Due to this scenario, we would like to circumvent the current politics. We are therefore reaching out to you, the Nicaraguan Navy. We believe this will be mutually beneficial.

"Who is *we*, the CIA?" said Espinoza.

"I'm not CIA, I'm a representative from the DEA."

"How do we know that?"

"One step at a time Admiral Espinoza, this is essentially an informal meeting. There is no written agenda. We will not be swopping business cards. There will be no official minutes from this meeting issued by the DEA. The meeting will not be recorded," said Madison.

"Again, how do we know that?" said Espinoza. Augusto felt the temperature in the meeting room drop ten degrees.

"The Mexican Police Federal Ministerial special services have swept the room for recording devices, there are none," said Reyes.

"Meeting participants could have devices concealed upon their person," said Espinoza.

"Admiral Espinoza, I acknowledge your natural mistrust. Can I suggest that we all switch off our cell phones and place them in the centre of the table?" said Weber.

Augusto thought that the larger Mexican guy, Franco, now seemed to be enjoying himself. People began to retrieve their cell phones from their pockets and bags and place them on the table.

"If this what is required to avoid a diplomatic incident, then let's go ahead," said Madison.

"Senorita Walker, you have the attention of the Republic of Nicaragua," said Espinoza.

"Thank you, please call me Madison."

"Gentlemen, Captain Weber and I both work for the Organized Crime Drug Enforcement Task force, shortened to OCD-ETF," said Madison.

"You Americans certainly enjoy your acronyms," said Espinoza, with a smirk.

"The OCD-ETF is a federal drug enforcement program in the U.S. and is overseen by the Attorney General and the Department of Justice," said Madison.

"And the Republic of Nicaragua is interested in this, because?"

"The program consists of eleven U.S. federal agencies that utilize their resources to accomplish our objectives."

"Including the CIA?"

"The CIA is not one of the eleven federal agencies," said Madison.

"But what are your objectives, Senorita Walker, to overthrow democratically elected governments?" said Espinoza.

Reyes said "Admiral Espinoza, if this informal meeting has unacceptable objectives or has a hidden agenda, then the Federal Government of Mexico would not be hosting the meeting."

"With all due respect Senor Reyes, there is no agenda, so it *is* hidden," said Augusto. There was muted laughter around the meeting room, even Madison smiled.

She continued, "The mission of the OCD-ETF program is to identify, disrupt and dismantle the most serious global drug trafficking and money laundering organisations and those primarily responsible for the drug supply to the United States of America."

"That is acknowledged, Senorita Walker," said Espinoza.

"Thank you."

"So, you are not CIA. You are DEA. You have the goal to reduce the illegal drug flows into your country. You are reaching out to the Nicaraguan Navy. How can the Republic of Nicaragua be of assistance?" said Espinoza.

Weber said, "As you are fully aware, the U.S. Coastguard and the Nicaraguan Navy have been cooperating for many years, with remarkable success. *Operation Martillo* was an achievement, as were the numerous joint training exercises that our two organisations have held around both the Pacific and Caribbean coasts."

"Yes, The Republic of Nicaragua has always held out the hand of cooperation. Unfortunately, due to the imposition of U.S. led sanctions upon the Republic of Nicaragua, our economy has suffered. Therefore, the Naval Force of the Nicaraguan Army has been unable to allocate the resources required to upgrade the Nicaragua Naval fleet. However, we have, during recent years, procured two additional Damen Stan 4207 patrol vessels from our friends in the Netherlands. The Republic of Nicaragua will continue to protect its Pacific and Caribbean coastlines," said Espinoza.

Reyes said, "Why don't we take this opportunity to have a break? Let's us enjoy the excellent coffee that is served in the Four Seasons."

Most of the meeting participants headed in the direction of the washrooms. Augusto was washing his hands when Weber entered the men's room.

"Now that your Admiral has gotten all of that off his chest, can we hopefully move on to the business in hand?" said Weber.

Augusto continued to wash his hands as he spoke, "The Nicaraguan people harbour a great deal of mistrust regarding the United States, especially on the subject of the CIA. The U.S. has invaded Nicaragua at least eight times, one of those invasions led to a 20-year occupation. The CIA supported the Contras, enabling them to wreak havoc on our country. Admiral Espinoza has a right to be sceptical."

Augusto dried his hands and walked out.

CHAPTER 6

Everyone seemed to have grabbed a coffee and reconvened at the meeting table. Madison spoke, "We have a PowerPoint slide that we'd like to share with you. In line with our mutually agreed meeting principles, we will not be issuing copies."

The slide was titled, *Cocaine trafficking routes in Nicaragua*. It was a map of Central America illustrating air, land, sea, and river routes that the narco traffickers were assumed to be utilising. The Pan American highway was clearly marked, with the Darien Gap shaded in red. The principal navy ports, on both the Pacific and Caribbean coasts, were highlighted.

As the Caribbean region was Augusto's responsibility, he looked closely at that specific area. It consisted of

Bluefields, Pearl Lagoon, Puerto Cabeza, the Corn Islands, and the Miskito cays. The map was detailed and impressive.

Madison continued, "Whilst the Nicaragua armed forces and police have seized a significant amount of cocaine over the last ten years, it seems that Nicaragua is still viewed by the narco traffickers as a refuelling or pit-stop. It is suspected that Indigenous groups, especially on the Caribbean coast, are providing logistics support to these narco traffickers. As the Indigenous groups on the Caribbean coast have few alternate forms of income, it is believed that the narco traffickers have a strong and reliable partnership with these groups."

Espinoza remained motionless in his seat, silent.

Augusto was fascinated by the presentation. He was familiar with these Indigenous groups and was, in fact, directly related to them. He was aware that occasionally the narco traffickers would make it as far as Bluefields and then progress north to the Honduran border. He knew that sometimes Nicaraguans would get involved in these narco networks.

Augusto was aware that the Gutierrez family, had moved cocaine shipments along the Nicaraguan Caribbean coast and provided services to international trafficking groups. But they were also alleged to have been involved in the massacre of six police officers in Bluefields. This incurred the wrath of the FSLN government in Managua. Three members of the Gutierrez family were shot dead by the National Army of Nicaragua just outside Greytown, close to the border with Costa Rica. On the same day, two family members were executed at their home in Bluefields. What people need to understand, thought Augusto, is that there are no large gangs in Nicaragua, the biggest and only gang is the FSLN government.

Augusto said, "Madison, may I congratulate you on your presentation, it is detailed and concise. The Nicaraguan Navy also has this information and therefore fully understands the challenges we face in our own country. To repeat the question tabled by Admiral Espinoza, how can the Republic of Nicaragua be of assistance?"

Madison responded, "our mathematical flow models, take into consideration the amount of cocaine that arrives on the streets of the U.S., minus the flow from identified narco routes through Mexico, fed by Guatemala, Honduras and El Salvador. The models also take into consideration the flows through Caribbean countries, such as Jamaica and the Dominican Republic. The DEA also investigates meticulously, the amounts of cocaine produced in South America, specifically Peru, Colombia, and Bolivia. Ninety percent of all cocaine that arrives on U.S. shores is from those three countries, with minor flows from Venezuela and Ecuador. Our point is that a significant flow of cocaine is reaching the U.S. and we cannot currently identify which route is being used. We know where it is being produced. We know how much arrives in the U.S. and hits the streets. We know how much enters mainland Europe through Spain and the other Mediterranean gateways. We have also identified and quantified the alternative, innovative routes, for example through West Africa. We have looked closely at all seizures across the globe. So much South American cocaine flows through Mexico and Central America that one would expect Mexico to be the leader in drug seizures, however our mathematical model indicates otherwise. Once cocaine arrives in Mexico the probability of that product being seized is small in comparison with seizures in Colombia or Peru themselves."

This comment roused Franco, "What are you trying to say, that the Mexican National Guard and the organisation of Drug Intelligence Operations is in some way incompetent or colluding with traffickers?" Augusto thought that the meeting was becoming interesting.

"Definitely not, Chief Inspector Franco, my point is that it is extremely difficult for the authorities in the U.S. and Mexico to track down the product once it arrives on our shores. The way forward is to stop it from arriving," said Madison.

"The fact is that a significant flow of cocaine from South America reaches the U.S. and we currently do not know how it arrives in our country. A piece of the puzzle is missing," concluded Madison.

"There is already an agreement between the United States and Nicaragua, signed in 2004. This is *the Narcotics Drugs, Cooperating National Information Exchange System* agreement," said Espinoza. All relevant information is being shared with the U.S. on a continuous basis."

"Yes acknowledged, however the main focus of that agreement is the use of light aircraft for illicit drug trafficking," said Madison.

"Is that not sufficient, Senorita Walker?"

"Admiral Espinoza, we suspect that the Caribbean coast of Nicaragua is a narco trafficking route, which leads to the Mayan Peninsula of Mexico via Honduras, and then ultimately to the United States."

The meeting participants were silent for a brief period. Espinoza glared at Madison.

Weber, Madison, and Franco continued with their discussions concerning the possible routes from Colombia through to Honduras and onward to the Mayan peninsula. There was an animated discussion centred upon methamphetamine and the trafficking of precursor chemicals through central America. Weber stated that this was the speciality of the *Sinaloa Cartel* in Mexico. Madison agreed and said that Acetone, Ethylphenyl and Methylamine had been seized in enormous quantities, however the preferred trafficking route for those products appeared to be the Pacific coast.

The meeting reached its natural conclusion with all parties agreeing to continue cooperation in principle, subject to approval from their respective governments. Espinoza said that he would have to report back to Ministry of Foreign Affairs in Managua. Reyes said he would be speaking to his superiors within the Executive Branch of the Federal Government of Mexico. Madison and Weber said that they would have to meet with their OCD-ETF directors in Washington DC. Augusto felt that there was a competition for who sounded the most important.

Finally, Espinoza said, "Don't forget your CIA colleagues in Langley, Senorita Walker."

. . . .

A Nicaraguan consular vehicle arrived at the Four Seasons and collected Espinoza. Before his departure, he informed Augusto that he had important duties to perform on behalf of their country, therefore he must depart.

Espinoza stated that he would forward his report to the Ministries of Defence and Foreign Affairs in Managua and that would become the definitive Republic of Nicaragua's official record of the meeting. Augusto must not formulate a secondary report, however he was authorised to discuss the meeting with his superiors in the Naval Force of the Nicaraguan Army, if ordered to.

Augusto was in no doubt that he was considered subordinate to Espinoza.

CHAPTER 7

Espinoza was driven away in a black BMW 7 Series, and Augusto was glad to see him leave. He walked across the lobby and checked in at the hotel reception.

"Welcome, Lieutenant Commander Romero. Your total bill will be paid in full by the Secretariat of Foreign Affairs, Federal Government of Mexico," said the smiling associate at the front desk.

He continued, "I would normally ask for a credit card to cover your extras, however in this instance it is not required. If we can take a copy of your passport or driving licence for our records, that will be sufficient."

Augusto went up to his room and put his overnight bag and laptop on to the bed. It had been a long day so far. He decided to go for a walk in the famous Chapultepec Park and get some fresh air.

. . . .

Augusto walked through the park. Everywhere there were people exercising. Joggers ran past him up a gentle slope. He noticed groups doing yoga in a grassy area and some determined Mexicans participating in a karate class. Augusto thought that it was unlikely that you would see such scenes in Managua, certainly not in Bluefields.

Augusto was enjoying his walk and he concluded that Chapultepec Park was a living tapestry of Mexican history. He was aware Chapultepec Hill was the site of the *Battle of Chapultepec* in 1847 between Mexican and U.S. troops. He grimaced when he recalled that the U.S. Marines Corps hymn still evoked that battle: *From the Halls of Montezuma*.......

Augusto ambled through the park. The sky-blue shade caught his eye. He recognised the Manchester City football shirt. He was surprised that someone would wear such English Premier League sports clothing in Mexico City. The guy wearing the football shirt was accompanied by a woman, they were looking around wide eyed. Obviously, they were tourists. Augusto had assumed that the couple were Argentinian, but as they walked past him, he could hear them speaking English. Augusto decided that he wouldn't become a detective.

He regained his self-belief, as a future intelligence operative, when he spotted her. "Hi Senorita Walker or is it, Agent Walker? Are you following me?" said Augusto, with a grin.

"Hi Augusto, obviously my spy training at the CIA hasn't been very effective," said Madison.

"I understand that the first thing they teach you at Langley is one hundred reasons you can use to explain why you are not a CIA agent."

"Where did you hear that?".

"I think Ben Stiller in *Meet the Parents*."

"I thought I would wander through this famous park and soak up the history," said Madison.

"Same here, my flight to Managua isn't until tomorrow morning. Where is the Linebacker Guy?" said Augusto.

"Who?" said Madison.

"Sir, Captain Weber, Sir, U.S. Coastguard, Sir," Augusto smiled.

"Craig has gone home. He caught the first flight back to Miami. Anyway, what are you up to? Deep cover surveillance?"

"I thought I would enjoy the hospitality of the Federal Government of Mexico."

"By hospitality, do you mean that the Mexicans are paying for your hotel?"

"Yes, Latino brothers stick together."

"U.S. Government agencies can't accept such hospitality. It's an absolute no-no," said Madison.

"I bet the Mexicans didn't even offer it to you," said Augusto.

"Not sure if they did or not."

"Would you like some company, that's if you do not deem it to be fraternizing with the enemy?" said Augusto.

"Sure, your perspective would be interesting, and you're not the enemy."

They wandered up to the Chapultepec Castle.

. . . .

"This is the scene of one of your many dastardly deeds," said Augusto.

"You mean General Winfield Scott's total defeat of Santa Anna?" said Madison.

"You know what it was all about. The U.S. annexed Texas, then captured Mexico City and put a gun against the Mexican government's head. It was a land grab; California, New Mexico, Arizona, Nevada, Colorado, Utah, all gone."

"Regarding the Treaty of Peace between Mexico and the United States, if it was such a disaster in the long term, why are millions of Mexicans trying to come to the U.S. for a better life? It's where their dreams and aspirations can become reality," said Madison.

"Maybe they just want to go home," said Augusto, "because they don't jump the border, the border jumped them".

"You should be thinking about the significant challenges you have in your own country, *Karl Marx*, and not being so obsessed with the USA."

"It's not possible to talk about Nicaragua, without discussing the USA."

"Whatever, this is not even funny anymore, in fact it's getting tiresome."

"Sins of your fathers," said Augusto.

. . . .

They wandered down *Avenue Paseo de la Reforma* and back to the Four Seasons hotel, in mutual silence.

"I'll tell you what, for me being such a pain in the ass, let me buy you dinner," said Augusto.

"You mean let the Mexican government buy *us* dinner."

"Come on, I am offering you my socialist hand of friendship."

Madison said, "I'm not sure I should be accepting Mexican government hospitality via the Nicaraguan Navy. Anyway, what kind of socialist are you? Enjoying all these capitalist, imperialist goodies? Obviously, the Marxist-Leninist brainwashing has not been effective."

"Last chance." There was a moment of silence.

"Ok, why not. Let's meet at 7:30pm. We can try the Zanava Restaurant. It was highly recommended by our Mexican friend, Senor Reyes," said Madison.

Augusto said, "Yeah, I suspect that he is, in fact, employed by the Four Seasons."

CHAPTER 8

The Zanava restaurant was busy, but they managed to secure a table in the courtyard. Madison was dressed in a blue blazer with two gold-buttons, tan chinos, and deck shoes. Augusto was going to tease her whether this was *Ivy League* attire. However, he knew that in any circumstances you should never comment negatively on a woman's dress sense, regardless of global politics. He also thought she might be a Mormon.

"Are you from Utah?" said Augusto.

"Nope, I'm from Louisiana, Go Tigers, crush the Razorbacks," said Madison, with a smile.

"Americans are very strange," said Augusto.

Augusto was wearing the same business suit; however, he had taken a shower, shaved and changed his shirt. He considered that he was the one who should be wearing the deck shoes, but he didn't own any. He decided, that was due to U.S. sanctions.

They both selected the signature dish, Zarandeado sea bass. They were offered it *Guajillo-style*, but neither of them wanted to admit they didn't know what that was, so they agreed to red onion, salsa, and tortillas. They were happy with a Californian Napa Valley wine. Augusto resisted the temptation to mention the Mexican American war and California. He was also getting tired of it.

Madison shifted into business mode, "So let's talk about the Caribbean coast and the narco trafficking route that passes straight through it."

Augusto said, "Most of the cocaine seized in Nicaragua is on the two main coastlines, Pacific and Caribbean. The Caribbean coast is economically undeveloped. There are rural villages populated by people that would identify as Indigenous. These are Miskitos, Garifunas, and other communities. They still tend to refer to the Spanish speaking mestizos as *Spaniards*," said Augusto.

He continued, "I have always thought that these communities were just providing help to narco traffickers on some type of opportunistic basis. The communities wouldn't want to anger the authorities in Bluefields and certainly not the central government in Managua, they would prefer to be low profile. These are not the real narco traffickers."

"What are your first thoughts regarding a plan of action?", she said.

"I need to reassess the seizures to date, when and where. I will also consult with my team regarding the tracking of smaller vessels and the ultimate stopovers and final destinations of said vessels."

"Would you be able to share that information with the DEA, once it's collated?"

"Only upon approval from my superiors in the Naval Force of the Nicaraguan Army, who would be directed by the Ministries of Defence and Foreign Affairs in Managua."

Madison's shoulders slumped. Augusto said "Come on, the U.S. have a history regarding Nicaragua, and especially the CIA. You can't expect us to be good buddies."

"I'm not CIA."

"That's what you say."

They ate in silence. The dinner was well prepared, and the wine excellent, in Augusto's opinion.

When they had finished the entrée, Augusto said, "Do you fancy a taste of Nicaragua as a dessert?" Madison was unsure what he meant.

"Excuse me, do you have *Flor de Cana* 10 years old?" said Augusto to the waiter.

"Senor, this is the Four Seasons Hotel, Mexico City, we have *Flor de Cana* 25 years old," said the waiter, with a broad smile.

As the drinks were being poured, Augusto said "Have you been to Mexico City before Madison?"

"Yes, I've been a few times. I attended an UNDOC conference, *UN office of Drugs and Crime,* in the Zocalo area of the city.

"Oh yeah, the *Plaza de la Constitution* and their gigantic Mexican flag."

"That's the spot. I managed to see the *Metropolitan Cathedral* and the *Palacio National*. The most interesting place was *Templo Mayor*, the Aztec temple. All the stone carved faces and heads. I imagined what it must have looked like before the Spanish Conquistadors gate-crashed the party."

"I thought the same when I was in Cusco in Peru. I wondered what the Inca towns and villages was like before Pizarro and his crazy brother came to town."

"All that pointless death and destruction, so that the conquistadors could live a life of luxury," said Madison.

Augusto couldn't agree more.

CHAPTER 9

They devoured their 25-year-old *Flor de Cana.*

Augusto said, "Would you like to adjourn to the *Fifty Mils* bar? Senor Reyes of the Four Seasons recommends the *White Rabbit* and the *Ant Man* cocktail." Madison laughed and they both agreed that was an excellent idea, especially as the drinks would be on the Government of Mexico's tab.

They wandered across the courtyard and sat by the bar. The dark wood and red leather lent an air of class to the place.

"So, it's cocktails all around?" said Augusto.

"Let's try a local mezcal," said Madison. The waiter nodded and poured them both a *Wahaka* mezcal.

"So, you have an interest in American history?" said Madison.

"I studied American History and Politics. I was at university in the UK for four years. I was lucky enough to obtain a full scholarship and attended Manchester University."

"Wow, that amazing, why the UK?"

"At the time, the U.S. colleges weren't too keen to give scholarships to a son of a Nicaraguan Sandinista."

"Did you try Berkley?" They both laughed. Berkley was well known to have a radical edge.

"My father was based in Puerto Cabezas, which was called Bilwi at the time. These were difficult years; my father was in the army and directed the local resistance against the Contra insurgents. There was a highly active *Nicaragua Solidarity Group* in Manchester UK. They managed to obtain support from the local council and their people came over to Bilwi."

"They were travelling into a war zone," said Madison.

"Yes, it was astonishing because it was extremely dangerous to travel in the region at the time. They supplied financial assistance for medical and hospital facilities in Bilwi. It was via one of these remarkable people that I, and others, were given the opportunity years later to study in Manchester."

"Sounds like you got a lucky break."

"I will be forever grateful to the people of Manchester. If it weren't for that opportunity, and the education they provided, I would probably be just sat in my panga boat tonight, trying to catch lobsters off the coast."

"That sounds okay to me." They both laughed. "What about the lousy UK weather?"

"When I first arrived in the UK, it felt as though the air conditioning was on full blast and that someone had turned a cold shower on every other day. But I had grown up in Nicaragua expecting a hurricane occasionally, so the rain didn't bother me."

"That's an amazing story, I now understand why you think you know so much U.S. history, although it does seem to have a kind of British-Limey left wing bias. The Brits still haven't gotten over 1776."

"That's the issue with you Americans, you think that world history began in 1776," said Augusto.

"You Americans? is that the mezcal kicking in?" said Madison, with a frown.

"I still have a great affection for Manchester and the British people."

"The British? The faded colonial empire. They've been the root cause of so many conflicts; Israel & Palestine, India-Pakistan, Ireland and before all that; slavery, pirates, opium smuggling. The British rap sheet has many volumes," said Madison.

"It's not the British government that I have an affection for, it's the people of the UK. The people in Manchester didn't really care who I was. If I supported one of the local football teams, drank lager until I fell over and didn't try to abscond with their girlfriends, they were cool," said Augusto.

"Did you manage it?"

"What?"

"Not to abscond with their girlfriends?"

"Most of the time," he said, with a smile.

"So, Senorita Walker, tell me something about yourself. You have managed to leverage out of me my UK adventure. To progress future Nicaraguan – U.S. relations you need to reveal yourself."

"I'm from Louisiana. I was born in Baton Rouge and went to LSU, Louisiana State University and studied Mechanical Engineering. I moved to New Orleans, after college. Because of work, I now live mostly in Washington DC. But my heart and soul, and the apartment I own, is in New Orleans. I drive a red *Mustang Mach-E*, which is my contribution to protecting the environment."

"A Mustang? Protecting the environment?

"Cos it's an electric vehicle, doh."

"That's all very routine stuff. Tell me something that people wouldn't expect."

"You are persistent, *Mr Karl Marx Trotsky Lenin*. Okay, I'll give you a clue."

Madison paused for a few seconds, "*Semper Fidelis*."

"What's that? It sounds Latin."

"Ten out of ten, it is. It means *always faithful*, to each other, to our country, and to our battles."

"Hang on, you're a Stonemason?" said Augusto, with a chuckle.

"You idiot. Now I know the mezcal is working," said Madison, "No, once a Marine, always a Marine."

"You were a U.S. Marine?"

"What did you expect? That I would have a shaved head and enormous biceps?"

"You are way too beaut-------."

"Whoa, guy from the Seventies. I'm not sure what goes for political correctness in Nicaragua, but what you are about to say is not acceptable in the United States of America."

"We are in Mexico City. However, accept my apologies, Senorita Walker, please continue."

"First Lieutenant Walker, United States Marine Corps to you, Mr Sandinista Karl Marx."

"I stand corrected, First Lieutenant Walker."

"There is a family tradition, going back over 70 years, that Walkers serve in the Marine Corps. This started with my grandfather, and then my father, uncles and two nephews. A Walker was present at Chosin reservoir, Hue, Mogadishu, Kandahar and the second battle of Fallujah."

"And you?"

"I served in Iraq. That's as much as you need to know, Mr Che Guevara," said Madison.

"I'm impressed, maybe one of your family shot at one of my family," said Augusto.

"Very possible."

"So why DEA?"

"It was a natural transition. I was fit and weapons trained to the highest level. If you can cope with Marine discipline, then the DEA is child's play."

"So, it must have been easy."

"To be honest, I used to consider catching narco traffickers a great deal safer than the Marines, but I've revised my thinking about that in recent years," said Madison.

"I'll drink to that, on Mexico's tab," said Augusto, and they both burst out laughing.

Augusto asked the bartender for two more large Wahaka mezcals. The drink had a smoky bouquet. The night was getting messy.

CHAPTER 10

Old Cartagena, Colombia

Cristiano and Danny met in a bar on Calle de la Iglesia, *Street of the Church*, in the historic centre of Cartagena. Danny was aware that the English pirate, Sir Francis Drake captured Cartagena in the 16th century. Drake was alleged to have stayed on this street, at a house now renamed *Casa Drake*. Danny considered it amusing that Cristiano and himself should be meeting, surrounded by the ghosts of pirates.

"What's the deal with the severed head?" said Danny.

"El Jefe is showing you he is a serious guy," said Cristiano.

"He's crazy."

"He can be vicious and cruel, but this is your chance to make serious money."

"It's not the normal thing you see at a job interview."

"This isn't going to be a normal job."

"I'm starting to have second thoughts, that guy is insane."

"You are the one who would be insane, if you didn't take this opportunity."

"Okay, then give me the details of this wonderful opportunity, which involves human heads in bags."

Cristiano told him that the 50-foot boat would be preloaded with bales of uncut cocaine. It would be fully fuelled, including back-up tanks and with sufficient drinking water. There would be three powerful engines totalling more than 1,000 horsepower. The boat would have Nicaraguan identification and numbering. It could easily accommodate five passengers, but Danny would be the only person onboard.

The route should be an approximate straight line between Cartagena and an area just north of Bluefields called Juticalpa Point. El Jefe's people would provide all the map co-ordinates and satellite information.

"The data will pinpoint exactly where you need to head for," said Cristiano.

"So, what else?" said Danny.

"Let's talk about the money."

"There's no other reason for me to risk twenty years in a Central American prison, or have my head carried around Cartagena in a holdall."

"They will pay you 30,000 U.S. dollars. $5,000 when you collect the boat, the balance when you return to Cartagena."

"I'm expected to take the $5,000 with me on the trip?"

"You may run into difficulties, having that cash could help you."

"How do I know they will pay me the $25,000 when I get back?"

"Anyone who can successfully pilot a go-fast boat, across the Caribbean to Nicaragua and return, is worth more than $25,000. They will see you as an asset."

"Yeah, probably," said Danny. He couldn't shake the image of the severed head.

"Definitely, in fact $25,000 is nothing to them, pocket change."

Danny knew Cristiano was taking a cut out of his fee. There was undoubtedly more than $30,000 on the table. Cristiano was probably picking up $20,000 for doing very little and taking no risk. Danny had only two choices, refuse the job and continue sailing around the Colombian coast with dumb tourists or take a massive risk and collect $30,000.

Although there was another option. He could just disappear with the product and never come back. Not sure how Cristiano would explain that to El Jefe and his cold-hearted bosses, thought Danny. He wondered whether Cristiano had also been spooked by the severed head.

. . . .

In the evening Cristiano collected Danny as arranged. He was over an hour late. Typical for a Colombian thought Danny, times are just suggestions to them. Cristiano drove them towards Pasacaballos, south of Cartagena.

"Reach inside the glove box," said Cristiano.

Danny opened the glovebox and pulled out a package. "What is it?" said Danny.

"5,000 U.S. dollars as agreed. Get the other package from underneath the seat."

Danny dragged the package out from beneath the seat. It was slightly heavier than the money. It was a handgun. Matt black and lightweight in the hand, like a toy, thought Danny.

"Do I really need this?"

"It's a Glock 17 generation 4, one of the best handguns in the world. I've included extra ammunition. I'm hoping you won't need it, but if you do, why not have the best?"

"I'm really getting in deep here."

"If you don't bring back the Glock, I'm going to deduct $2,000 from your money," said Cristiano.

"That is the least of my worries," said Danny.

. . . .

When they arrived at the Pasacaballos dock area, El Jefe and his people were stood at the dock.

"You are very late," said El Jefe. Danny thought that he looked angry.

"Sorry, but it's still not ten, we aren't too late," said Cristiano.

"Idiot, you were supposed to be here at 9pm, you are an hour late. He needs to get going, right now," said El Jafe.

Danny said, "I'll need to familiarise myself with the boat. The Caribbean is not a duck pond, it's a dangerous place."

"Indeed, it is very dangerous," said El Jefe. Danny noted his crooked teeth. "What have you got there?" He pointed at Danny's bag.

"I have binoculars and a telescope," said Danny. He didn't mention the Glock or the $5,000.

El Jefe stared at Danny.

Cristiano and one of El Jefe's people guided Danny through the controls and navigation systems on the boat. It was all standard equipment, and nothing raised any concerns for Danny.

"Okay, get moving, you need to make up time. You have a schedule," said El Jefe. He handed Danny a slim folder, which included locations, maps, and co-ordinates.

"Good luck Danny," said Cristiano.

Nobody else on the dock spoke.

"Thanks, that's it, I'm gone. See you in a few days," said Danny.

Danny edged the boat out of the mooring and into the strait. He glanced back at the dock; he thought that El Jefe and Cristiano looked worried. Danny had a quiet chuckle to himself.

Once Danny was out of site, El Jefe stepped directly behind Cristiano. He then reached around and, with a boxcutter, slit Cristiano's throat. Blood sprayed from the carotid and jugular arteries as he slumped to the floor of the dock.

CHAPTER 11

The Caribbean Sea

The rumble of the boat's engines. The crashing of the waves. The constant forward movement. The go-fast boat could travel over eighty knots in calm waters, but for safety reasons, Danny needed to maintain 30 knots in the pitch-black night of the Caribbean Sea. He was as relaxed as he could be transporting bales of cocaine across the Caribbean Sea, at night.

The journey from Cartagena to Bluefields was over five hundred nautical miles. The immediate problem was the daylight, which was already appearing. The go-fast boats were difficult to identify on a radar; however, they could be spotted in the bright Caribbean sunlight.

The monotonous drone of the engines. The heat and humidity were barely noticeable as the boat surfed across the waves. Time was passing and inch by inch, mile by mile, progress was being made. He was starting to get tired and thirsty. He gulped a bottle of water and peered into the void. He could feel the heat of the rising sun behind him. His anxiety increased as he sighted the coastline in the far distance. Danny was astounded that he had gotten himself into this situation. $30,000 wasn't enough.

. . . .

He saw it floating in the sea. Danny slowed the boat. A large bale bobbed in the water. He noticed another item floating close to the bale. Danny brought the boat to a dead stop. It was a body. There was a large hole where the person's chest should have been. Without the breeze created by the boat's movement, the rising sun and humidity pounded him. He suddenly felt sick and frightened.

When the nausea subsided, Danny decided not to take the bale on board. He had his own cargo and enough issues. He was so close to the coast that he believed he had reached Nicaraguan territorial waters. Then he spotted activity on the horizon.

Danny grabbed his Seamaster binoculars and scanned the horizon, they provided a wide field of view. He could see two Nicaraguan Navy patrol boats. There were also several smaller go-fast boats in their vicinity. He quickly changed over to the telescope. The Ocean-Viewer 1905 provided Danny with higher magnification. He focused the telescope on the scene, trying to keep it dry and not drop it. He could see that one of the navy vessels was large and had deck guns. The other navy vessel was a type of patrol boat armed with cannons. For a coastal naval force solely focused upon smugglers and refuges, this was serious firepower, if not slow. Danny rapidly reached the conclusion that the navy vessels had tried to apprehend the go-fast boats and that there had been an altercation. Smoke lingered in the air. One of the go-fast boats had overturned and another one was on fire. Rapid machine gunfire could be heard. His only advantage was speed, so he decided to rush for the coast. He gunned the engines and headed west towards land. Danny spotted a small inlet on the coast. He accelerated away from the chaos.

An ice-cold shiver tracked down Danny's spine.

CHAPTER 12

Aquila Creek, Nicaraguan Caribbean Coast

As Danny steered the boat into the inlet, he could see numerous huts scattered across the inlet edge. A group of people, including children, came to look at him. They watched him without speaking. Danny assumed that these were Indigenous Miskito people.

One of the old men shouted out to him in Spanish, "Can we help you?" Danny slowly steered the boat toward the makeshift wooden pier.

Danny replied with the traditional greeting of the Miskito people, "*Naksa*."

He continued in the jagged Miskito language, "I have boat trouble, I come ashore?"

"*Naksa*, we thought you Spaniard."

"I'm from Pearl Lagoon. What is this place?"

"Aguila Creek."

"Help me and I will help you."

"Go other side of creek, we help you."

Danny edged forward to what could be, very loosely, described as a berth. Danny was approached by the old man, who seemed to be a headman. He wore a tattered t-shirt, baggy cargo shorts and rubber flipflops.

"Hello Senor, can we help you fix your boat?" said the headman, in Spanish.

"I just need the engines to cool off for a while, can I cover the boat with something, so that it is not in the sun?"

Danny knew that the headman had deduced that the boat was carrying some type of heavy cargo. Because Danny had wanted to quickly hide the boat, it was obvious that the headman fully understood what was going on.

"I will make it very worthwhile if you can help me hide from the Spaniards."

"Yes, we help you, you will then help us."

"Absolutely, please can you help me hide from the Spaniards until dark?"

"This is very dangerous for my village."

"I will help you," said Danny.

"You are blood to us, you speak some of our language, you are one of us." The headman called to his people, to bring sheeting, ropes, and wood.

Danny retrieved his personal stuff, binoculars, telescope, his cash bag, and the Glock. There was no point in trying to unload the boat. He didn't want the Miskito people to see the bales, they may get ideas.

The villagers covered the boat in canvas sheeting and then tied it down with ropes. Then they quickly stacked wood and corrugated sheet metal around the boat. It was now a ramshackle, dilapidated dwelling. It was ingenious. It was obvious to Danny that they have done this before. The headman approached Danny and directed him to one of the huts at the back of the village. Although it was hot and humid, Danny was shivering.

. . . .

About fifteen minutes later, Danny heard a steady rumble. It gradually increased in volume. He peaked through a small hole in the hut. Initially he couldn't see anything. Then a navy boat came into view. Danny recognised it as a military zodiac-type Rigid Inflatable Boat, usually called a RIB. There were four Nicaraguan Navy people in the vessel, all dressed in blue camouflage. They were carrying automatic weapons. Danny suddenly became aware of his bowels, they were churning. A combination of hunger and panic, but mostly fear.

Three of the navy guys jumped out of the RIB and waded through the water towards the villagers. The navy guy with three yellow stripes on his arm pointed his automatic weapon towards the villagers. Danny assumed this navy guy was their leader.

"*Buenas tardes*, Senor Sergeant, how can we help you?" said the headman.

" A boat entered this creek, where has it gone?" said the Sergeant.

"Senor Sergeant, I can assure you we have not seen anything."

"You are lying, all you Miskito people lie and cheat."

"It has been very quiet today."

Pointing towards the village panga boats, the headman said "Senor Sergeant, as you can see, we have just returned from fishing. We are now preparing the afternoon meal. You and your men are welcome to join us."

"I am not interested in your disgusting native food," said the Sergeant.

He then slapped the headman across the face. Some of the Miskito villagers cried out. A child began to weep. The Sergeant pointed his weapon into the face of the headman. The Sergeant raised his voice, so that all the villagers could hear him "The boat that entered into your creek is a narco trafficker. You know what will happen if we discover that you are hiding this boat. We will arrest you all and burn your village."

The headman spoke, "Please Senor Sergeant, be assured. We have not seen this boat. If we see these boats, we always report it to the authorities, we do not want narco in our village."

The Sergeant strode over to the group of villagers, who were watching the events unfolding. He grabbed a small girl and held a pistol to her head. The villagers began to howl. All the women were crying. Danny felt the guilt rise in his throat like vomit. He was bringing terror upon these innocent Miskito people. And for what? He felt ashamed. He wanted to step out and give himself up, but he was too afraid. Guilty, shamed and a coward. That is what he thought he had become, or who he always was.

"Tell me where the boat is, you god-damned savages, now," shouted the Sergeant. The small girl was hysterical.

The headman stepped forward "Senor Sergeant, if we saw anything, we would tell you. We know you are a powerful man. You are the boss of the Caribbean Coast. You protect us from the Narcos and their evil drugs. You make sure our young people do not start to use these drugs and become ghosts. We honour and respect you."

The Sergeant released his grip on the girl, she ran back crying to the group of villagers. The Sergeant scowled at the headman. "Yes, we are here working long hours, in this god forsaken place, so you can be safe. The Indian and Creole people on the coast, we protect you."

"Yes, we understand Senor Sergeant and we thank you for your protection. Senor Sergeant, we have caught many fish this morning. We have too much. Please take some fish. We have red snappers, rainbow bass and even lobster. Take however much you want," said the headman.

The Sergeant waved his men over to the fish baskets. They took most of the morning catch and tossed the overflowing fish basket into the RIB. The men boarded the RIB, reversed the engines, and edged away. The Sergeant looked directly at the headman; He then fired a volley from his automatic weapon into the panga fishing boats. The villagers were frightened and shocked. Children began to cry. The headman stood on the water's edge and watched the RIB as it eased out of the creek.

. . . .

Once the RIB was out of sight, the headman walked over to the hut where Danny was hiding. "Now, we shall eat and drink," said the headman. Danny apologised to the headman for the problems he had brought to their village. He was suffering from a terrible guilt that had washed over him. The headman said "The Spaniards are a problem. But that Sergeant, he is a *Chele*, they are the worst". Danny had not heard the term *Chele* for many years. *Chele* meant a white or pale-skinned person. It was derived from *leche* meaning milk. Danny struggled to stop laughing.

Danny began to relax. The guilt and shame slowly faded, but an ache remained in his stomach. The headman's people came into the hut with red snapper, plantains, and green bananas. The headman poured Danny a drink he called Mishla, made from ripe plantains and bananas.

"You are very welcome in our village, my brother," said the headman.

"Thank you very much for your hospitality, do you still have enough fish to spare?"

"Yes, the sea is bountiful, we Miskito people are blessed."

"Thank you, it is appreciated. You are helping me; I will help you," said Danny.

"Eat my friend, we talk later about the help you will give my village. Let us now have food and drink."

The food was excellent and reminded Danny of the meals that his mother prepared when he was a child.

As they ate the headman said, "You are hiding from the navy?"

"Yes, I am taking my cargo up the coast. If the navy discover me, I will be in trouble and the cargo will be confiscated," said Danny.

"You are carrying the Colombian cargo, no?"

Danny paused, then said "Yes, I take it north of Bluefields."

"This is an extremely dangerous game, Senor. There are many people on this coast who would like to take your cargo from you."

"Are you going to try to take my cargo?"

"No, you are our blood brother. We will help each other. If you were a Spaniard, we may look at you through different eyes."

"Thank you. I would like to stay here for a while, maybe sleep. I will leave your village once the sun goes down."

"You are welcome to stay as long as you wish."

"I would like to give you 1,000 U.S. dollars. This I could give you when I am leaving."

"Let's talk about this later when we know you are safe. Please rest now."

The headman left the hut. Danny was concerned, but after everything he had seen with the navy, he felt that the headman was genuine.

. . . .

Danny woke wondering where he was. His dreams had been filled with floating bodies and bullets. His legs were itchy, and he tried to resist scratching them. Sand flies had bitten him. Danny looked over towards the temporary ramshackle dwelling, it didn't look as though it had been tampered with. He briefly relaxed. Danny saw the headman and beckoned him over.

"My friend are you rested?" said the headman.

"Yes, thank you very much for your hospitality," said Danny.

"We Miskito people always welcome strangers, especially ones who try to speak our language."

"I learnt the language from my mother, she could speak Miskito and Rama."

"Rama? We have Rama people in our village, from Rama Cay. In fact, Aguila Creek was a Rama village. We were invited to come and live with them."

"That explains why you are here. I was surprised to find a Miskito village this far south of Bluefields."

"Yes, we are the most south of all Miskito villages. The last you will find before you reach Costa Rica.

"Rama or not, it appears be a traditional Miskito village."

"We are sustained by the sea. We catch many fish. We catch the spiny lobster. We also sometimes catch green turtles, but please do not tell the Sergeant." said the headman, with a grin.

Danny smiled.

"Let us now talk about how you will help our village," said the headman.

"I would like to give you 1000 U.S. dollars," said Danny.

The headman ignored Danny's offer, "You have seen what our villagers have done for you. We have disguised your boat and we have hidden you. The Sergeant has threatened our children, his people have taken our fish, and he has damaged our boats."

"Yes, and for this I feel very guilty. I am ashamed. You deserve a great deal for what you have done for me. How can I help you?"

"We want you to give us one bale of your cargo."

"Why do you want it? It is poison. Better to keep it away from the villagers and their children."

"We will sell it. We have our own connections."

"But if I give you that, the Colombians will blame me, and I will be in serious trouble."

"My brother, you are already in serious trouble, you are now trying to get *out* of serious trouble."

Danny didn't want to hand over any of the cargo. But the Glock was no protection against a whole village. The Miskito villagers might take all the cargo. They could kill him if they wanted to. They may even inform the Sergeant of his whereabouts. He had underestimated them. They held all the cards. "Okay, I will hand over one bale of the cargo, when I am about to leave," said Danny.

CHAPTER 13

The sun was setting in the west as Danny prepared to leave. The villagers had dismantled the temporary dwelling. He thoroughly inspected the boat for any damage. The seaworthiness of the boat was everything. He could see no obvious damage. He removed the cargo protective sheeting and struggled to lift one of the bales out. He placed it on the passenger seating. It was heavy. The villagers were watching him. No secrets here.

Danny started the engines and they burst into life. The light was fading rapidly. He slowly reversed the boat and then aligned it with the creek thoroughfare. Ready to go. He beckoned the waiting villagers and pointed towards the bale. They jumped onboard, carried it to the shore and started to rip open the bale. Danny waved to the headman and eased the boat towards the creek outlet.

As he picked up speed, he heard shouting. Bullets crashed into the boat. Gunfire was all around him. The windscreen on the boat exploded into a thousand of pieces. He then felt as though a baseball bat had hit him on the back of his shoulder. He had been shot. It hurt like hell. Danny didn't know what was happening. Was it a trap? He would have returned fire with his Glock, but he couldn't see who was shooting at him. As he sailed through the creek outlet into the sea, he expected to see the Sergeant and his men, but there was no one there.

His shoulder felt like it was on fire. He could feel blood running down his back. Weapons were still being fired from the village. What was going on? Had the villagers decided that they wanted all the cargo? His shoulder was now throbbing. He gunned the engines and headed away from the coast and then northward, as fast as he could.

CHAPTER 14

He could see the twinkling lights along the coast. The engines droned and he kept moving north. Danny's shoulder ached and he felt tired and weak. The bright lights of Bluefields were on his left, so he was confident that the Corn Islands were on his immediate right.

Once Danny had passed Bluefields, he continued north towards Pearl Lagoon. He knew people there and had spent many days and nights drinking at the *King Marlin*. However, sailing into Pearl Lagoon with a cargo of uncut cocaine was a recipe for disaster. Regardless of his family connections and his numerous friends, the piranhas would be out, and he wouldn't last the night.

The boat started to lose power.

Fear rose into his throat.

He stopped the boat and grabbed a flashlight. He saw his blood on the floor and also splattered on his shoes. But his immediate concern was the boat. All three engines couldn't be faulty. He inspected the boat in a state of mild panic. After ten minutes he discovered the problem. The villager's bullets must have damaged the fuel lines and it had leaked into the sea. He had spare fuel, but he had nothing with which to repair the lines. He envisaged a situation where he was apprehended by the psychotic Sergeant and his merry men, or the Pearl Lagoon piranhas discovered him.

The boat drifted for around 30 minutes; the tide was carrying him away from the coast. It gave him time to think. If he could get to one of the remote islands, then he may be able to get help. He also needed assistance with his shoulder, simple painkillers may not be enough. It was very sore and stiffening up. He had lost a significant amount of blood.

Danny noticed a speck of light in the distance. The boat was drifting in that direction. He decided to take a gamble. He poured fuel into the tank; his shoulder was stiff and painful.

He then restarted one of the engines and headed towards the light. The boat was groaning and protesting. He considered that there had been more even damage to the boat than the fuel lines. As the boat got closer to the light, Danny could see it was an inhabited island. Hopefully, a fishing village and not a small navy base thought Danny.

    The boat spluttered towards his fate.

CHAPTER 15

Manchester, England U.K.

Paul was certainly having buyer's remorse. His wife, Charlotte, was apprehensive about Nicaragua as a holiday destination. She had started researching Pelican Island online and specifically personal safety in Nicaragua. She was vaguely aware that Nicaragua had often been in the news over many years regarding civil wars and earthquakes. Charlotte scoured the internet.

Her immediate concerns became focused upon the recent public demonstrations across Nicaragua, related to taxes and pensions. It was reported online that there had been marches by students and opposition parties. The marches had been harshly curtailed by government forces.

There were estimates alleging sixty-three deaths and over four hundred wounded. Charlotte said to Paul that Nicaragua may not be the place for them.

Paul spoke to the travel agent acting on behalf of Pelican Island. The agent tried to reassure him.

"Pelican Island is a very safe place and far away from the problems on the west coast."

"Yes, you had to transit through Managua, the capital of Nicaragua. It is a small airport and easy to find your way around."

"The flight to Bluefields from Managua is early morning, so you needed to be at Augusto C. Sandino Airport, Managua at 7am. It is essential, that you stay over one night minimum in Managua," said the agent.

"Occasionally there are military and police roadblocks between the airport and the city centre. But you can stay at the Best Western hotel at the airport. Yes, it's very safe."

"If you are travelling in via Mexico City, then please look closely at the flight schedules. Due to the recent disturbances, AeroMexico has a reduced schedule between Mexico City and Managua."

"You could consider flying via San Salvador, capital of El Salvador or Guatemala City, capital of Guatemala. However, these are both renowned for their high murder rates, so best avoided."

"No, Managua is very safe, as is Nicaragua as a whole. There is an extremely low level of crime. Just please do not get close to any political demonstrations."

"I have been informed that waving the Nicaraguan flag can sometimes be deemed provocative."

Paul doubted that it was the dream Caribbean holiday that they had imagined.

Paul said to Charlotte that he hadn't met anyone who had been to Nicaragua. She said that the UK government website Foreign & Commonwealth Office website had detailed potential issues in Nicaragua related to crime, the political situation, and natural disasters. Paul declared that official UK Government websites were typically paranoid regarding most countries in the world.

Charlotte said she couldn't understand why people still lived in Nicaragua if it's all true. She concluded that if tourists were concerned about every event over the last fifty years, then people wouldn't go anywhere, including New York, London, or Manchester.

They decided to be adventurous, and maybe even foolish.

CHAPTER 16

Mexico City

Paul and Charlotte began their trip to Nicaragua with an AeroMexico flight from Heathrow to Mexico City. They stopped over in the city for two days. They stayed in the *Gran Hotel Ciudad de Mexico*. It had an iconic Tiffany stained-glass roof and the first panoramic elevator ever installed in Mexico. But that wasn't what impressed Paul.

"This is the hotel used in the James Bond movie, *Spectre*. The movie which showed the Mexican *Day of the Dead* parade," said Paul, "The movie shows the interior of the hotel, James Bond entering a bedroom and climbing out onto a balcony. Brilliant." Charlotte was bemused.

They gorged themselves on special tacuba-style enchiladas with mole poblano sauce and beef tacos with guacamole and refried beans.

Charlotte said, "I'm never going to fit into my clothes ever again."

Paul said "Yeah, the food is great, but it's very filling. I've noticed that all food in Mexico seems to end in an A or an O."

They spent time visiting the Templo Mayor Museum of Tenochtitlan. It held stone carvings of strange gods and spirits, such as *Eagle Cuauhxicalli* and sculpture of god *Xoloti*. There were bizarre skull masks and ceramic pots modelled on skulls.

Paul said "The conquistadors made a serious attempt to destroy this culture. The Spanish even built directly over the Aztec temples."

"The Aztecs did seem to be rather war-like though," said Charlotte.

"Yeah, but I'm not sure it justifies a type of ethnic cleansing," said Paul.

They went to the Xochimilco area, which was a neighbourhood outside the city. The place consisted of Aztec canals, a floating garden, Mexican gondola rides and spooky plastic dolls. They also spent time at the Teotihuacan pyramids and saw the carved jaguar heads. They were being real tourists.

They wandered around the Roma district of the city. Charlotte had wanted to go there because she had seen the multiple Oscar winning movie *Roma* recently.

"I'm not sure what you saw in that movie. It was in black and white, in Spanish and with English language subtitles," said Paul.

"It was a movie with depth, unlike James Bond," said Charlotte.

"I didn't see the point of it," said Paul.

"It revolves around class, families, the semi-madness and chaos of Mexico City," said Charlotte. Paul didn't think the movie was up to much and thought that the walk around Colonia Roma was uninspiring, like the movie.

They spent half a day wandering around the Chapultepec Park and castle. They scrutinized the castle and studied the paintings and statues. There was a unique mural on the ceiling. Paul asked a guide what the significance of the mural.

The guide said "These are the Los Ninos Heroes, the Child Heroes. When the Americans invaded, there was a significant battle here, the battle of Chapultepec.

"Yes, I am aware of that battle," said Charlotte.

"The Americans were advancing, and the Mexican cadets refused to retreat. One of the heroes, Gabriel Flores, grabbed the Mexican flag, wrapped it around himself and jumped off the castle point," said the guide.

"Very brave," said Paul.

"Yes, the recruits are national heroes," said the guide.

"Seems rather sad," said Charlotte.

"I doubt they'll be making a Hollywood movie about that incident," said Paul.

As they walked back down the hill and through the park, Paul noticed a man looking at him. The man seemed to be a local. He was smartly dressed in a business suit. He didn't seem to be a vagrant or some type of thief, but this was Mexico City, who knows? thought Paul. When Paul and Charlotte walked past the man, he was observing them both, looking intently at the Manchester City football shirt that Paul was wearing. Nothing came of it, and it was a false alarm. A touch of paranoia thought Paul.

. . . .

They returned to the *Gran Hotel Ciudad de Mexico* and went up to the Terraza Restaurant and bar overlooking the Constitution square. They ordered margaritas from the waiter. He said, "I suggest that, as you are in Mexico City, you have a margarita with mezcal, and not tequila". Paul asked what the difference was. The waiter provided an elongated explanation that revolved around the agave plant, the geography of Mexico and aging oak barrels. All that Paul remembered was that all tequilas are mezcals, but not all mezcals are tequilas.

"That will teach you to ask too many questions," said Charlotte. They obliged and ordered two mezcal margaritas.

Paul was silent for a few minutes sipping his drink, then said, " Nothing ever happens to me."

"What is that supposed to mean? I might be insulted," said Charlotte.

"No, you don't understand what I mean."

"You mean your wife doesn't understand you, can't you be more original?"

"Give me a break for a minute."

"Ok, go ahead, you have five minutes to recover from your *foot in the mouth* moment."

"It's just that I breeze through life, I'd even call it sleepwalking. I've never witnessed any significant, recordable, historical moment in my whole life. People had been in wars; others had seen the sinking of the Titanic or the Hindenburg crash and burn. Others had been present when Paris was liberated, they have watched helicopters lifting off from the roof of the U.S. embassy in Saigon. People were there when Churchill or JFK spoke."

"Aren't most of those people dead now?" said Charlotte.

Come on, you know what I mean."

"No, I'm not sure what you are getting at."

"It's just I'm always somewhere, someplace after the event.

"Considering some of the terrible things that can happened in the world, isn't that a good thing?"

Paul said, "Look at Mexico City. There are thousands of places with historical significance, but that's all they are to me, historical. Am I destined to go through life and not have that moment, that instance, that event which defines me, that distinguishes me? *Wow, there goes Paul, you know he was actually there when -------------- .*"

"So, you want to be present at a world changing event, something that is going to be in the history books?" said Charlotte.

Paul nodded but felt foolish.

"You were at Manchester City's Etihad stadium when City won the Premiership for the first time in over 40 years, isn't that enough?" said Charlotte, laughing.

"Very funny Charlotte. I mean something that's serious."

"City is not serious to you? That's news to me, I'm shocked." She grinned.

Paul said, "The Welsh poet, Dylan Thomas, wrote a poem *Do not go gentle into that good night*. The poem can mean differing things to different people, but for me it says, do the maximum with your life, keep going, do not accept your destiny."

"Well, as you are quoting literature, I think it was originally from *Aesop's Fables*, I paraphrase, *you really need to be careful what you are wishing for.*"

CHAPTER 17

Managua, Nicaragua

The sunshine spilling through the aircraft window didn't help. Augusto's brain, or whatever remained of it, was in a vice. Madison drank like a marine, a marine on shore leave. He felt sick. He resolved never to drink mezcal again, ever.

Upon arrival at Augusto C. Sandino Airport, Managua, he entered the airport building and headed towards passport control. He went to an immigration desk with no queue. Augusto was still wearing the same business suit. It smelt of stale alcohol and looked as though he had slept in it. Maybe he had, he wasn't sure. The Nicaraguan immigration officer gave him a blank look. Augusto's immediate thought was whether all immigration officials around the world went to the same training centre. They all looked miserable. Without exception, they were all poor representatives of their countries. Nicaragua desperately needed the revenue from tourism. This guy didn't care. The immigration guy looked at Augusto as though he had just found acne on his nose.

"Passport," said the immigration guy. Augusto handed it over, with the photo page open. The immigration guy started blinking rapidly and said, "Lieutenant Commander Romero, welcome home". If it wasn't for his hangover Augusto would have felt a moment of self-satisfaction, but he just felt nauseous.

"Lieutenant Commander," I have a message for you on my system."

Augusto didn't have a clue what he was referring to. His head hurt.

"Sorry?"

"I have a message from the office of the Capitan of the Navy, Pablo Colindres on my computer. There is an order to contact his personal assistant, on an urgent basis."

Augusto took back his passport and switched on his phone. As Augusto walked into the public arrivals area, his phone burst into life, alerts, messages, and emails flooded in.

From the deluge of messages, he figured out that there had been an incident on the Caribbean coast, just south of Bluefields. Several narco go-fast boats had been intercepted and a firefight had ensured. Some of the boats had been destroyed. Other boats had escaped north. There was a navy fatality and several injuries.

Augusto called his second-in-command, Lieutenant Amander. There was no answer. He left a message. "Josue, call me immediately, I want an update now."

. . . .

As ordered, Augusto called the Nicaraguan Navy headquarters in Managua.

"Office of the Captain of the Navy, how may I help you?"

"Good afternoon. This is Lieutenant Commander Augusto Romero, Nicaraguan Navy, Caribbean Coast

Region. I have been requested to urgently contact the Office of the Captain of the Navy, Pablo Colindres. Please may I speak to the personal assistant of Captain Colindres?"

"I will put you through, Lieutenant Commander," said the person. Augusto waited for what felt like a long time, he even considered that he may have been cut off.

"Lieutenant Commander Romero?" said another voice.

"Speaking" said Augusto.

"Sir, we have been trying to contact you, without success," said the person. "I have been out of the country on official business. My cell phone struggles to receive overseas calls," said Augusto.

"Captain Colindres demands to meet you, today."

"Certainly. I am at the airport. I will come directly to the office of Captain Colindres."

"The captain has requested that you meet him at the Intercontinental Hotel at 3pm."

"I will get a taxi and meet him upon his arrival."

"Perfect. I will inform the captain that the meeting is confirmed."

Augusto thought that this must have something to do with the meeting in Mexico City. Colindres was a very senior person within the navy. Espinoza had been the Captain of the Navy before his sidestep over to the diplomatic post at the Nicaraguan Consulate in Mexico City. Colindres was his replacement, based in Managua. He was probably angry at Augusto because he couldn't contact him. Augusto would soon find out. He felt ill.

CHAPTER 18

Augusto arrived at the Intercontinental Hotel, Managua City and took a seat in the reception. He suddenly became aware that he was inappropriately dressed. No uniform, his suit was a mess and he realised that he smelt bad. Colindres would be in his uniform, all spit and polish. Colindres was his superior, he could charge Augusto with *manner unbecoming of an officer*, *disrespect to a superior* or even worse.

Augusto walked rapidly to the hotel washroom. He took his toothbrush from his overnight bag and cleaned his teeth. He then splashed water on his face. That's a start thought Augusto. He grabbed some paper towels and buffed up his shoes. He combed his hair and instantly wished he had shaved that morning. Augusto realised that the shirt, that he had worn for the meeting in the Four Seasons, would be in better condition than the one he was wearing. He changed shirts. He wiped stains off his suit. When he had finished, he looked in the mirror. He was distraught. The U.S. Marine Corps had fucked him up.

A black BMW arrived outside the hotel reception. A muscular guy, who was sitting in the front passenger seat, jumped out. The guy opened the rear left-hand door. Colindres eased out of the BMW. He was not in uniform. His hair was obviously dyed black, and he was wearing an expensive designer suit. When Colindres approached him, Augusto stood to attention and saluted. Colindres did not return the salute.

"Lieutenant Commander, let us retire to the terrace café" said Colindres.

"Certainly sir, it is a pleasure to meet you again," said Augusto.

Colindres had visited the Caribbean Coast Region occasionally. Augusto had recently given a presentation to Colindres and his team in Bluefields regarding violent crime, civil disturbances, and the smuggling of narcotics. Augusto had been ordered by Colindres to come to Managua and deliver the same presentation to the Ministries of Defence, Finance & Public Credit, and senior officers in the Nicaraguan Army.

"So, Lieutenant Commander, I understand that you have just returned from a meeting in Mexico City," said Colindres, as he sat down.

"Yes, Sir. Admiral Espinoza also attended the meeting. The Mexican Government hosted the gathering. Representatives from the U.S. Coastguard and the DEA attended."

"Senor Espinoza has submitted a meeting report. It is very interesting," said Colindres. "Lieutenant Commander, do you believe the CIA participates in this smear upon the Republic of Nicaragua?"

Straight to the point, thought Augusto. "It seems unlikely, there appears to be a genuine desire on behalf of the DEA to identify this *missing piece of the jigsaw*, as they call it, said Augusto.

"Oh yes, the DEA. This Senorita Walker, no?"

"Yes Sir. She seems focused on the task in hand."

"Yes, I'm sure she is. Did you extract any additional information from her?"

"Sorry Sir, what do you mean exactly?"

"Lieutenant Commander, you spent extensive time with her in Chapultepec Park. You had dinner with her in the Four Seasons and then drinks in the cocktail bar. It sounded like a wonderful evening. The life of a Nicaraguan Navy playboy. Sandino must be turning in his grave."

"Sir, I was being followed?"

"Lieutenant Commander, if the Nicaraguan Intelligence Services believe that the CIA have an agent in Mexico City, who is masquerading as DEA, then we will follow them. The fact that one of our navy officers spends the evening with said CIA-DEA agent, this is of interest to us."

"Sir, I did not divulge any information that would endanger the Republic of Nicaragua."

"And now we can progress to what is important. Whose side are you on?"

"Sir, this cannot be a serious question."

"It most certainly is. Maybe you are one of *Ian Fleming's* MI6 people, a kind of Hispanic James Bond."

"Sir, you know from my files that I studied in the UK. However, my loyalty is to the land of my birth, Nicaragua."

"Your father. He was a brave man. A revolutionary. He pushed back the Contras in Bilwi. They were murdering bastards, funded, and armed by the CIA. Your father and his brigade propelled those bastards back across the border."

"Yes, Sir. I am from a revolutionary family. We are loyal to the Republic of Nicaragua."

"But are you loyal to the party? Are you loyal to the FSLN and *Comandante Daniel*?"

This was the acid-test question, his loyalty was to the democratically elected government. For Augusto, regardless of who was the President; Daniel Ortega or someone else, his loyalty was to the Republic of Nicaragua.

But nothing was simple in Nicaragua.

"I am led by the spirit of my father and my grandfather before him. I am a revolutionary, I am a Sandinista, until death."

"Which is what I would expect from you."

Colindres paused for a moment.

"Within the last 24 hours, there has been a major incident within your region of responsibility," said Colindres.

Augusto was still struggling to catch up with the information. Damn pathetic navy phone.

"Yes Sir," said Augusto.

Colindres continued, "I have been reliably informed that at approximately 13:00 hours yesterday, five go-fast boats entered Nicaraguan territorial waters. They were duly engaged by two navy vessels. One was a Damen Stan 4207 with deck guns. The other patrol vessel was a Dabur-class patrol boat, armed with two Oerlikon 20mm cannons and two 12.7 mm machine guns. I am certain you are aware of these vessels" said Colindres.

"Yes Sir. In my post as Lieutenant Commander Caribbean Coast Region, I am responsible for the deployment of said vessels, Sir".

"You most certainly are. Yet they were deployed without your knowledge."

"Sir, Unfortunately I was not contactable whilst in Mexico City."

"So, while you are dining and drinking mezcal with the CIA, Nicaraguan Navy vessels under your command were deployed and brought into action, without your knowledge?"

"Sir, I nominated my second-in-command to take over my responsibilities in my absence."

"You, Lieutenant Commander, are responsible. You cannot delegate such significant responsibility or authority."

"Yes Sir, fully understood."

"I want a full report on my desk tomorrow morning."

"Yes Sir."

Colindres extracted a pack of cigarettes from his pocket and lit one. Obviously, the rules of the hotel were not applicable to him.

"Lieutenant Commander Romero, you need to understand our national strategy."

Colindres elaborated, "Within Central America, Nicaragua is a special place. The government of Nicaragua has placed a protective firewall around our country. We will not allow narcotics to be transported throughout our country. We seize all cocaine that is transported on our roads. We imprison all narco traffickers apprehended on our road network. We will not allow unidentified light aircraft, to illegally smuggle narcotics, to land in our country or to use our aviation infrastructure. Because of this protective firewall strategy, we have no drug gangs or cartels in Nicaragua. We have an exceptionally low murder rate by international standards. This is a major achievement when one considers the slaughterhouses that are Honduras, Guatemala, El Salvador, and Mexico."

"Sir, our government has protected the people from this nightmare," said Augusto.

"Yes, and the people of Nicaragua are grateful that we have implement this approach. We have stopped cocaine and its evil twin, crack cocaine, from contaminating our barrios."

Augusto recalled that when crack cocaine had been brought to the poor Managua neighbourhood of barrio Vargas Mendoza, the National Guard had ambushed the main dealers and killed them all. That was the end of crack cocaine in the barrio.

Colindres continued, "In Cuba, Castro had a no-tolerance approach to cocaine trafficking. Even though illegal U.S. sanctions were strangling Cuba and they desperately needed foreign currency, he did not waiver. Castro tracked down the cocaine traffickers, captured and then executed them on the beach. One strike and you are out. We have adopted this strategy and made it our own. A Nicaraguan narco strategy, a protective firewall. The U.S. has tried to infer that the Nicaraguan government, and therefore the FSLN, are in league with the narco traffickers. Nothing could be further from the truth. We will stamp on this evil trade, and we will not allow this poison to enter our country."

"Sir, I am confident that the people of the Caribbean coast of Nicaragua are grateful to you for protecting them from this curse."

"Lieutenant Commander, I have taken the time to meet you personally, so that I can explain our national strategy."

"Thank you, Sir, it is greatly appreciated."

"It is imperative that you understand that your duty is to protect the Republic of Nicaragua."

"Yes Sir, I am 100% committed to serving the Republic of Nicaragua. I will work tirelessly to ensure illegal narcotics do not enter our country."

"That is excellent Lieutenant Commander. You now are fully aligned with the protective firewall strategy of our government."

"Yes Sir. I am honoured that you have taken the time to highlight my failings."

Colindres leaned back into his chair. He continued smoking his cigarette.

"Augusto, I knew your father. He was a brave man, a great hero, a Sandinista. He dedicated his whole life to Nicaragua, and his family.

"Thank you, Sir."

Colindres continued smoking and leaned further back.

"Is your mother still with us?" said Colindres.

"No Sir, she passed away four years ago."

"I was a junior officer, an Ensign seconded to Bilwi. Your father was my commanding officer. He introduced me to your mother many years ago. She was a beautiful woman. I understood why your father married an Afro-Miskito woman.

Augusto swallowed the veiled insult, "My mother always considered herself a *Mestizo of the Caribbean Coast*.

She was a magical blend of Indigenous Miskito, African Garifuna and White British," said Augusto.

"And yet you have risen to a high rank in the Nicaraguan Navy. said Colindres. Another insult.

"This meeting has ended," said Colindres.

Colindres stood, threw his cigarette butt on to the hotel floor, and began to stride to his waiting vehicle. He stopped and spun around and said, "Your duty is not to protect the United States of America. We cannot seize every shipment of narcotics that passes through our territory. However, we can stop the narcotics entering our society. In that way we will protect our citizens and ensure that law and order is maintained in our republic."

"Yes Sir."

"Ensure that a full report of the incident is on my desk tomorrow morning".

"Yes Sir."

"And one final order, Lieutenant Commander, ensure that if we meet again, you are dressed accordingly. You are attired like one of your Caribbean Miskito vagrants."

CHAPTER 19

When Colindres left in his BMW, Augusto called Lieutenant Amander. After a few rings, the Lieutenant picked up.

"Josue, where have you been? I've been trying to contact you. What's been going on?" said Augusto.

"Sorry I missed your call Sir. It's been a nightmare here. I have been trying to contact you for over 24 hours. I left messages at the Four Seasons hotel, Sir."

Augusto remembered that he hadn't checked out of the hotel. He had no bill to pay, so he just left. He'd been so drunk and then hungover in the morning; he wouldn't have noticed any notes pushed under the door or flashing messages on the in-room phone. There could have been a message spray painted on the hotel room wall and he still wouldn't have seen it.

"I'm on the line now. Tell me everything."

Josue described the events of the previous day. The only airworthy plane still operated by the Nicaraguan Airforce, a Cessna 337 Skymaster plane, was on training duties out of Bluefields. It was probable that the pilots were enjoying themselves and showing off to trainees. Fortuitously, they spotted five go-fast boats approaching the coast around the area of Punta Gorda, south of Bluefields.

Josue mobilised the Damen Stan 4207 and the Dabur-class patrol boat. That was at 09:08 hours yesterday. All five go-fast boats were spotted visually and identified by the crew of the navy vessels at 09:57. The go-fast boats were in Nicaraguan territorial waters and therefore were duly engaged by the two navy vessels.

Three of the go-fast boats immediately began firing light automatic weapons at the navy vessels. Josue was on board the Damen Stan 4207 and returned fire with her deck guns. Two of the go-fast boats were critically damaged and both immediately began to sink. The Dabur-class patrol boat turned her weaponry onto the third go-fast boat that was firing automatic weapons. This go-fast boat then caught fire. During the engagement, the fourth and fifth go-fast boats gained speed and avoided the engagement. They fled the scene and headed north.

"Narco traffickers body count?" said Augusto.

"Five dead, none captured," said Josue.

"Our casualties?"

"Unfortunately, Seaman Rafael Centeno serving on the Dabur-class patrol boat was hit in the upper body by gunfire and was killed instantly. Three other sailors serving with me on the Damen Stan 4207 received minor injuries from shrapnel," said Josue.

"Have you sent the injured for treatment?"

"Yes Sir. They have received treatment at the Clinica Medica Hospital in Bluefields.

"Have you informed the family of Seaman Rafael Centeno?"

"Yes Sir. I have spoken to his wife. They have two small children."

"It is a tragedy. I will go and speak to his wife personally. Please inform me when the funeral has been confirmed. Both of us should attend," said Augusto.

"Yes, Sir. Can I speak plainly, Sir?"

"Go ahead, Josue."

"I'm not sure why we are dying so that Mexico and the United States can keep cocaine out of their countries," said Josue.

"Yes, Josue, I fully agree. Nicaragua is caught in an absolute *no-win situation*." said Augusto, "and nobody seems to care."

. . . .

Josue explained that his crews had spotted a possible sixth go-fast boat on the horizon. It could have been a tailender to the narco convoy said Josue. It was observed heading towards Aquila Creek, a remote southerly Miskito village. He had sent Sergeant Gamboa in a navy RIB, launched from the Damen Stan 4207, to investigate. Sergeant Gamboa reported that there was no sign of this sixth go-fast boat. He did report though that the Miskito villagers were very uncooperative.

"Any thoughts where it went, Josue?" said Augusto.

"It's possible that this go-fast boat didn't enter Aquilla Creek. It could have entered the mainland at Punta Gorda. If it did, then it would be difficult to find on the river network and within all those mangroves".

"Ok, listen out for any local information that may arise on that vessel. We don't want all that cocaine making its way into the depths of our country," said Augusto.

"No Sir, bad for the villagers, and their sons and daughters."

"Josue, the priority is to keep this evil away from our people."

"Absolutely Sir."

"What about seizures?"

"There were three bales found floating south, with five bodies entangled in the wreckage of the go-fast boats or floating in the sea. Other bodies could have sunk and might wash up in the next few days."

"The three bales?"

"I've had them secured within the armoury at Bluefields, under armed guard," said Josue.

"Three bales seems a small number. Do you suspect someone has subsequently hidden any of the bales?"

"Definitely not any of the crews of our vessels. I was always present."

"What about the fisherman around the coast?"

"Sir, as you know, that's very possible. The local fishermen and the beachcombers will be aware of this incident. They will start acting as though they are sharks and piranhas themselves. It could rapidly develop into a feeding frenzy.

"That's what White Lobster does to people," said Augusto.

CHAPTER 20

Augusto had to get himself over to the Caribbean coast. But he had no chance of travelling over to Bluefields and completing the report for Colindres at the same time. He also needed a shower, so he went to look around the hotel for Tico. He found him berating the swimming pool attendants.

"Hey, Senor Tico, please don't be tough on our Nicaraguan people. It takes time to learn everything that a Costa Rican knows already," said Augusto.

"Yes, but it is important that we Costa Ricans should drag Nicaragua into the 21st century," they hugged each other.

Tico was the Costa Rican General Manager of the Intercontinental hotel. He had been born and raised in Limon on the Caribbean coast of Costa Rica. He was an ambitious soul. When he was young, Tico had managed to secure a luggage porter job at the Holiday Inn in the capital of Costa Rica, San Jose. He spoke and wrote perfect Spanish and English. Tico worked hard and was soon in charge of the hotel concierge desk and all the other porters and drivers. The group, which owned the Holiday Inn and Intercontinental Hotels, were always on the lookout for local talent. Tico was difficult not to notice. He embarked on their management training course with the same gusto he embraced life. Augusto and Tico were kindred spirits and real friends.

"So, Lieutenant Commander, why do we have the pleasure of your company?" said Tico.

"I have just been shafted by my boss, so I'm feeling pissed off."

"You have come to the right place; a cold beer should help."

"It certainly would and if you could assist me with a room that would be even better."

"We can sort that out for you," said Tico.

"I have my navy ID, so a discounted rate shouldn't damage my imaginary trust fund."

"Augusto, my friend, I have a room for you, free of charge. Just keep away from the mini-bar and don't charge anything, I mean *anything*, to your room."

"You're my hero. You've saved me once again. Regarding the mini bar, don't worry, I'm still recovering from a heavy night in Mexico City."

"Mexico City? I want the full details; locations, liquor consumed, food eaten, and ladies entertained."

"I can brief you only when I see that beer."

"It's on the way. So, who's been a naughty boy then?" Tico began laughing.

. . . .

After a few beers and the de-briefing session with Tico, Augusto walked slowly to his room. The gait of a defeated athlete. He put his overnight bag on the bed and glanced at himself in the mirror. He looked terrible. Augusto opened his bag and realised crucial personal supplies were exhausted.

He would have to walk over to the Metrocentre Mall and buy underwear, socks, and a shirt. He knew that the prices in the Metro centre Mall were at least three times the price of the local market but needs must. Augusto left his room and meandered over to the mall, which was directly across from the hotel.

Augusto bought what he needed and then decided to have a coffee at one of the *Italian style* coffee places. Why Central America needs *Italian style* coffee places, he wasn't sure. As he sipped his coffee and felt sorry for himself, he saw the colour again. The sky-blue shade caught his eye. He again recognised a Manchester City football shirt. It was the same English-speaking couple whom he had seen in Mexico City. As they walked past the coffee place, he spoke to them,

"You don't see many of those football shirts in Nicaragua," said Augusto.

The couple stopped walking, surprised to be spoken to in their own language. The English-speaking guy said "Yes, I'm flying the flag for Manchester City in Central America."

"They're my European football team," said Augusto.

"Why is that? I thought you all supported Barcelona and Real Madrid."

"Many do. But I was in Manchester for four years. City are my adopted team."

"Why City and not Manchester United?"

"City wore light blue like the Nicaraguan flag, and anyway you were the underdogs in those days, just like Nicaragua."

"A lot has changed, the Arabs in Abu Dhabi bought our club, now things are going from great to fantastic."

"Maybe we should encourage Abu Dhabi to buy Nicaragua," laughed Augusto.

. . . .

Augusto invited the couple to join him for a coffee. They seemed reluctant, even wary, thought Augusto. He impressed upon them that in Nicaragua you need to slow down, relax, and take your time. The couple decided to join him at his table and Augusto ordered *Italian coffees.* They all introduced themselves.

"Why were you in Manchester?" said Paul.

"I studied at Manchester University," said Augusto.

"What did you study?" said Charlotte.

"American History and Politics."

"Very useful for this part of the world," said Paul.

"I'm not sure I've put my degree to proper use. I am an officer in the Nicaraguan Navy."

"That's impressive," said Paul.

"Not really. It's not the U.S. or British Navy, it's a small outfit really."

"Where did you live when you were in Manchester?"

"I lived just off Princess Parkway, close to the big white German engineering building."

"Just near Didsbury? I know where that is."

"As people always say, It's a small world. I noticed you both in Mexico City yesterday. I'm not following you, honest."

"Yes, I remember you, in the large park in the centre of the city," said Paul.

"Chapultepec Park. I would be a terrible spy."

"A Nicaraguan James Bond," said Paul. Charlotte sighed.

"Where are you headed now? Nobody comes to Nicaragua to visit the Metrocentre Mall," laughed Augusto.

"We're going over to Pelican Island on the Caribbean coast."

"Oh yeah, I know that area very well and I'm familiar with Pelican Island."

"Is it safe?" said Charlotte.

Augusto chuckled, "Absolutely. In fact, if you spend all your time in the luxury of Pelican Island, you won't meet any people other than guests and locals who are working at the resort."

"We were worried about visiting your country. If Nicaragua is in the news in the UK, it's never good news." said Charlotte.

"I know what you mean. When Hurricane Eta hit the Miskito coast recently, that was very destructive."

"I was thinking more of the student demonstrations," said Charlotte.

Augusto fell silent. He was ashamed of what had happened, and that ordinary citizens had lost their lives. He considered that you could have a reasonable debate when you were discussing the situation with Nicaraguans, but when speaking to foreigners it felt reprehensible.

"Managua is a very safe for tourists. Do you have any plans?" said Augusto, changing the subject.

"No. We thought we'd decide now that we are here," said Paul.

"Are you staying across the road at the Intercontinental?" said Augusto.

"Yes" said Paul.

"Right then. I will speak to my friend Tico. He's the manager of your hotel. He can arrange a momentous day out for you. To the lakefront, the museums and to the volcano."

"Are you sure? Will it be expensive?"

"For a tourist, with U.S. dollars, Euro or British pounds, not much is expensive in Nicaragua."

"Thank you very much. It's appreciated," said Paul.

"Just one thing, Tico is a Costa Rican. They're very dodgy characters. Keep him away from your wife," said Augusto. Paul wasn't sure how to take the comment. Charlotte beamed.

Paul and Charlotte continued their walk through the MetroCentre Mall. Augusto headed back to the hotel. He looked around for Tico but couldn't spot him. He was somewhere in the hotel persecuting the housekeeping staff. Augusto sent him a text message outlining the tour for the British tourists and left it with him. Tico was notoriously efficient. Augusto was confident that Paul and Charlotte would see the sights and have an enjoyable time. *Gringos on tour.*

CHAPTER 21

Little Pelican Cay, Caribbean Coast

The boat burrowed into the sand. Danny's momentary relief was overwhelmed by fear. Whoever was on the island would have heard the boat approaching. It had been difficult to land quietly on the island with the engines grinding away. He jumped from the boat onto the sand. It was challenging to see in the dark. He considered hiding in the mangroves or the palm trees but decided that there was realistically nowhere to run.

It was inevitable. After around fifteen minutes Danny saw two figures moving in the dark. They were walking towards him along the beach. This is it, thought Danny;

assaulted, imprisoned even murdered. He reached in the darkness for the Glock and kept it close.

The smaller of the figures shouted in Creole, "Who are you, what are you doing here?"

"My boat has problems; I have landed on your island by accident," said Danny.

The larger person said, "He also asked who you are?"

"I'm Danny McCoy from Pearl Lagoon," said Danny, trying to sound upbeat.

The two figures came closer, and Danny could just see their faces through the darkness. They were both of Creole descent.

The smaller person spoke, "I'm Kenner, I'm from Awas." His sweater stretched tightly across his chest. He was small, however his leg muscles bulged in the twilight.

The larger person spoke, "I'm Ruben, from Pearl Lagoon. I don't recognise you." Ruben was much taller and skinnier than Kenner, his t-shirt and shorts appeared to be two sizes too small for him.

"I left many years ago. Maybe you know the McCoy family, we lived on Central Avenue, close to the *King Marlin*," said Danny.

Ruben looked at him. "I vaguely remember the McCoys, didn't some of them speak the Miskito language?" said Ruben.

"Yes, my mother taught me and my brothers and sister," said Danny.

"Yes, I remember them. When I was young, people sometimes used to ask for their help when they wanted to talk with the Miskito people," said Ruben.

"Yes, it was usually about buying and selling stuff, or disputes," said Danny.

"It doesn't happen too much these days, as they all seem to speak Spanish," said Ruben. Danny thought that Ruben seemed the more communicative of the two of them.

Kenner said, "I am from Awas Tingi, I speak Garifuna, Miskito, Creole, standard English and Spanish." Ruben and Danny both stared at Kenner through the darkness.

Ruben interrupted the silence, "That's great Kenner, thanks for that. So, Danny, what is going on? What are you doing floating along the coast?"

"I'm transporting goods to Juticalpa Point," said Danny.

Ruben and Kenner looked at each other and then back at him.

"You are in a very dangerous place, Danny," said Ruben.

"What do you mean?"

"Kenner and I are not idiots. We know what you are doing."

"What am I doing?"

"You are smuggling cocaine up the coast to Honduras, this is very dangerous. I hope they are paying you a great deal of money because the risk is massive." There was a momentary silence between them.

"Where am I? What's the name of this place?" said Danny.

"This is *Little Pelican Cay*. We are the only people here. If you look over there to the west, you will see Pelican Island."

"So, who's on Pelican Island?"

"That's a luxury holiday resort, catering for rich Americans and people from Europe. Kenner and I both work on Pelican Island."

"So, what are you doing here?"

For the first time, Ruben didn't speak. Danny knew there was something going. Kenner said, "Ruben and I were fishing, our fishing gear is over there on the beach, next to our panga." Danny wasn't convinced; however, it was irrelevant what they were up to.

"I need your help. I have been shot in the shoulder and the boat is damaged. The windscreen has been shattered, but more important is that the fuel lines have been severed by gunfire," said Danny.

"You are in big trouble. The main problem you have is that the navy regularly patrols this area. They are not friendly. The navy will see your boat and will land here. They will arrest you. You will go to prison for a long time," said Ruben.

"I have cash, I can pay you."

"If we take your money and they find it, we will go to prison as accessories. You know that prison in Nicaragua is no joke," said Ruben.

"I can give you 2,000 U.S. dollars if you help me. I just need to get the boat repaired and medical attention for my shoulder."

Ruben and Kenner glanced at each other, then took a few steps back and started whispering to each other out of the earshot of Danny. The sun was rising. The fear and panic within Danny also started to rise.

"If you do not get treatment your wound will become infected," said Kenner.

"So, will you help me? I am not a stranger. I was born in Pearl lagoon. My home language is Creole. Please help one of your own," said Danny.

Kenner said "We both need to go back to work this morning. I am the groundsman and Ruben is a waiter on Pelican Island".

"Barman and Waiter," said Ruben.

"Sounds like Batman and Robin," laughed Kenner.

"Can I get over to Pelican Island?" said Danny.

"If you abandon your boat here it will definitely be spotted by the navy," said Ruben.

"I can't leave the boat. If I follow you across to Pelican Island, is there somewhere we could hide it?"

"$2,000?" said Ruben.

"Yes, I can hand it to you when the boat is fixed and my shoulder has been treated," said Danny.

"You will have to pay for the boat repairs and the medical treatment separately from our $2000," said Ruben.

"Yes, agreed, 100%."

"I have an idea where we could hide the boat on Pelican Island," said Kenner.

"The maintenance shack?" said Ruben.

"No, I have a better idea, one of the buildings," said Kenner.

"Ok, let's do this," said Ruben.

CHAPTER 22

They all walked over to the panga boat. Danny noticed that their fishing gear consisted of a few reels of fishing line, a bucket, and a bag of spark plugs. Children on the Miskito coast used spark plugs as weights for fishing. Danny glanced inside the bucket and saw that there were two small red snappers and one rainbow bass. A poor return for a night's fishing, thought Danny.

"We need to start heading towards Pelican Island. The sun is coming up fast. Let's get over there and hide the boat before anyone sees us. Your go-fast boat is very noisy, so only use one engine, keep the revs down and just follow us," said Kenner.

Danny watched their panga move slowly away. He had been fortunate. Little Pelican Cay could have been a small naval base and he would have been arrested, or worse. He was also lucky that Ruben and Kenner were willing to help him. He could have run into some dangerous people, who may have done him serious harm. Danny pushed the boat off the beach and into the sea, his shoulder was aching. He started one of the engines, and then followed the panga. His boat was in a bad state due to the villager's gunfire. Danny was desperately hoping that the boat could make it across to Pelican Island. The image of him drifting aimlessly across the Caribbean until the navy, or the piranhas, found him was his worst nightmare. The fear returned to his throat.

. . . .

The journey across to Pelican Island took twenty minutes, but to Danny it seemed like an eternity. As they approached the north of the island, Kenner waved and pointed in the direction of a group of buildings. The panga moved towards the water's edge, it beached, and Kenner and Ruben jumped out. One of the buildings was a covered mooring. It was exactly what Danny needed. He guided the boat straight into the building.

Kenner ran up to the boat and rapidly secured it to the dock pilings. The building was part of a floating dock.

Danny climbed out of the boat, making sure he had his binoculars, telescope, cash bag and the Glock. His shoulder was painful and stiff.

"You must show me which parts are needed for the boat. It's going to take time to arrange for these items. We should be able to go and buy them in Bluefields," said Kenner.

Ruben walked over to Danny.

"The main issue is your medical attention. Neither Kenner nor I have any knowledge in these matters. My friend on Pelican Island has had three years medical training, she may be able to inspect your wound and decide what is needed. The problem is that we will have to involve her in this situation. That's dangerous for her and for all of us. I'm not completely sure how she will respond, when I tell her what's going on," said Ruben.

"We are going to have to take a chance. Offer her $500," said Danny.

"Okay, I will speak to her. The further challenge we have is hiding you on the island for the next few days. The other staff cannot see you," said Ruben.

Kenner fully secured the boat and covered it with sheeting. He then walked back over to them.

"He can sleep in the building, right next to the boat. Nobody will come over here. I'm sure Danny wants to protect his valuable cargo," said Kenner.

"Yes, and we can bring you food and drinks whenever I can borrow them from the kitchen," said Ruben.

"You can wash in the large sink at the back of building. There is also a toilet." said Kenner.

"What a team," said Danny.

"We are your saviours, Danny, don't forget that," said Ruben.

As Danny walked back to the building, he caught site of Ruben and Kenner on the dock. They were standing close to one another, their faces nearly touching and whispering to each other. Danny suddenly realised why they had been on Little Pelican Cay, alone together.

CHAPTER 23

Intercontinental Hotel, Managua City

Augusto spotted Tico in the hotel lobby. He was fawning over a couple of well-healed guests. Once Tico had stopped licking their boots, he walked over to him.

"Hey Dude, how's the brownnose business?" said Augusto.

"If you look up the word *sycophant* in the Oxford English Dictionary you will see my photo," said Tico. They both laughed and shook hands.

"You certainly seem rested, but you look like a flood victim," said Tico.

"I know, I'm going home to Bluefields. I'll dump these clothes and put on a laundered and pressed navy uniform."

"I suggest you burn the clothes you're wearing."

"Thanks for the room. It gave me time to complete that urgent report. I've just emailed it to my boss."

"So, now you are a happy man, Senor."

"Nearly, I need one of your guys to drop me at the airport," said Augusto.

"Your photo is in the dictionary, next to the word *Pest*," said Tico.

. . . .

Augusto boarded the flight from Managua to Bluefields. It was an ageing propeller driven plane, with too many seats jammed inside. The pilots were sat directly in front of the passengers, with no screen to separate them. It was always an experience, thought Augusto.

As the flight progressed across Nicaragua, He looked out of the window. He could see Lake Nicaragua, a massive freshwater lake, the largest in Central America. He remembered that in the distant past, the *Sweet Sea*, as it was called, was infested with pirates. Augusto considered his homeland a beautiful country, with a fascinating history, and many ghosts.

When the battered old plane landed at Bluefields, Augusto thanked the pilots and headed towards his parked car. He drove to his house in the Old Cotton Tree district. When he arrived, he showered, shaved, cleaned his teeth, and changed into his clean uniform. He inspected his shoes, his belt buckle and combed his hair. He looked at himself in the full-length mirror and saluted,

"Sir, Lieutenant Commander Augusto Romero, Nicaraguan Navy, Caribbean Coast Region, Sir," hollered Augusto at his reflection.

CHAPTER 24

El Bluff, Nicaraguan Navy Base, Bluefields

Augusto boarded the navy patrol vessel at Bluefields harbour and disembarked 15 minutes later at El Bluff. As he entered the navy HQ office complex, he spotted a familiar face.

"Just the person I want to talk to. Good day Lieutenant Amander," said Augusto.

"Sir, Good day Lieutenant Commander. You have a visitor in your office," said Josue.

"In my office? Who?"

"Sir, your Uncle Dereck," said Josue, with a smirk.

"I'll catch up with you later Josue, after I've dealt with this troublemaker."

Augusto entered his office. It felt as though he had been away for weeks, not three days.

"*Naksa*, uncle, what a nice surprise," said Augusto.

His elderly relative rose from his seat. They hugged.

"*Naksa*, my nephew. Well, if it isn't the head of the Nicaraguan Navy himself, all dressed up and nowhere to go," said Uncle Dereck.

They exchanged friendly banter for the next ten minutes. Augusto thought it was nice to see his old uncle, however meetings with Uncle Dereck were never accidental.

"So, what brings this elder statesman to the madness that is Bluefields?"

"As you know nephew, I have strong connections to the rural areas. I am welcome as far as Monkey Point, Rama Cay and the Corn Islands."

"Yes uncle. All the people in the region hold you in high regard for all you have done for them. You are appreciated for the voice you have given them for many years."

"Thank you, nephew. Yes, I will speak truth to power," said his uncle. Augusto liked his Uncle Dereck, but Augusto thought that he was rather melodramatic, at times.

"I am here to inform you of an incident on the south coast," said Uncle Dereck.

"I'm up to speed on the current issues," said Augusto.

"The crew of one of your navy RIB boats assaulted the villagers of Aguila Creek."

"What? That's not true."

"Oh yes, I have reliable information."

"Is this reliable information or typical village gossip?"

"Nephew, you have the power. I will provide you with the truth. It is your decision what to do with that truth." He then gave a detailed account, beginning when the RIB entered the creek, until the RIB left.

"Okay, I have a few questions."

"Please proceed nephew, I will try to answer all your questions in full."

"Who was the Sergeant?" said Augusto, although he knew.

"Sergeant Gamboa, he is a menace."

"Apart from taking the fish, which was a gift according to your detailed account, did any of the other navy personnel do anything illegal?"

"No, only the Sergeant. He hit the headman and threatened to kill the child. He then fired his weapon at the panga boats, they are now severely damaged."

"He wasn't really serious about killing a child, was he?"

"Grabbing a child and putting a loaded pistol to her head is, without doubt, serious, nephew."

"Did a narco boat enter the creek?"

"Not as I am aware."

"That is an elder statesman's diplomatic answer."

"*Diplomacy is the art of saying nice doggie until you can find a rock*, that's a quote by a Cherokee Indian, Will Rogers." said Uncle Dereck.

"Yes, uncle, very smart. They were either hiding a narco boat or they weren't," said Augusto.

"Nephew, there is no honest work in this region. There is deep poverty here. There have been decades of neglect by the Spaniards in Managua. This has caused widespread resentment in the villages, in the lagoons and in Bluefields itself. Can you blame the communities for providing sustenance to the narco traffickers, for U.S. dollars?"

"Uncle, they do not understand the harm they are doing. The government of Nicaragua has placed a protective firewall around our country. Because of this protective firewall strategy, we have no drug gangs or cartels in Nicaragua. We have a very low murder rate, by international standards."

"Nephew, I understand that you are a senior man in the navy. But you need to see the facts. Aguila Creek is the most southernly of the Miskito villages. Why is it there? Miskito people cannot suddenly move south, into land that is not historically Miskito land. The government in Managua would not allow it. So, who encouraged them and gave the Miskito people permission to move south? There are stronger currents in the water than even you are aware of. They may inform you in Managua of these strategies, of how they are protecting all of these helpless people on the Caribbean coast, but you need to look at the facts."

"Which facts? Such as?"

"Drug addiction has become a growing problem, particularly in this region. In Bluefields we see drugs sold openly on the streets. There are crack houses in the town, you must know that."

"But that's what I mean, we need to catch these boats, seize their cargo, and keep cocaine out of Nicaragua."

"You and who's army? or should I say navy?"

Augusto knew that the traffickers were better equipped than the navy. They had satellite communication and night vision binoculars. The navy had a dilapidated bunch of vessels on the Caribbean coast, which were always breaking down. In fact, the navy was underfunded. The traffickers had go-fast boats that were powered by multiple three hundred horsepower motors, giving them a top speed of over 80mph. The navy patrol boats could never catch them.

They spoke about the villages in the north and their extended families for a while and then both hugged and shook hands.

Uncle Dereck left, having *spoken truth to power.*

Augusto was determined to deal with Sergeant Gamboa.

CHAPTER 25

"Lieutenant Amander, please can you come into my office?" said Augusto. Josue sat down in Augusto's office.

"Tell me again about Aquila Creek," said Augusto.

"Sir, as outlined in my report, we saw a sixth go-fast boat on the horizon. We guessed that it was heading towards Aquila Creek. So, I sent Sergeant Gamboa and his team in a RIB to investigate. Sergeant Gamboa reported that the Miskito villagers were very uncooperative. They said that they had not seen the go-fast boat."

"Is that it? Nothing else?"

"That's it, Sir. As I informed you previously, I therefore concluded that the go-fast boat had entered Punta Gorda, not

Aquila Creek. There was little opportunity to track it, so I returned my focus upon the go-fast boats that we had previously engaged. It's possible that this sixth boat had nothing to do with the five narco go-fast boats. It wasn't even in the convoy; it was much further behind."

"Ok Josue, fully understood. You did exactly what was required. Please can you locate Sergeant Gamboa and bring him to my office?" said Augusto.

. . . .

Thirty minutes later, Sergeant Gamboa and Lieutenant Amander were sat across from Augusto in his office.

"Sergeant Gamboa, tell me about Aquila Creek," said Augusto.

The Sergeant paused and then spoke, "Upon the orders of Lieutenant Amander, I investigated Aquila Creek. This was an attempt to locate the go-fast boat, that we thought had entered the creek. The villagers were unhelpful. We could not see any evidence of the go-fast boat, so we left."

"Is that it, Sergeant?" said Augusto.

"Yes Sir."

"What about the fish?"

"Sir?"

"If the Miskito villagers were uncooperative and unhelpful, how is it that they gave you their morning's catch?"

"Sir?"

"Yes, as I am the Lieutenant Commander, you should address me as Sir. However, you are also supposed to tell me what happened."

"The Indians offered us some of their fish."

"Before or after you threatened to shoot a child in the head?"

"Sir?"

"You are starting to piss me off Sergeant."

"Sir, it was just a tactic, to encourage the villagers to inform us about the boat."

"Tactic? Putting a loaded pistol to the head of a child? Tell me about when you hit the headman in the face. Was that also a *tactic*?"

"Sir, that was in response to him attacking me."

"An old Miskito headman attacked you? An armed navy Sergeant?"

"Yes Sir, he tried to wrestle my firearm away from me."

"Why would he do that?"

"I have no idea what these Indians are thinking about most of the time, Sir."

"These Indians?"

"Sir, you are local here, born and raised. You may understand them Sir, Me? I have no idea what they're thinking or what they even want, Sir."

"Tell me about the panga boats."

"Sir?"

"Sergeant, if you respond again with just Sir, you will be seconded to the remote navy pontoon at Maria Cay for seven days. Do you understand Sergeant?"

"Yes Sir, I understand."

"Good, let's try again. Tell me about the panga boats."

"Sir I have no knowledge of the panga boats at Aquila Creek, Sir."

"I am reliability informed that you fired bullets into the panga boats, therefore damaging them."

"No Sir, that's a lie."

"Lieutenant Amander will conduct a full investigation into these alleged incidents. He will interview the crew of the RIB on that day. He will go to Aquila Creek and interview the villagers, including the headman."

"Sir, with all due respect, Sir, that's a waste of navy time and resources, Sir. Would you believe these Indians and not me, Sir? A Sergeant Primo?"

"You Sergeant Gamboa, will go to the navy stores and collect rations for seven days. You will then go directly to

Bluefields harbour, sequester a navy RIB and go immediately to the remote navy pontoon at Maria Cay. You are seconded to Maria Cay for seven days. You will observe and monitor sea traffic, making copious notes related to possible narco go-fast boats in the vicinity. You can also record the weather and tide times if you so wish."

"But Sir, I answered fully, as you requested."

"Sergeant, I just don't believe you. When you are on Maria Cay you won't be able to influence the statements of the RIB crew. Once Lieutenant Amander completes his report, we will meet again. I'm already looking forward to it. Now, go directly to Maria Cay, do not pass Go, do not collect $200."

"Sir, this is unfair. I am doing my duty and having to deal daily with all these Indians and blacks."

"Sergeant Gamboa, I do not like your attitude. All the people on the Caribbean coast are Nicaraguans, and they will be treated as such. You are here to serve and protect. We are not an army of occupation."

"Sir, with all due respect, it is different for you. You are one of them. I just want to go back to my home city of Masaya. I didn't ask to be sent here, into the middle of nowhere. I was happy dealing with all those student demonstrations in the west."

"So, Sergeant Gamboa, we have you and your colleagues to thank for hundreds of dead and wounded?"

"They were protesting, spitting at us and then throwing petrol bombs. They attacked police stations. We dealt with them, they stopped rioting, Sir."

"So, Sergeant, you think an appropriate level of force was used upon the students?"

"Sir, yes Sir. They were being paid by the CIA to protest."

"Ah, the bogeyman that is forever the CIA."

"Sir, if it's not the CIA, it's probably some anti-FSLN dissidents or blacks and Indians behind it all."

"This is certainly a country with a distinct social, political and racial hierarchy. Everyone is equal, but some are more equal than others. I paraphrase Mr Orwell."

"Sir? Mr who?"

"George Orwell, Animal farm, the book," said Josue.

"Sir, I would like to apply for a transfer back to Masaya," said the Sergeant.

"Sergeant, a full report on the events at Aquila Creek will be prepared by Lieutenant Amander. If the report clarifies the situation, as I expect it will, you can then go back to Masaya as a citizen, because your navy days will be over."

CHAPTER 26

Masaya Volcano, Nicaragua

Espinoza peered over the rim of the volcano. The gases stung his nostrils, and he tasted sulphur on his tongue. He could see the fire inside the volcano cavern, the molten lava swirling and the acidic smoke rising.

He was aware that the volcano had always been a place of death. The Indigenous people believed that demons dwelt within the volcano. They had hurled people down into the boiling lava lake, to placate the malevolent spirits. Spanish conquistadors had positioned a Christian cross to face the yawning orifice of the volcano, to blockade the devil.

The place was locally known as *the Mouth of Hell*.

Espinoza was always amazed when he visited the area. He reflected that to see this dramatic site in its glory, you had to visit the volcano at night. Then you could see the swirling lava glow in the darkness. He struggled to comprehend that it was only twenty minutes' drive from Managua. Espinoza thought it was a wonderful day when the Nicaraguan government convinced the European Community in Brussels to fund the construction of a sealed road up to the volcano. Masaya was now one of the most accessible live volcanos in the world; you could reach the volcano rim by car, bicycle or even by foot. Espinoza continued to be in awe of the vista.

Espinoza wasn't surprised when he was requested by Colindres to come to Managua. Even so, he had to rapidly formulate a bogus reason for travelling. He certainly couldn't just inform people that he was meeting Colindres in Managua. It would raise too many questions. Although the navy and the Nicaraguan consulate in Mexico City were in regular communication, there was no official reason for Espinoza and Colindres to be meeting privately.

Only tourists came to the volcano; therefore, it was an ideal place to meet.

Espinoza saw Colindres arriving. He was driving his black BMW. Colindres obviously didn't even trust his own driver, thought Espinoza.

"A familiar face, in a familiar place," said Colindres as he walked over to Espinoza. He was dressed in a casual designer shirt, expensive imported jeans, and Italian leather shoes. Forever the Nicaraguan womaniser, thought Espinoza.

"It is great to see you again Pablo," said Espinoza.

"Likewise, Antonio," said Colindres.

They shook hands.

"I believe I know why you have dragged me back from the joys of Mexico City to our wonderful socialist republic."

"Careful, your sarcasm is starting to show."

"DEA, CIA, United States Coastguard, OCD-ETF. Where shall we begin?"

"Do we have anything to worry about regarding Senorita Walker, and her gang?" said Colindres.

"I doubt it. It's unlikely she is CIA; she's too open and communitive. She obviously forwards her reports to the CIA, but she's probably not guided by Langley."

"Yet, you still had her followed?"

"Yes, as my report states, she spent the afternoon and evening with Lieutenant Commander Augusto Romero. They just talked socially, discussing their backgrounds, but nothing of interest."

"Did they fuck?" said Espinoza.

"Highly probable. That doesn't interest me. She has identified the Caribbean coast route; how does this affect us?"

"I'm not sure it does."

"You must be concerned?" said Colindres.

"No, I have confidence that you will manage any issues that arise here in Managua."

"Well, yes, I've already met with our Lieutenant Commander. I challenged him regarding his loyalty," said Colindres.

"I don't think that's an issue. His family were true devotes to the Sandinista cause".

"Yes, I agree. I fed him the *protective firewall strategy*."

"Did he swallow that?"

"Yes, hook, line and spark plug sinker."

"It sounds as though he is one of Vladimir Lenin's *useful idiots*," said Espinoza, with a grin.

"Yes, I expect him to loudly espouse the protective firewall strategy, whilst chasing shadows and silhouettes up and down the Caribbean coast."

"Then he is definitely our man."

"The navy is so threadbare, lacking capital and operational funding, even Haiti could invade us and we wouldn't be able to defend ourselves" said Colindres.

"Maybe the CIA can arrange that."

They both smiled and suppressed their laughter. "So, what is happening in our villages?" said Espinoza.

"We have three and they are rapidly becoming fully operational. They're already refuelling boats and two of them are providing simple maintenance. They provide fresh water, local food and can store the cargo, if needed at short notice. The travellers can rest and recuperate after their difficult journeys."

"It seems to be working well. Any problems?"

"We had an incident a few days ago in Aguila Creek."

"That's the Miskito village south of Bluefields? The one we had to do *personal deals* to get established?" said Espinoza.

"Correct. The problem was that an unscheduled go-fast boat entered the creek, and the navy pursued them."

"So, what happened?"

"The villagers said that they had seen nothing."

"It's what they have been instructed to say. What happened then?"

"The navy intimidated the villagers, shot up their panga boats."

"That is stupid. What does that achieve?"

"Nothing, it just pisses off the villagers. The navy didn't catch the go-fast boat. It left a few hours later, undetected."

"Was it one of ours?" said Espinoza.

"I'm looking into it. It could just be miscommunication from Cartegena."

"They need to get fully organised. We don't want any issues with the villagers."

"It was reported that there was a shoot-out between the villagers and the go-fast boat as it departed. Nobody is talking."

"What? Was our village compromised in anyway?"

"No, it doesn't seem to be. The unidentified go-fast boat left the village without being observed by the navy."

"It's a mystery. We cannot let any other narco traffickers operate off our coast."

"Our coast? I thought you were from Granada?" said Colindres, with a smirk.

"It's our coast, we own it. We just make the appropriate personal deals."

"Yes, if they are not associated to us, then our navy takes them out. Simple as that."

"*Protective firewall strategy,*" said Espinoza.

They both laughed. The remaining tourists viewing the volcano looked over at them. Espinoza peered again into the volcano. "There is an urban myth that the Somoza regime used to drop dissidents, from a helicopter, into the volcano."

"Not sure it was a myth."

"Their death would have been very quick, no time for pain. But being aware what was about to happen to you, the dread, the terror. That must have been the real torture," said Espinoza.

"Better them than me," said Colindres.

CHAPTER 27

Intercontinental Hotel, Managua City

Tico spotted Paul and Charlotte heading towards the hotel reception desk. "My friends from Great Britain. How was your VIP tour of Managua?"

"It was fascinating, thank you for organising it," said Paul.

"No problem, my friends. Did you go to the lake?" said Tico.

"Yes, there weren't many people around. I was told by the guide that no one goes fishing in the lake," said Paul.

"Lake Managua is the most contaminated lake in Central America. The lake has been severely polluted by all the sewerage dumped into it over many years," said Tico.

"That's unbelievable," said Paul.

"Nothing is unbelievable in Nicaragua. Some local people do still fish in the lake. However, I would not recommend eating any fish caught in Lake Managua."

"We will try not to," said Charlotte, with a grimace.

Where else did you go?" said Tico.

"We saw the Old Cathedral," said Paul.

"Yes, that's quite spectacular. It was devastated by an earthquake in 1972."

"We also visited the National Palace of Culture. I was astonished that they didn't seem to consider the Spanish colonial period as being worthy of elaborating upon," said Paul.

"Nicaraguans came directly from heaven, the Spanish weren't involved," said Tico.

"We also went to the volcano, which was amazing," said Paul.

"I assume you went to Masaya Volcano. Nicaragua has nineteen active volcanos; the country is close to uninhabitable."

"Yes, Masaya. It was incredible. To see all the molten lava, the smoke and to smell the sulphur. There were two guys poised on the volcano rim and they were both laughing. I couldn't believe it. They were a few steps from oblivion," said Paul.

"They were probably Nicaraguans. When your lake is polluted, your cathedral is wrecked and your socialist revolution has run out of steam, I suppose that standing on the edge of a live volcano is amusing. It might be a case of *we have nothing left to lose, so why worry*?"

"Tico, I'm rather doubtful that you should apply for any future job with the Nicaraguan Tourist Board," said Paul.

. . . .

Tico arranged a taxi to take Paul and Charlotte to Managua airport. Porters were loading their luggage into taxi, and Tico said,

"Have a great time over on the Caribbean Coast, it is the most wonderful part of Nicaragua."

"We're really looking forward to visiting Bluefields and then going over to Pelican Island." said Paul.

"Pelican Island is fantastic, but Bluefields? It's an absolute car crash. I'm not sure what Augusto has told you, but there is nothing to see in Bluefields."

"Augusto? Who?"

"Lieutenant Commander Romero, Mr Navy."

"Oh yes. We met him in the Metrocentre Mall. We also noticed each other in Mexico City," said Paul."

Tico said, "Interesting. Just one thing about Augusto, He is a Bluefields Caribbean guy. They are very dodgy characters. Keep him away from Mrs Charlotte."

"That is exactly what he said about you," said Paul, with a smirk on his face.

CHAPTER 28

Paul and Charlotte boarded the flight to Bluefields. They wedged themselves into one of the twelve cramped plane seats. Throughout the flight they both looked nervously towards the pilots, who were almost sat next to them. The aircraft was old, however all the local passengers seemed unaware or unconcerned with the potential for imminent death. Another case of *we have nothing left to lose, so why worry*? thought Paul.

The plane landed and came to a sudden halt at the Bluefields airport terminal. Paul and Charlotte disembarked from the plane. They both laughed when they saw a crate containing live chickens being retrieved from the aircraft hold.

They saw a guy carrying a Pelican Island sign, so they waved to him. He was wearing a baseball cap on backwards. As he approached them they noted that he was wearing Oakly reflective sunglasses, that were badly scratched.

"Hi I'm Ruben. Welcome to Bluefields. You are Mrs Charlotte and Mr Paul?" said Ruben. Paul noticed that Ruben spoke with a Jamaican, Bob Marley-type of English accent.

"Hi, Yes I'm Paul, this is my wife Charlotte," said Paul. They all shook hands.

"I'm going to drive you through Bluefields, on the way to the harbour. Once we arrive, we'll board a panga boat. A panga is a local and very safe form of transport. Then we will make our way to Pelican Island, where your real vacation begins," said Ruben.

Ruben drove them through Bluefields towards the harbour. Many of the houses and shops had corrugated roofs. The roads were jammed with people walking around. Vendors were selling fresh fish in the street. Schoolchildren, all dressed in their uniforms, crammed the sidewalks.

Occasionally, Paul spotted a horse drawn cart. He noticed that the banks had armed guards, with shotguns, stationed outside their front doors. He observed that the population was much more diverse than Managua. Music was playing everywhere, houses were painted in bright bold colours, there appeared to be a strong Afro-Caribbean influence here. Paul loved it.

When they arrived at the harbour, Paul and Charlotte seemed to be an attraction themselves. Local people called out to them saying *Hi* and *Welcome*. Local children came up as close as they dared and studied them.

Ruben ensured that the luggage was loaded on the panga boat and that Paul and Charlotte put on their lifejackets. As they eased out of the harbour, Paul saw that there were several rusting and grounded ships in the harbour. The vessels appeared to have been stranded there for many years.

The sea was a beautiful cobalt colour. They passed numerous palm strewed islands, which seemed to be uninhabited. More islands were dotted across the horizon and brightly coloured birdlife was everywhere. Sea salt coated their faces as the panga gathered speed. The mainland on their left, seemed a foreboding and threatening place to Paul. The sun beat down relentlessly on the uncovered panga.

After about an hour, the boat glided towards Pelican Island. Paul and Charlotte spotted people stood on the pier. As the boat got closer, they could see that it was a group of employees in their white uniforms. They were all waving.

"It is my co-workers. They are welcoming you to Pelican Island," said Ruben.

"That's very lovely," said Charlotte.

Ruben said, "Yes, I know that they are waving to you, because they are never that happy to see me." Charlotte laughed.

This is going to be an experience of a lifetime, thought Paul.

CHAPTER 29

Pelican Island, Caribbean Coast

Beads of sweat trickled down Danny's neck. He didn't feel well, he felt sick. As he lay on the dirty mattress that Kenner had provided, he contemplated the nightmare he was in.

He was on this remote, God-forsaken Island, with a gunshot wound in his shoulder. He was sleeping next to a boat holding bales of cocaine. He had $5,000, a Glock handgun, a pair of binoculars and a telescope to his name. His actions had nearly gotten the Miskito villagers killed by a crazy Nicaraguan Navy Sergeant. The villagers then decided to shoot him and rob him. His boat was damaged, and worst of all, he couldn't escape this place.

Danny feared that the navy would appear at any moment and arrest him, that would lead to at least 10 years in a hellhole of a Nicaraguan prison. He was terrified that other narco traffickers would arrive, kill him, and take his cargo. Also, they could come to the island and just steal the bales. This would result in him being murdered by El Jefe and his men, if he ever got back to Cartagena. They would also kill Cristiano. Their heads would be used as props at the next narco traffickers' recruitment seminar.

He was now subject to the whim of two young guys, who could betray him at any moment. They might also try to kill him, although he did have the Glock. He was now waiting for a visit from a semi-trained nurse to save his life.

He had never felt so alone or vulnerable.

. . . .

There was a knock on the building door.

"Hello Mr Danny, this is Ruben here, don't shoot."

"Come in Ruben."

He walked into the building, closely followed by a young creole woman. Danny estimated that she was about twenty-eight years old, maximum. Her dark hair pulled back and clipped tight to her head. She was slim and was tiny compared to the height of Ruben. Danny thought that she was very pretty.

"This is Fiona. She has medical training; she will look at your wound," said Ruben.

"Hi Fiona, thanks for helping me. It's appreciated," said Danny.

"Mr Danny, please sit down and show me where you are injured," said Fiona. Danny sat on the chair and then started to remove his shirt delicately.

"I assume Ruben has spoken to you about the $500?" said Danny.

"Mr Danny, I do not want your money. I am inspecting your wound because I have taken an oath, I have devoted myself to the welfare of those committed to my care," said Fiona. Danny thought it was an inconvenient time to ask why a well-trained and ethical nurse was working on Pelican Island.

Fiona put on a pair of green, thin rubber gloves. She insisted that Danny sit very still as she looked closely at his shoulder. She took her time and inspected the wound.

"Am I going to die Nurse Fiona?" said Danny.

"We all die one day, Mr Danny."

"A comedian, that's all I need."

"And please don't call me Nurse Fiona," she said.

"Ok, whatever, Doctor Fiona."

"Fiona is fine. A gunshot to the shoulder is dangerous and can be lethal. Shoulders contain the subclavian artery, which feeds the brachial artery. The brachial artery is the main artery of the arm. I do not need to explain to you what would happen if you were on a remote island in the Caribbean and your brachial artery was pierced," said Fiona.

"I'm assuming that we wouldn't be talking right now."

"The shoulder also contains the brachial plexus, which is a large bundle of nerves that controls your arm. Mr Danny, please clench you fist."

Danny made a fist and groaned.

"That hurt."

"Please move your arm and bend it simultaneously, Mr Danny."

Danny did as he was instructed. Sharp pangs of pain shot through his shoulder and upper back.

"Oh God," said Danny, as beads of sweat appeared on his forehead.

"Okay, no serious nerve damage or muscular injury, as I can see. If the brachial plexus were damaged, you would need surgery. If the bullet had hit the joint between the humeral head and the glenoid fossa, it would certainly need replacement or repair. That is not a procedure we offer on Pelican Island, even with medical insurance."

"Now she *is* a comedian," said Danny.

"The Nicaraguan prison system may offer you this procedure, but I doubt it," she said, with a grin.

"She likes to tell it as it is," said Ruben.

"Okay, good news then bad news Mr Danny. With my very limited visual assessment, I would say that there does not seem to be any damage to the subclavian artery. If there was, then there would be a much greater loss of blood. There also does not seem to be much, or any, damage to the brachial plexus, because you seem to have full functionality and movement of the arm."

"The bad news?" said Danny.

"Looking at the wound, I would say it was a .22 calibre bullet. If it was a 9mm or a .45, there would be much more damage and maybe an exit wound. Yes, I would say a .22, from a hunting rifle, it's difficult to say. It's all immaterial now. You got shot."

"You talk more like a detective, than a nurse. Anyway, that doesn't sound too bad," said Danny.

"The bad news is that the bullet is still embedded in your shoulder. Ideally, it should be extracted, if it is not situated close to an artery or crucial nerves."

"Won't he get lead poisoning if it stays in?" said Ruben.

"That's the least of his worries, lead poisoning takes a very long time. The biggest risk we have here is infection," said Fiona.

"So, what happens next, Fiona," said Danny.

"I can clean and dress the wound, but you need antibiotics and proper pain relievers."

"That's typical, I've just come back from Bluefields. I could have bought that stuff there," said Ruben.

"When are you planning to go back?" said Fiona.

"Tomorrow, I have to collect some more guests," said Ruben.

"Is Kenner planning to go home to Awas?" said Fiona.

"No, but we were going to Bluefields to buy some parts for the boat," said Ruben. Fiona glared at Ruben; she didn't blink. A stone-cold stare. Ruben looked away.

Danny sensed the tension. "I'm just an honest guy, who is having to do something dishonest, to get a break," said Danny.

"Aren't we all?" said Ruben.

Fiona turned around to Danny, "Mr Danny, I will make you as comfortable as possible. Ruben and Kenner will buy the medical items tomorrow from Bluefields," said Fiona.

"I feel as though I am in safe hands," grinned Danny.

"Mr Danny, please do not underestimate what has happened to you. Acute injury to the shoulder can lead to the loss of the arm. Infection is a major complication in gunshot victims, especially when there is an incomplete removal of foreign bodies."

"Now you are talking like a doctor," said Danny, with a grin.

"That's a different story, for another day, Mr Danny," said Fiona.

CHAPTER 30

Bluefields

Augusto looked out across Bluefields Bay. He could see El Bluff receding in the distance. Visiting grief-stricken families was dreadful, thought Augusto. He disembarked from the navy patrol vessel at Bluefields harbour and walked over to his parked car. He then drove to the Santa Rosa district, to fulfil his duty.

He located the house. It was close to the Malecon in Santa Rosa. He noticed that the house had a corrugated tin roof, and the exterior walls were bright yellow, and were peeling. He walked up and knocked on the door. A woman, in her late twenties with a weary face, observed him through the door mesh.

"Mrs Centeno? I'm Lieutenant Commander Augusto Romero, Nicaraguan Navy, Caribbean Coast Region. Your late husband's commanding officer." She looked at Augusto blankly. Her long unkept hair drooped into her eyes and across her face, slightly concealing her faint creole features.

"Please come in," said Mrs Centeno.

Mrs Centeno invited Augusto to take a seat and offered him a drink.

"I am happy with anything, water is fine," said Augusto.

Mrs Centeno returned from the kitchen with two plastic bottles of mineral water. Mrs Centeno had the physique of a woman who had recently been through childbirth, thought Augusto.

"I understand that you have two children Mrs Centeno," said Augusto.

"Yes, Jareth is at school and baby Francisco is with my mother today."

"Two boys, they must be a handful."

"They certainly are, and it is going to get more difficult now that Rafael has passed."

Augusto spoke "Your husband, Seaman Rafael Centeno was bravely serving on NN-89678, a Nicaraguan Navy vessel stationed at El Bluff. The vessel he was serving upon had an engagement with several go-fast boats, that we suspect were being used by narco traffickers. The engagement was south of Bluefields, around Punta Gorda. The suspected narco traffickers open fire upon the two navy vessels. Tragically, your husband, Rafael, was shot in the chest by gunfire from the go-fast boats. The wound was fatal, and he died instantly. I have been assured that he did not suffer."

Mrs Centeno was silent. She just looked down at the floor.

"Mrs Centeno, the Nicaraguan Navy is in your debt. Your husband has given his life for the Republic of Nicaragua, he will not be forgotten."

Mrs Centeno did not move. She continued looking at the floor, she resembled a statue, thought Augusto.

"Mrs Centeno, the navy will pay for all of your husband's funeral costs. You will be given, within 30 days, an ex-gratia payment that equates to three months of Romero's basic pay. You will also receive a monthly pension that begins the end of next month. Any issues or difficulties you may have receiving these payments, please contact me directly," said Augusto. He offered his business card to Mrs Centeno. She remained very still, frozen. He placed the business card on the battered table in front of them.

After a period of silence, she spoke, "Lieutenant Commander, Rafael has died for nothing."

"Mrs Centeno, He was serving his country. I know he was proud to be a navy sailor; I spoke to him occasionally, when we on manoeuvres."

She responded, "I have an education, I graduated from Managua University with a degree in Sociology. Rafael didn't get the opportunity to study at a higher level. He could not get a job anywhere else. In Nicaragua, a man's choices are baseball player, construction work or repairing boats. All the well-paid jobs here on the Caribbean Coast are illegal jobs, smuggling, stealing, unlawful fishing and prohibited logging."

Augusto said, "Tourism is increasing and that will bring many jobs. I expect your children's generation to benefit from tourism."

"The tourists have stopped coming to Nicaragua since the government in Managua shot all the students in Granada and Managua." Mrs Centeno continued, "these demonstrations and killings have frightened away the tourists. There are thousands of our own people hiding in Costa Rica. One of the senior protestors said that the government was hunting them, like deer."

"The government response to the student protesters was an over-reaction," said Augusto.

"Over-reaction? Hundreds dead and wounded," said Mrs Centeno. "In May 2018, Mother's Day, thousands of people marched to honour the mothers of the dead students. The marchers were attacked by the police shooting into the crowd and snipers firing from the roof of the national baseball stadium. Sixteen killed and many injured," she said.

Augusto remembered the incident; it had been called the *Mother's Day Massacre*. Augusto recalled rumours that the government forces progressed from using tear gas and rubber bullets, to real bullets and then finally military-level weapons.

"Nicaragua is two countries. The Pacific people over there in Managua, Granada and Leon, they have all the money, all the jobs, all the government benefits. Us, the people on the Caribbean coast, we have no money and no jobs. The authorities always ignore us," said an angry Mrs Centeno.

"We now have the Carretera Highway between Managua and the Caribbean coast, which should open things up," said Augusto.

"The government in Managua are only interested in the fish and seafood from over here. They have polluted their own lakes, they now wanted to take our livelihood."

"The Carretera will provide business opportunities and jobs for our people here in Bluefields and the surrounding region."

She responded, "The government in Managua wanted the Carretera so that they can move illegal drugs. The drugs find their way to the Pan-America Highway and then on to Mexico. You are an smart man; you know this is true."

"It is not government policy to assist the narco traffickers. It cannot be the reason the government sought funding from the Inter-American Development Bank and the World Bank. What? To build a Carretera across our country, to assist the South American drug cartels? That's from some internet conspiracy website, I'm sorry Mrs Centeno," said Augusto.

"Some people in the government are in league with the drug cartels. It is staring you in the face. Rafael told me that the navy vessels based at El Bluff are a joke. He said they are old, keep breaking down and that they have no spare parts. He said that you couldn't catch the go-fast boats, even if you wanted."

"It is true that we are underfunded. But money is tight in Nicaragua, we still have USA and OAS *Organisation of American States* sanctions against us," said Augusto. "Mrs Centeno, I am a public servant, an officer in the Nicaraguan Navy. My position is to continue and do that the best I can, with the resources I have been provided with."

"I understand your position. You should understand mine. My husband is dead. I am not sure what he died for."

"I am very sorry. I understand your grief and anger," said Augusto.

Mrs Centeno said, "Maybe you do. But listen to this and listen well; The only opportunity for the poor and forgotten people on the Caribbean coast, is that we assist the narco traffickers or we go fishing for White Lobster."

CHAPTER 31

Outside Mrs Centeno's house, Augusto sat exhausted and silent in his car. He stared vacantly at the dashboard. Then his mobile phone vibrated suddenly. It shook him from his stupor. It was a message on WhatsApp.

hi, it's me, mustang. u got time to talk?

He was pleased that she had reached out to him, he liked her. However, communicating unofficially with her, via any medium, could seriously damage his career. But he was intrigued as to what she wanted to talk about.

hi mustang. call me now. karl marx

He waited. His phone buzzed.

"Hi Karl Marx, how's it going?" she said.

"Another happy day in our socialist paradise, Mustang. How's it up there in your Imperialist Empire?"

"I'm actually down in your *hood*. I'm in Costa Rica."

"Costa Rica? Where? San Jose?"

"Nope, I'm very close to your homeland, you should have picked up my scent," she chuckled. "Greytown is on your turf, isn't it?"

"It most certainly is, Mustang. New Greytown is in the Caribbean Coast Region, we call it San Juan de Nicaragua."

"Whatever Karl Marx, call it what you want, let's meet there."

"When do you want to get together?"

"Let's meet tomorrow. Head down to the border and I will contact you regarding the exact place for our liaison."

"I could come down their tomorrow. But why should I, Mustang?"

"I have some information that will enhance your perspective."

"Why can't you tell me now, on the phone?"

"Listen Karl Marx, this could go on all day and night, it's always questions with you. Come down to Greytown, or San Juan, or whatever you are calling it this week. I'll share this information with you directly, face to face."

"So, it's ok for me to inform my Commanding Officer and tell him that the DEA have contacted me, and are offering to provide me with key information?"

"I don't recommend you do that, for your own safety."

"My own safety, Mustang? What do you mean by that?"

"Come down to Greytown, Karl Marx. Then you can figure out if you're in danger or not. But you are, I'm certain."

Part Two

White Lobster

CHAPTER 32

Pelican Island

Paul and Charlotte clambered out of the panga boat, helped by the Pelican Island employees. They were handed cocktails and their luggage was carried to dry land. Paul observed that Ruben had already left them and was running towards some huts in the distance. From within the group of Pelican Island employees, a man burst forward with his hand outstretched.

"Good afternoon, welcome to Pelican Island. I am Jannie van Rensburg, the Manager," said Jannie. He had a very friendly and courteous manner. His red bulbous nose, combined with his Afrikaans accent, revealed him as a potentially hard drinking South African.

Jannie ushered Paul and Charlotte to the bar next to the swimming pool. He ordered more cocktails. He explained that there were only three guest suites on the island, numbered 1 to 3. Paul and Charlotte had been allocated Suite 3. He informed them that their luggage had been taken to their suite and shouldn't worry. Jannie explained that dinner would be served at 7pm at the Astral restaurant. They could now rest and unwind until this evening.

Jannie's final comment was, "and don't forget, it's a free bar, so enjoy yourselves."

Paul was even more convinced that they were going to have a fun time on the island.

CHAPTER 33

Paul and Charlotte arrived at the Astral restaurant at 7pm. Jannie invited them to have pre-dinner cocktail at the restaurant bar. Jannie introduced them to two other guests, who were seated at the bar.

"This is Todd and Becky from the United States, they arrived yesterday," said Jannie. Everybody shook hands and exchanged pleasantries. Todd explained that he and Becky had been on vacation in Costa Rica and that on an impulse decided to cross the border and visit Nicaragua. They had taken a bus from Liberia in Costa Rica to Managua. Todd said that it had been quite an experience.

"The bus broke down before we even reached the border. I'll be honest, we had serious thoughts whether we were doing the right thing," said Todd. They made it to the border and then managed to plough through the dual nation bureaucracy at passport control and customs.

"I'm not sure the Nicaraguan immigration officials are that keen on American tourists," said Becky.

They had dinner together and it was an enjoyable evening. Todd was a freelance TV broadcast engineer in the United States. He was a technical guy dealing with outside broadcasts, microwave, and satellite communication. He explained that his *alma mater* was the University of Georgia and that is where Becky and he had met. They had married and now lived in Colliers Hills, Atlanta. Becky was a geography teacher for 11th & 12th grades in Midtown, Atlanta.

Once the serious drinking began, Todd and Becky burst into the song *Glory, Glory,* and a butchered version of something called the *Battle Hymn of the Bulldog Nation,* plus random shouts of *Go Bulldogs*. Paul responded with the songs *Blue Moon* and an equally indecipherable, *the best team in the land and all the world*, both well-known songs to Manchester City football supporters. Charlotte was embarrassed and bemused. Jannie kept drinking and was enjoying himself. "This is lekker," said Jannie. Paul had no idea what that meant.

. . . .

When Ruben served them all breakfast in the morning, there were a few sore heads. Charlotte thought that both Todd and Becky looked a little green around the gills, whilst Paul picked at his breakfast and drank copious amounts of mineral water.

A cheerful and energetic Jannie appeared. Paul pondered why is it that people who drink the most seem to never have hangovers?

"So, my valued guests, what are your plans today? You can visit our sports hut, grab a kayak and row around the island. Or you can go snorkelling, or fishing. You could go on a trek with Ruben to Bluefields for a coastal cruise and view the Miskito coast villages along the way. So, wat se jy?" said Jannie.

"I'm assuming you are asking what we want to do?" said Paul.

"Ya, that's correct."

Charlotte and Becky decided that they were going to sunbathe and enhance their tans. As neither Paul nor Todd fancied laying in the heat with their hangovers, they opted to *trek* with Ruben to Bluefields.

"You will need to take your ID with you," said Jannie. "You may be stopped by the police at the harbour. It's no big deal, just routine. Passports are preferred."

Although he had a hangover, Paul was excited to have the opportunity to explore Bluefields. He expected it to be authentic Nicaragua, the real deal.

CHAPTER 34

Ruben edged the panga away from the Pelican Island pier. He seated Paul and Todd in the front of the boat, suitably attired in lifejackets. It would not be acceptable for paying guests to drown on his watch. Kenner was also on-board and sat next to Ruben.

Fiona had given Ruben the list of items she required. He would therefore have to go to the Pharmacy Genna, which was just off Calle Cabezas. Kenner and Danny had agreed upon which parts were necessary for the boat repairs.

. . . .

The Sergeant was furious about being marooned on Maria Cay. That officer Romero, he was a Creole, Black, Indian, half-breed bastard. He took another swig of *Flor de Cana*. The Sergeant scanned the horizon through his navy binoculars.

He spotted the panga too late. He would have jumped into the navy RIB and intercepted them. However, he was not dressed. He didn't have his boots on and was stripped to the waist. He deduced that the panga had left from Pelican Island or Little Pelican. He took another swig of *Flor de Cana*, snorted a small amount of pure cocaine, and bided his time.

He would intercept them on their return journey.

CHAPTER 35

Bluefields

They docked at Bluefields harbour. Ruben explained to Paul and Todd that he must visit the pharmacy and that Kenner had to collect items from the marine hardware store. He said that he also would have to go and collect two guests, who were arriving at Bluefields Airport.

Paul suggested that, if Ruben considered it sensible, Todd and himself could wander around town and have a beer, or a coffee, somewhere. Ruben reassured them they were very safe, their plan sounded fine and that they could all meet in two hours at the harbour.

. . . .

Ruben entered Pharmacy Geena and looked for a pharmacist. He identified a young woman called Maria Elena. He vaguely knew her from school in Pearl Lagoon. She smiled at Ruben and ask how she could help him. Ruben passed her the list of items that Fiona had requested; Antibiotics; Ampicillin, and Clindamycin. He also needed bandages, sterile gauze, tape, disposable gloves, and pain medicine; Celerex or Ultram.

Maria Elena looked at the list and then asked Ruben to step into a separate area, where they could talk privately.

"Who and what wound are you trying to treat with these items?"

"Out at Pelican Island, one of the guests has had a minor injury."

"This doesn't seem minor; antibiotics, painkillers?"

"Our nurse has assessed the injury. If she can obtain these items, then she has said that the patient will be okay."

"Nurse? Which nurse? This patient needs to see a doctor."

"I am just a bartender and waiter; I don't know anything about medicine. I have just been requested to collect these items."

"You said it was a guest. An overseas guest? A foreigner?". "Yes, a tourist, an American," said Ruben.

"Ruben, this is serious. If an American tourist has been hurt, then we could all be in trouble. We need to do the right thing. Have you reported this to the police?"

"Maria Elena, let's not involve the police. I just need to purchase these items and take them back to Pelican Island."

"Ruben, you shouldn't get involved in this situation. It is dangerous."

"Maria Elena, I am already involved. Please help me."

Ruben saw that she was scanning the pharmacy, in a hushed voice she said, "You came into the pharmacy. You handed me the list. I gave you the items. You paid and left. That's it. We did not have this discussion, understood?"

"Yes, understood. We did not have this discussion. Thank you very much, Maria Elena."

"Ruben, you are swimming in treacherous waters," she said.

. . . .

Paul and Todd wandered around Bluefields. There wasn't too much for a tourist to see. Paul thought that The Moravian Church was quite interesting. They grabbed a couple of cold beers at the Hotel Oasis overlooking the Ferry Terminal.

"This area is quite different from Managua. It seems bizarrely like a Caribbean Island tacked onto Nicaragua. It could be another country," said Paul.

At a table close to Todd and Paul some local guys were drinking beer. One of them spotted Paul and Todd, "Hi guys, where are you from? Are you tourists?"

"Yes, we are staying on Pelican Island. Todd here is American, I'm from the UK," said Paul.

The oldest of the local guys spoke " It's nice that you are here. Welcome to Bluefields."

"Thanks for your kind words. I was just saying that Bluefields and the Caribbean Coast seems like a different country from Managua," said Paul.

"That's because it was," said one of the men. "Bluefields is named after a Dutch pirate called Blauvelt. Pirates lived on this coast for some time. The Dutch, French and English pirates who lived on this coast gave the Spaniards hell for many years."

"That's very intriguing," said Paul.

Another of the men said "Then the Americans came. The U.S Marines kept invading and occupied the region for so long, that the Nicaraguan national sport became baseball. You can still hear country music to this day being played by the people on the Caribbean Coast."

"That's amazing. It's like a neglected piece of history," said Paul.

"Yes, we have been forgotten by the British, the Americans and now our own government," said one of the other guys, they all started laughing.

"Let's all drink to living in the moment," said the old guy.

They all said cheers. Paul bought a round of cold beers, which he passed to them, with smiles all around. They drank the beers and shared local stories. Just before Paul and Todd left for the harbour, one guy asked, "Have you heard about White Lobster?"

'No, what's that? Is it a delicacy?" said Paul. The local guys burst out laughing.

"Ask the employees at Pelican Island."

"We will. Hopefully, we can try it," said Paul.

The local guys roared with laughter.

CHAPTER 36

Paul and Todd strolled back to Bluefields harbour. The beers had made them lightheaded and giddy. Paul spotted Ruben and Kenner stood next to their panga. There was a European couple talking to them.

"Mr Paul, Mr Todd, please can I introduce you to Mr Graham and Mrs Beverley, they are Pelican Island guests who have just arrived from the UK," said Ruben.

Graham was even taller than Ruben. Paul noticed that an extra hole had been amateurly punched into his belt to cope with his girth. He was a big man. Beverly was minute in comparison. Paul felt sympathy for her.

"I'm Graham and this is Bev, my girlfriend. We're from Yorkshire, England, God's country," said Graham. Paul suppressed the urge to laugh. They all greeted each other and shook hands.

Ruben insisted that everyone wore lifejackets. Ruben helped Graham to fasten his lifejacket. Paul noticed that Ruben positioned the passengers strategically, ensuring that Graham's weight was counterbalanced by Todd, Kenner, Bev and himself. Ruben gunned the panga away from the harbour and Bluefields started to rapidly fade into the distance.

Paul was captivated by the cobalt-blue Caribbean Sea and the scattering of the remote deserted islands. He felt that he was meant to be here, it was his destiny.

. . . .

They were approximately twenty minutes from arriving at Pelican Island when a vessel appeared on their right-hand side. It was still quite a distance away, however Ruben slowed down.

"Why are you slowing down?" shouted Graham, over the noise of the engines.

"It's a navy vessel, Mr Graham. Nothing to worry about. They just want to speak to us," said Ruben.

"Speak to us about what?" said Graham.

"Please Mr Graham, let me deal with this."

The navy RIB edged towards the panga. The Sergeant spoke in Spanish. "Who are you? Where are you going?"

"I am Ruben Downs; I work at Pelican Island. My passengers are overseas tourists, guests at Pelican Island."

"I know you from Bluefields. You are one of those gay guys," said the Sergeant.

"Sergeant, I am transporting these overseas tourists to Pelican Island. We need to ensure that they are safe and that no harm comes to them," said Ruben.

"Follow me to the navy base at Maria Cay," said the Sergeant.

"But Sergeant, I need to get these overseas tourists safely to Pelican Island."

The Sergeant raised his AK47 and pointed it directly at Ruben. "You will follow me, now."

CHAPTER 37

Maria Cay, Nicaraguan Caribbean Coast

Paul studied the small island as they got closer. There was large wooden sign, with a background of blue paint peeling in the salty sea air; *Armada de Nicaragua 1er Batallon de Marina de Nicaragua. Orgullo, Partiotismo, Honesto.* There was a skinny brown dog sleeping beneath the sign.

The Sergeant beached his navy RIB and promptly jumped out on to the sand, AK47 in one hand. He wore a blue camouflaged uniform, with three yellow stripes prominent on both his shoulders. As Ruben steered the panga towards the beach, the Sergeant pointed at everyone, and then gesticulated to indicate that every passenger should vacate the boat.

"What is this all this about?" said Graham.

"Mr Graham, please do as the Sergeant says. I will deal with him and then we can be on our way," said Ruben.

All the passengers disembarked the panga. Ruben and Kenner walked over to the Sergeant and engaged him in conversation. To Paul, it sounded as though they were speaking in Spanish.

"I used to be able to speak Spanish fluently," said Graham. Paul was having doubts about Graham.

Ruben returned to the four guests. "He wants to see your passports," said Ruben.

"Why does he want to see our passports?" said Graham.

"He just wants to inspect them," said Ruben.

"This is a pain. Mine and Bev's are in the suitcase," said Graham.

"Just do as he says, Graham," said Paul "He's the one with an automatic rifle."

"I'm a British Citizen. He can't push me around," said Graham.

"Please Mr Graham, gather your passports and then you and Mrs Beverley can proceed to Pelican Island and have cocktails," said Ruben.

Graham reluctantly waded out to the panga and retrieved their passports. Ruben passed the four passports to the Sergeant. He studied them intensely.

The Sergeant then spoke "puedes hablar espanol?" Paul knew what that meant. There were various calls of, "No" or "Sorry No." Paul noted that Graham also said no, obviously fluent means a different thing in Yorkshire, thought Paul.

The Sergeant approached them. As he got close to the guests, Paul could see that his eyes were bloodshot and that there was a distinct smell of alcohol. The Sergeant looked at the photo page of each of the UK passports and handed them back to each specific person. When he handed Bev's passport to her, he smiled. Paul thought it was more of a lecherous grin. He noticed that the Sergeant needed significant dental work.

The Sergeant held Todd's U.S. passport in front of him.

"CIA?" said the Sergeant to Todd.

Todd started to laugh "Definitely not, Sir."

"Why you think this funny?" he said in English.

"I'm not CIA. I work in broadcasting."

"Broadcasting? Spy satellites?"

"No, TV. CNN, global news, that type of genre."

"I no comprehendo. Fox news?"

"I have done freelance work for them, sure," said Todd.

Paul thought that the Sergeant was struggling to understand English.

"How you enter Republic of Nicaragua?"

"We came on a bus from Liberia, Costa Rica," said Todd.

"Where did you cross border?"

"I think it was called Pen Blanks."

"*Penas Blancas*. Show stamp in passport."

Todd leafed through the passport until he found the page. The Sergeant inspected the stamp.

"None will leave your Pelican Island without my permission," said the Sergeant.

"He can't do that, who does he think he is?" said Graham. The Sergeant glared at him.

The Sergeant pushed past the tourists and waded over to the panga. He half-heartedly rooted through the luggage. Paul could see that that Graham's face was now bright red, he seemed furious.

"Our luggage has already been checked by immigration at the airport," said Graham.

"This is a narco trafficking region, a Marine Sergeant can search any item he wishes," said Kenner.

"Narco trafficking region?" said Graham.

"What is this?" said the Sergeant in Spanish. He was looking at the items Ruben and Kenner had bought in Bluefields.

"They are medical items requested by our nurse on Pelican Island," said Ruben.

"And some parts to repair one of the boats," said Kenner.

"What has happened?" said the Sergeant.

"Nothing Sergeant. It is our nurse restocking her medical supplies. Just in case, with all the new overseas tourists arriving," said Ruben.

"And we need to carry out repairs on our boats," said Kenner. Although Paul couldn't understand the conversation, he thought that Ruben and Kenner appeared like a comedy double act.

Paul saw Ruben approach the Sergeant and speak in a whisper to him. Ruben then coaxed the Sergeant away from the panga, Kenna and the four guests.

Paul could see that Ruben was in deep discussions with the Sergeant, and then Ruben swiftly passed the Sergeant a handful of banknotes.

"Hey, he's bribing him," said Graham. Everyone turned around and looked at Graham.

"Mr Graham, please keep quiet. Let Ruben deal with this," said Kenner. Ruben strode back to the guests and then handed the U.S. passport to Todd.

"Everybody please re-board the panga. Let's get this holiday party started," said Ruben.

. . . .

The Sergeant watched them as they departed. CIA, gays, foreigners, all enemies of Nicaragua. He took a long swig from his bottle of *Flor De Cana* and inhaled a thick line of cocaine. He was determined to trap the CIA agent. Then he would be a hero. He would be promoted and transferred back to Masaya, in glory. Officer Romero could kiss his backside.

CHAPTER 38

It was approximately sixty-five nautical miles from El Bluff to New Greytown, therefore the journey would only take a couple of hours, thought Augusto. He had brought Lieutenant Amander along with him for the trip. His local knowledge could be useful. Josue had been born and raised in Greytown, or San Juan de Nicaragua. Whatever we were calling it this week, thought Augusto, and then laughed to himself.

The navy had a small detachment based at the entrance to the San Juan del Norte Bay. Augusto instructed Josue that upon arrival he should inspect the detachments depot, equipment, and state of readiness, whilst he dealt with other issues. The detachment's purpose was to monitor the border with Costa Rica. The area was a significant place for smuggling and for unauthorised people to move across the border illegally. To say the border was porous would be an understatement.

Augusto had requisitioned the Dabur-class patrol boat. This was the vessel on which Seaman Rafael Centeno had been killed. He recalled the discussion with Mrs Centeno. She was obviously grieving for her husband. Still, she was an educated woman, who was knowledgeable and passionate regarding the wrongdoings of the government, and the economic pressure that the region was facing.

It was true that there weren't many honest jobs available in the region. The steady increase in tourism had stopped abruptly, once Sergeant Gamboa and his accomplices dealt with the student protesters, with M16 rifles and grenade launchers. That tragic news spread around the world via social media.

In Augusto's opinion, on the positive side the road from Managua over to the Caribbean coast was a marvel of civil engineering. It was the first time in modern history that the west coast had been permanently linked to the Caribbean coast. It was progress. Augusto knew that the old bush road was certainly not dependable and, most of the time, not even driveable. Bluefields and Pearl lagoon would now have access to cheaper products. Augusto concluded that Mrs Centeno had spoken a great deal of truth, but he was certain that her theory that the government was in an alliance with the Colombian cartels was an internet conspiracy.

. . . .

Augusto and Josue were stood on the deck viewing the coastline. On their right they saw the entrance to Aguila Creek in the distance.

"Before you ask, Lieutenant Commander, I had planned to meet with the headman this week and get his side of the incident," said Josue.

"No problem, Josue, let's call in to the village on our return journey."

"Yes Sir, let's find the truth."

"I was thinking, Josue, why did you leave Greytown?"

"I was born in Greytown. I wanted to go somewhere else."

"What? Bluefields?" Augusto started laughing.

"I was raised as child of the sea, always out on the boats."

"Fishing for White Lobster?"

"Never caught any," said Josue.

"That's what you say, you probably have an 8-bedroom, 10-bathroom mansion in San Juan de Nicaragua," said Augusto.

"If I did, I wouldn't be limping along the Caribbean Coast, in this leaking rust bucket," said Josue. They both laughed and Augusto slapped Josue on the back.

When the joviality subsided, Augusto peered into the distance towards Greytown. Reality kicked in, what was Madison going to tell him? What information did she have? What danger was he in? He felt it was a game of chess and he was an expendable pawn.

CHAPTER 39

Greytown, Nicaraguan Caribbean Coast

Lieutenant Amander guided the navy patrol boat from the Caribbean Sea and into San Juan del Norte Bay. The navy depot was positioned to face the bay entrance. Josue brought the vessel into a berth directly at the navy depot. The detachment seemed surprised that a navy vessel had arrived. When they realised that Lieutenant Commander Augusto Romero and Lieutenant Josue Amander were onboard a minor panic began.

Josue ordered that they fall in, button up their uniforms and stand to attention. Augusto suppressed a chuckle. Whilst Josue was terrorising the Greytown detachment, his phone vibrated. It was message from Mustang.

karl marx, nice to see that you have arrived

greytown airport in 30 mins, see you soon x

Augusto took possession of the detachment's only RIB. He informed Josue that he was off on a tour of the bay. Josue vaguely acknowledged him. Augusto noticed that he was busy enjoying himself tormenting the detachment. Augusto saw that one sailor was jogging on the spot, with a rifle above his head. He boarded the RIB with a broad smile.

. . . .

The new airport was unique. The only method in which passengers could get to the airport was by boat. Typical Nicaragua, thought Augusto, you had to get a boat to board a plane. He navigated the RIB from the navy depot into the bay and then manoeuvred his way into the airport dock. He secured the RIB, and then his phone vibrated.

follow the signs to the old greytown cemetery

He soon spotted the sign: *Antiguo Cementerio de Greytown*. Augusto followed the directions.

As he entered the cemetery, he saw a woman dressed in a purple Louisiana State University t-shirt, tight jeans, and a yellow backpack. She was disguised as a tourist, hiding in plain sight.

CHAPTER 40

Old Greytown cemetery

Madison was studying the old gravestones. Augusto thought that she would see the gravestones with more clarity if she removed her sunglasses.

"I am assuming that you are an illegal alien?" said Augusto, smiling.

She returned the smile. "For sure, I've jumped the border to come and soak up the Nicaraguan colonial history."

"So, not only am I fraternizing with an agent of an adversarial nation, but I am also aiding and abetting an illegal immigrant."

"Illegal alien is preferred, nobody is an illegal immigrant in Nicaragua. Who would want to emigrate to Nicaragua?" laughed Madison.

He managed to laugh, "It's similar to *Hotel California* by The Eagles, *you can check out any time you like, but you can never leave*," said Augusto.

"You could jump the border with me and escape to Costa Rica."

"I can't. My country needs me."

"More than you will ever know."

They toured the colonial graveyard together. Augusto had visited the cemetery before and was aware that there were in fact, four separate cemeteries: British, Catholic, Freemasons and one for North Americans. The graveyards were overgrown by grass, weeds and sporadically, flowers; even so, many gravestones were still visible. Diplomats, captains, sailors, and other residents of the original Greytown, even a representative of the old German Empire, were all buried there.

The new airport had been built remarkably close to the cemetery, to such an extent that the main street of Old Greytown was now the paved airport runway.

"Don't you think it is suspicious that the Nicaraguan government decided that this small airport was a funding priority. That it was more important than dredging the inlet to the San Juan River or ensuring the town had a reliable electricity supply?" said Madison.

"Don't say that you have convinced me to commit an act of treason, so that you can share your wild conspiracy theories?"

"Just wondering out loud. Why does Greytown need an airport?"

"Can we move on to the real world? What is this information that you deem so important?"

Madison reached into her tourist backpack and retrieved an iPad. She then balanced it upon the ancient tomb of:

Capt. Ebenezer F. Oswald born 27th Jan.1823 Port Antonio, Jamaica and died 29th May 1879 Grey Town, Nicaragua, aged 55 and 4 months. Blessed is the merciful, for they shall obtain mercy.

Augusto saw that the iPad display showed a map of the Caribbean Coast of Nicaragua. "So, what great insights are you going to provide to me today, surrounded by your ancestors."

"Not sure they are *my* ancestors," said Madison.

"Ok, let's not get into that. What's so important that you dragged me here?"

Madison explained that the U.S. Coastguard, the DEA and other nominated U.S. government institutions, under the direction of the OCD-ETF, had established a major multi-task force narcotic tracking program. Utilising satellite data and imagery, plus innovative leading-edge IT algorithms, the OCD-ETF had tracked every vessel, over the last nine months. Specifically, vessels that had left from the Northern Colombian coast, which had then ultimately arrived on the Honduran Caribbean coast.

"It's amazing what can be achieved when you have multimillion dollar budgets," said Augusto.

She explained that the route from Cartagena, Colombia to Puerto Lempira in Honduras was over 750 nautical miles. This couldn't be completed as a non-stop journey in a go-fast boat. The go-fast boats must therefore stop somewhere on route. They need fuel and ideally rest, fresh water and food.

"Here we go again, conspiracy time," said Augusto.

Madison continued. The countries of Costa Rica and Panama were fully cooperating with the DEA, and their respective coastguards have the latest technologies and weaponry with which to thwart the narco traffickers. The narco traffickers had to avoid these countries, therefore having to maximise their journey in international waters. The only region which is therefore accessible to them is the Caribbean coast of Nicaragua.

"It is the largest national coastline in Central America. It is sparsely populated. The inhabitants on the coast have been abandoned by central government. There are few jobs, the economy is in tatters and sporadic hurricanes have just exasperated the problems. There is negligible law and order," said Madison.

"Tell me something new," said Augusto.

"Therefore, the area is ripe for exploitation."

"Thank you for your World Bank economic dissection of the Nicaraguan economy, and your point is?"

"If you look closely at the map on the screen, you will see three red marks. These are the location of the logistics hubs that operate as *highway truck stops, pit stops, motorway service stations*, depending upon your vernacular. These hubs aid the narco traffickers on their journey from Colombia to Honduras, via Nicaragua," said Madison.

Augusto stared at the screen.

She expanded the map on the iPad, Augusto could clearly see the three red marks indicated on the map; Puerto Kiabrata, Juticalpa Point and Aquila Creek. They were evenly spaced along the Nicaraguan Caribbean Coast.

"How confident are you that this is correct? Or are you about to pull a coin out from behind my ear?"

"100% confident."

"No problem then, I occupy all three locations and round up all the usual suspects. I arrest and charge the obviously guilty. I closedown their operations, easy. Thanks for the information. I feel a significant promotion coming on," said Augusto.

"Not so fast, Karl Marx, who do you think is behind the establishment of these logistics hubs or pit stops?"

"The narco traffickers. The cartels in Colombia, that's obvious."

"You need to look at these photos."

Madison pulled up three photos on the iPad, which was still balanced on Ebenezer's tomb. Augusto studied them. The first was a photo of Espinoza and Colindres. They were in a park, appearing to be having a discussion. The second photo was of Espinoza and two people. They were in a restaurant, having lunch or dinner, Espinoza was smiling. The third photo was Colindres with a grey-haired guy, who was wearing a baseball jacket embroidered with the letters LBPN, *Nicaraguan Professional Baseball League*, on the front. They look as if they were in a coffee shop, their faces were relaxed and calm.

"Do you know these people?" said Madison.

"Let's do this the other way around, Mustang. What do you know about these people?"

"No problem" she expanded the first photo on the iPad. "In this photo we have Admiral Espinoza, my friend from the Four Seasons, Mexico City, with the Captain of the Nicaraguan Navy, Pablo Colindres," said Madison.

"So what? these guys know each other. I'm certain they have a great deal to talk about."

"I'm sure they do. Wait, two more photos to go, all will be revelled. In the second photo, Admiral Espinoza is having dinner in Mexico City, in an upmarket restaurant. The other two people are emissaries of the Colombian *Los Pelnino crime gang*. These nasty characters are responsible for all the narco vessels that depart Cartagena in Northern Colombia," said Madison.

"Maybe he's requesting them not to use Nicaraguan territorial waters for transportation of their cargo."

"Yeah, right. Even you, Mr Naïve - Nicaragua 2022, doesn't believe that. Let's go to photo number three. This shows Pablo Colindres having coffee in Managua."

"What's so special about that?"

"The man with Colindres is the architect behind the establishment of the three logistics centres."

"Are you certain about the grey-haired guy, the baseball fan?"

"We've tracked him for a month, it's him."

"Who is he?"

"He's very cautious, we don't have a name yet."

"If you knew all this, what was the Four Seasons meeting all about?"

"To look Admiral Espinoza in the eyes and sound him out. You were a bonus, a welcome surprise. We have concluded you're one of the good guys. We're confident that you'd want to dismantle this malevolent infrastructure, for the good of your country."

"You mean for the good of *your* country."

"I know you hate what Espinoza and Colindres have established. You're fully aware what cocaine can do to your local communities. Crack cocaine in Bluefields and Managua, gang warfare, murders, exploitation of young people. There isn't one country in Central or South America in which the illegal narco business hasn't had an overall negative effect. If they play with fire, they will get their fingers burnt."

"We don't have gang warfare in Nicaragua and the murder rates are significantly lower than our neighbours."

"That's because in Nicaragua, there are no *Bloods and Crips*. No Medellin or Sinaloa cartel. No Los Extraditables. There's only one gang in Nicaragua, and you know who they are."

"This is a David and Goliath situation, what am I supposed to do?" said Augusto.

"Well, I've just provided you with some stones for your slingshot," said Madison, with a smile.

CHAPTER 41

Pelican Island

Ruben docked the panga at Pelican Island. The employees, dressed in white, were waiting to greet the new arrivals. Ruben and Kenner helped the four guests to scramble out of the boat. Jannie van Rensburg performed his usual role and greeted them all.

Graham was having none of it.

"It is outrageous what has just happened. We were threatened by an armed police officer and man handled. He rummaged around in our personal belongings and demanded to see our passports," said Graham.

Graham continued "The Sergeant says that we cannot leave the island without his permission. This is not the holiday I booked. I am demanding a full refund."

Jannie said "Mr Graham and Mrs Beverly, please go over to our pool bar, cocktails will be served immediately and will be continuous. Your luggage is being forwarded to Suite 1, so please don't worry about them. I will join you at the bar and we can drink cocktails together and resolve this issue. Please Mr Paul and Mr Todd join us for cocktails at the bar and we can also ease your concerns."

Graham reluctantly headed towards the bar, grumbling at Bev that he would obtain satisfaction. Paul and Todd decided that after all the excitement a cocktail would be perfect.

Kenner grabbed the medical supplies and boat parts. He went to find Fiona.

. . . .

Ruben moved behind the bar and started preparing mojito cocktails. Jannie started his routine,

"My VIP guests welcome to Pelican Island. Cocktails, rum, whiskey, beers, everything, is available 24 hours a day. We serve excellent dinners at our Astral bar and grill on the east side of the island, every evening from 7pm. We can serve Nicaraguan and international breakfasts either in your room or at our relaxed diner, the Stingray café, which is just here on the west side of the island," said Jannie.

Graham interrupted " What's a Nicaraguan breakfast? It sounds dodgy."

"A Nica breakfast is *gallo pinto*, which is cooked rice with either black or red speckled beans. You can then add scrambled eggs, sour cream, a slice of hard, salty cheese and a sweet fried plantain, it's wonderful," said Jannie.

"*Gallo pinto* is named after the local spotted rooster, as the beans are speckled," said Ruben.

"I'll stick with bacon and eggs," said Graham. Bev agreed.

Ruben served mojitos to all the guests, plus Jannie. Continuing in guest pleasing mode, Jannie told the guests of the *Mojito legend*.

"In the 16th century, Francis Drake, the English pirate, raided Cartagena in Colombia. He then began his journey back to merry England with his loot."

"Good old Francis Drake, what a hero. Those bloody Spanish," said Graham.

Jannie continued, "However, his crew were suffering from scurvy. He was told that the people in Cuba had a medicine, so he stopped in Havana to acquire these local remedies."

"Like a kind of jungle juice," said Graham.

Jannie dodged the interruption, "The concoction consisted of fermented sugarcane, lime juice and mint. The locals understood that lime cured scurvy and mint reduced sea sickness. Rum was added to the drink years later and it was known in the western world as *El Draque*."

Ruben said, "The Spanish word *mojadito* means *a little wet* and a Cuban lime-based seasoning is called *mojo*. Therefore, it has the famous name, Mojito."

"It's a load of nonsense," said Graham.

"I don't care if the Francis Drake story isn't true, it's sounds good to me," said Paul. Todd agreed and ordered two more mojitos from Ruben. "Dos mojitos por favor."

"Cheers to Sir Francis Drake, a true English hero," shouted Graham.

"More mojitos for everyone," said Jannie.

"This is all well and good, but let's talk about the act of terrorism that we had to endure this afternoon," said Graham. Bev nodded in agreement.

Ruben summarised the events. Graham interrupted numerous times. Nevertheless, Jannie managed to understand what had occurred.

"My valued guests, please let me apologise on behalf of Pelican Island for any inconvenience and worries that may have arisen due to this incident."

"Inconvenience? I was nearly shot," said Graham.

"Mr Graham, please can you allow me to bring clarity to the situation? It will be helpful for all our guests and employees," said Jannie.

"Yes, clarity is what I need," said Graham. Bev nodded her head in agreement.

"The Nicaraguan Navy has the right to stop any vessel that is traveling within Nicaraguan territorial waters. There have been minor issues with drug trafficking on both the Pacific and the Caribbean coast of Nicaragua, for many years."

"Oh my God," said Graham. Bev was close to tears.

"There is nothing to worry about. In fact, the presence of the Nicaraguan Navy is a reassuring factor," said Jannie.

"It's not reassuring when they threaten to shoot you," said Graham.

"They wanted to check our identification and inspect our cargo. This is routine," said Ruben.

"We should contact the British Embassy in Managua," said Graham.

"I'm sorry to say, there isn't one. Your contact would be the British Consulate in San Jose, Costa Rica," said Jannie.

Bev was now crying.

"What's all this about not me being able to leave the island?" said Graham.

"That is not typical. I will speak to the head of the Nicaraguan Navy in Bluefields. I know him well, he's a good guy. I'm sure he will sort this out."

"I have to be honest, I thought it was quite exciting," said Paul.

"Me too" said Todd, "Though, when the Sergeant began waving my U.S. passport in front of my face and accusing me of being CIA, Bill Stewart and ABC news did flash through my mind."

"Bill who? What's that all about?" said Graham.

Todd offered to explain the background to the *Bill Stewart incident*, to a now attentive audience around the bar.

Todd said "Bill Stewart was an experienced ABC news journalist. In 1979, he was in Managua to cover the vicious civil war between the Sandinistas and the Somoza regime."

"And he got shot?" said Graham.

Todd continued, "Bill Stewart was travelling in a marked press vehicle with his camera and crew. Members of Somoza's National Guard stopped them. They ordered him and his interpreter to lie down in the street. A National Guard then shot Stewart and his local interpreter, dead."

"Oh my God, why have we come here?" said Bev, on the verge of hysteria.

"It's just history, Mrs Beverley, please don't get upset," said Jannie.

Paul glanced at Graham and thought that his head was about to explode. "See, we could have been killed," said Graham.

"The whole incident was captured by fellow journalists in the press convoy. The video tape and photos of the incident were secretly transported back to the U.S. and appeared on prime-time news. President Jimmy Carter condemned the Somoza regime, accusing them of the murders. The regime subsequently collapsed, and Somoza fled Nicaragua," said Todd.

Graham slumped into his seat, grim and red faced. Bev was sobbing loudly.

"We're all going to die," said Bev.

CHAPTER 42

"I'm not even sure why we came here. I won the holiday in the *Ice Cream and Gelato corporate dinner* in Batley, Yorkshire. There was a charity auction." said Graham.

"I also picked up the package from an auction, in Manchester," said Paul.

"Are you in ice cream?" said Graham to Paul.

"Err no" said Paul, he suppressed his laughter, "Airport systems".

"I'm in ice cream toppings. We supply all the major outlets on the east coast of Yorkshire; Scarborough, Bridlington, Whitby and Withernsea."

"That's interesting," said Jannie. Paul doubted it was.

"Yes, I have a fatherly approach to my employees. If people ask me what I do for a living, I always say I'm helping people pay their mortgages. Then I provide details about the ice cream toppings."

"So how did Mrs Beverly and you meet?" said Jannie.

"In an ice cream parlour?" said Paul, with a smile.

"No, I was doing my magician tricks in the pub, when I saw the most beautiful woman I have ever seen. I knew I had to be with her."

Bev smiled for the first time. Paul noticed black mascara had run down her cheeks. Graham kissed Bev's hand. She smiled again.

Ruben served another round of mojitos. Paul noted that Jannie seemed pleased to receive a double *Flor de Cana* with cola.

"Hey Ruben, we were having a few drinks in the bar in Bluefields, and the guy said we should ask you about White Lobster," said Paul.

Ruben smiled, "Can I tell them, Mr Jannie?" said Ruben.

"Sure, why not? No secrets here on Pelican Island," said Jannie, as he drained his rum and cola.

Ruben laughed and then addressed the group. "As Mr Jannie has already explained, the Caribbean coast is sometimes used by the narco traffickers. When they get tracked down by the navy, occasionally they throw their cargo overboard. These bales of cocaine have a type of floatation devices attached, so that they are buoyant in the water," said Ruben.

"That's awesome," said Todd.

"That's White Lobster," said Ruben.

"When news of a *narco incident* reaches Bluefields, Pearl Lagoon, Net Point and surrounding areas, the fishermen and beachcombers come out in their hundreds. Everybody wants to catch White Lobster," said Ruben.

"That's incredible" said Paul, "So White Lobster is worth a great deal of money?"

Jannie said "Finding a bale of White Lobster is life-changing for the local families on the Miskito Coast. If you look around the villages, you will see many traditional homes and residencies with corrugated tin roofs. But occasionally you will spot a large, newly built, modern house that could easily fit into the wealthy suburbs of Cape Town, London, or Miami. These are the fortunate few who have caught White Lobster."

"But what do they do with the White Lobster once they find it?" said Paul.

Ruben didn't offer any insight into that part of the process. However, Jannie was enthusiastic about the subject.

"Finding White Lobster is just the beginning. The fishermen offer it back to the narco traffickers if they can find them. The local people can also sell it to dealers in the region, who will transport the bale to Managua for sale. But it's a dangerous business. I mean, let's be honest, who wants to deal with drug dealers and narco cartels from Colombia?" said Jannie.

Ruben added, "Also who wants to be captured by the Nicaraguan authorities and be accused of being a narco trafficker yourself? Nicaraguan prisons are very nasty places."

Bev had become very pale, contrasting Graham's red complexion.

Ruben shifted the conversation away from the narco dealings, "On the coast here we have a unique combination of ocean currents and trade winds. Our grandparents have known about these forces of nature since they were children. Every item floating in the Caribbean Sea tends to wash upon the coast of Nicaragua," said Ruben.

"It sounds as though it's a combination of weather and geography," said Paul.

"Once the conflict between the government and the Contras ended, the narco traffic through the Caribbean steadily increased year on year," said Jannie.

"The official national sport of Nicaragua is baseball. But our real national sport is White Lobster fishing," said Ruben. There was general laughter from the guests.

"I know what White Lobster is" said Graham, "It's when you ejaculate over a woman who has sunburn."

Everybody burst out laughing, except Bev, who remained pale and stony-faced.

CHAPTER 43

Fiona finally lost her patience waiting for Kenner to arrive with the medicines from Bluefields. She decided to check on Mr Danny and make sure he was okay.

She stepped quietly into the building. She was welcomed with sudden shouting, "Who's there?". There was a recognisable odour in the room.

"Hi, its only me, it's Fiona," she said.

"Who? What do you want?"

"It's me, Fiona. I've come to see if you are ok."

"Oh, Nurse Fiona. Yes, yes, I remember."

Fiona walked towards the direction of Danny's voice. She turned the corner and saw him. The chair he had been sat upon when she had initially examined him, was laying on its side. He was slumped on the old mattress, his face a deathly grey. There was a handgun in his lap.

"Mr Danny, how are you feeling?" she said.

"Nurse Fiona, nice to see you again." His speech was slurred.

"How is your shoulder?"

It's sore, where is the medicine?"

"It's on the way. Ruben and Kenner have just arrived, they will be bringing it here. Now let me have a look at your shoulder."

Fiona carefully removed Danny's shirt and looked at his back. There was a dark red swelling all around the wound. She knew this was a type of blood infection. The recognisable odour detected when she entered the building was sepsis, thought Fiona.

. . . .

"Hey, Fiona, I've got the stuff," said Kenner. Fiona was startled, as Kenner was stood directly behind her. He handed over the medical supplies.

"Did you have to creep up on me like that?"

"Wow, what a journey we had. I felt like I was a secret agent, yeah, like *Mission Impossible*."

Fiona turned around and glared at him. Why do young guys always act like children? she thought.

She inspected the medical supplies. Fiona put on a pair of new disposable rubber gloves. She then ensured Danny took the antibiotics and pain medication. Fiona informed Kenner that Mr Danny needed to take the tablets three times a day and that he should check daily that Mr Danny had taken them. She began to clean and redress the wound using the new supplies, sterile gauze, bandages, and tape.

"We've also got the parts to repair the boat. I can start on that tomorrow," said Kenner.

"You and Ruben have to give Mr Danny some space. He needs to let the medication do its job. What's happening about his food?" said Fiona.

"I'll bring him some early dinner in a couple of hours. Is fish, eggs and galle pinto ok, Mr Danny?" said Kenner. Danny didn't respond. He had a glazed, distant look in his eyes.

"Kenner, just bring him the food, it's not the Intercontinental," she said. Kenner wandered off. Fiona thought that he was expecting a medal for his efforts.

Fiona was aware that gunshot victims could suffer from a type of trauma, acute stress disorder or paranoia. She engaged Danny in conversation to see how he responded.

"So, Mr Danny, how have you been sleeping?"

"Bad, I keep … having nightmares," said Danny. His speech was slurred.

"What are your nightmares about?"

"I'm …. being chased. Everyone is …. out to get me. Vultures are …. circling."

"Mr Danny, that's not surprising really, when you consider where you are, and what you are doing."

"Yeah, I …. suppose so. I feel that danger is …. around every corner."

"Yes, just because you are paranoid doesn't mean people aren't really following you."

Danny managed to laugh.

"So …... Nurse Fiona …. tell me about yourself."

"What do you want to know?"

"I see…. you're wearing …... a wedding… ring, are …you married?"

"No, I'm not married. I wear that to stop the guys from hassling me."

"Does …... it work?"

"Obviously not."

" Nurse Fiona …. your education is …. being wasted on …. Pelican Island. Why …. are you here?" he said.

She was happy to keep him talking. She wanted to assess his mental state.

"Where to begin? That's the question."

"Start at …… the beginning."

CHAPTER 44

Fiona Alston had been a brilliant student. Her examination results were in the top 2% in the country. This allowed her to progress to higher education. She was accepted as a student at the American University in Managua to study medicine. However, it was a private university, so funding was a major issue.

In what appeared to be a miracle, Fiona was offered one of only three annual places for Nicaraguan students at the Latin American School of Medicine in Cuba. These were fully funded scholarships, which included tuition, dormitory housing, three meals a day, textbooks in Spanish and medical uniforms.

Fiona seized the opportunity and started her 6-year studies at the medical school, located twenty-two miles outside Havana. She was told, by a fellow student, that preference for scholarships was given to students from the Americas that were low-income applicants, from African and Latino descent.

Fiona thought that it was the first time in her life, and maybe the last time, that being black, and poor, gave her an advantage.

She enjoyed the university and living in Cuba. The people were friendly and genuinely interested in where you were from. The campus was far enough from Havana, that the city retained its excitement whenever she visited.

After three years of successful study, Fiona was enjoying life. She had become accustomed to living in Cuba and was progressing well in her studies. She made friends on campus and managed to avoid getting distracted by the parties and wild nights in Havana. Fiona's goal in life was to become a surgeon.

. . . .

Then the phone call came.

She received a phone call in the university dormitory. She was informed that her father had suffered a heart attack. When she arrived in Bluefields two days later, her father had passed away. Her mother had a form of Alzheimer's and her father had been the sole carer for her mother.

Fiona never returned to Cuba.

. . . .

Fiona saw that Danny was falling asleep, she did consider that it was her boring story that sent him to sleep. She decided it was the medication. If the infection didn't improve, he would need to be treated by a doctor, not a half qualified one.

She then noticed that he had fallen asleep, with his handgun by his side. She covered him with a blanket and whispered a prayer, he would need both.

CHAPTER 45

Aguila Creek, Nicaraguan Caribbean Coast

As the navy patrol vessel approached Aguila Creek, it was obvious to Augusto that the inlet was narrow and was not deep enough for the vessel to enter. He ordered the crew to prepare one of the navy dinghies and launch it into the sea. Augusto and Josue would go across to the village in the dinghy, accompanied by one of the crew as a pilot. All of them would be armed.

Augusto and Josue disembarked from the dinghy and strode towards the village. There didn't seem to be many villagers around. Augusto spoke in Miskito to a young boy,

"*Naksa* child, where is headman?" The boy seemed startled but then said, "I will show, follow."

"I didn't know you could speak Miskito," said Josue.

"My mother used to speak to me in Miskito when I was a child. Father spoke Spanish and Creole English. I was a very confused child," laughed Augusto.

Josue said, "My father is fluent in Miskito, and he used to give me grief for not being able to speak it. But I settled with Spanish and English." The boy led them along a path though the mangrove swamps. He was taking them away from the village.

"Where you take?" said Augusto.

"To headman," replied the boy. They trudged on through the vegetation. An opening in the swamps appeared before them. It was a construction site.

It was obvious to Augusto that this was one of the narco traffickers' logistics centres. Madison had been correct.

They walked towards the partly constructed buildings. There were workers beavering away on several buildings.

There was two large excavators and four scissor lifts, plus a heavy-duty forklift. There was a large power generator and three light towers. This was a serious construction project, thought Augusto.

Augusto caught sight of a construction worker that looked familiar. He walked towards him, and the worker recognised Augusto.

"Hey Officer Romero, how are you? Long time, no see," said the worker.

Augusto couldn't remember his name. But he played along, "Hi, how are you? What are you doing down here, so far south?"

With a shrug of the shoulders, he said, "We go where the work is these days."

"It looks like a major project."

"Yeah, an accommodation block, fuel and water storage tanks, warehouse, small school and a sports ground."

"A sports ground? For what? Baseball?"

""Yeah, baseball, basketball, football, whatever. I didn't even know the Indians liked sports."

"This looks very expensive, all the heavy construction equipment."

"Don't get me started. As you know, there are no reliable roads from Bluefields to Aguila Creek. We had to ship all the equipment down here by sea. We even brought our own power generation, lighting, and our own drinking water. Why these people want to live here is beyond me," said the worker.

"What about the cost of all of this?"

"I'm not involved in the overall project costs; I just have specific budgets to work to. Do you know my boss, Colin Martin, owner of Martin Construction in Bluefields? He should be able to give you the details." Colin Martin was a wealthy local businessman. Augusto knew Colin, he had some dodgy business connections.

As Augusto was talking to the worker, the headman appeared. He spoke abruptly to the young boy,

"Why brought them here?" The boy looked towards the ground.

"Because I asked," said Augusto, in Miskito. The headman seemed alarmed, thought Augusto.

"Oh, I didn't know you have my language," said the headman.

"*Naksa*, it is our language," said Augusto.

"You not Miskito."

"My mother call us Mestizo's of Caribbean Coast."

"She was wise woman. How I help, Sir?"

Augusto asked that they converse in Spanish, so that Josue could understand. The headman obliged. Augusto and Josue introduced themselves and informed the headman that they wanted to discuss the recent visit from the Sergeant and his men.

The headman invited them into the accommodation block, so that they could sit down and be comfortable. They entered the block and Augusto noted that it was being built to modern specifications. There were several bathrooms, electrical outlets, and a large kitchen.

"It will be very nice when it is all completed," said Augusto.

"Yes, there is still a lot to do. We need to get the school completed, so that we can provide our children with an education and a future," said the headman.

"It must have cost a great deal of money," said Augusto.

"Yes, all the villagers have pooled their money for the future of our children.

"Impressive," said Josue.

"Now, you wanted to know about the Sergeant?" said the headman, changing the subject.

They asked for the headman to recollect the events of that day. Josue informed the headman that they just needed the truth. The headman provided a detailed description of the events of that day. However, he did not mention the arrival of the narco boat.

"So, you were assaulted by the Sergeant and then he threatened a child. He stole your catch and then went ahead and damage the pangas?" said Josue.

"That's mostly correct; he cannot be accused of stealing the fish, we offered them to him and his crew," said the headman.

"Under duress, though," said Josue.

"Let's keep it simple Josue, assault and wilful damage," said Augusto.

"So, you and your villagers did not see a go-fast boat enter the creek?" said Augusto.

"No, and I told the same to the Sergeant."

"Do you ever see go-fast boats enter the creek?" said Augusto.

"We are a simple village, why would they come here?"

"Fuel, water, food."

"We have little to spare."

"Obviously, you've got fish to spare," smiled Augusto.

"Will the village be compensated for the damage?"

"Please leave that with us. We will charge the Sergeant with these offences. Once found guilty, we will apply for compensation on your behalf," said Augusto.

"We will need a written statement from yourself," said Josue.

The headman agreed and asked if an email was acceptable.

"You have a computer?" said Augusto.

"Yes of course. The village has a data communications link. We have a 4G network and ultra-broadband internet access. We are hoping to upgrade to 5G," smiled the headman.

"But I thought you had no mains electricity?" said Augusto.

"We don't. We have our own diesel generators and solar power. We prefer solar as it is a green technology and sustainable," said the headman.

"I'm not sure what's going on in this world," laughed Augusto.

CHAPTER 46

Old Cotton Tree district, Bluefields

Augusto disembarked from the navy patrol vessel at Bluefields harbour. He then drove back to his house in the Old Cotton Tree district. It had been a long day. His head was spinning with Madison, Espinoza, Colindres, the mystery guy, Aguila Creek, the construction site, the headman, the Sergeant. It was all too much. He needed to microwave something, drink some *Flor de Cana* and have a good night's sleep.

He was checking his phone and saw there was a missed call from Jannie van Rensburg, the South African manager over at Pelican Island. He decided to return his call.

"Hi, Jannie, it's Augusto."

"My friend, thanks for calling me. How are you?"

"Busy, but never too busy for you, how can I help?"

"I'm sorry to say, we are having an issue with one of your guys."

"My guys? Who?"

"The Sergeant that you have sitting on Maria Cay. He is causing issues with the tourists. That's not good for any of us. You need to reprimand him."

"Why? What is he doing?"

"Demanding passports, opening their luggage and pointing weapons in my employees faces. He even accused one of my American guests of being CIA."

"Is he?" chuckled Augusto.

"Come on Augusto, you know how important tourism is to the government and the region, this can't continue."

"I agree. I'll sort it out. I'll stop by Pelican Island."

"That would be perfect. You are always welcome to visit us. We can have a beers' together."

"You're my kind of guy, Jannie."

. . . .

In the morning, Augusto felt tired after a night of restless sleep. He forced himself to call the construction company owner, Colin Martin.

"Martin Construction, Mr Martin's office, how can I help you?" a young woman said.

"Hello, this Lieutenant Commander Augusto Romero, Nicaraguan Navy, I would like to speak to Mr Martin."

"He is in a meeting at the moment."

"Please interrupt the meeting and tell him I am on the phone."

"I'm not allowed to disturb him."

"Just do it, please. Tell him it is Lieutenant Commander Augusto Romero."

The young girl reluctantly conceded and went off the line. After a moment there was a voice,

"Hi, Augusto, Colin here. Is there a fire somewhere?"

"Hi Colin, I need to speak to you urgently. Can we meet this morning in Bluefields?"

"I have a number of meetings scheduled, but for you, I'll rearrange. Can you give me a clue what it's all about?"

"All will be revealed, 11am at Hotel Casa Royale."

"See you then, I'm intrigued," said Colin.

CHAPTER 47

Hotel Casa Royale, Bluefields

Augusto strolled into the lobby and made his way towards the swimming pool. The hotel had a modern swimming and exercise area. Colin was sat at a table, talking on his phone. Augusto noticed that Colin hadn't missed any meals recently, he had gained a lot of weight since they last met.

When he saw Augusto, he ended the conversation, stood up and shook Augusto's hand.

"So, Lieutenant Commander, what's happening?"

"I know you are busy man Colin, so I will cut to the chase."

"Please do, Augusto, as I said, I'm intrigued."

"Tell me about your construction project at Aguila Creek."

Augusto noticed that Colin started to spin his mobile phone around in his hands, "Not sure what you want to know. I thought you were navy."

"Colin, don't screw me around. I want to know what you are doing down there."

"Martin Construction has a contract to build a complete turnkey project. This consists of an accommodation block, fuel storage area, clean water storage and pumps, a warehouse with workshop, a school, and a sports ground with hard core asphalt and grass areas. Period of on-site construction is eighteen months."

"How much will it cost?"

"That's confidential. Not sure why the navy needs to know that."

"Who are you in contract with?"

"That's also confidential."

"You're not being very helpful."

"Confidential is confidential."

"I could get my friends in the police, or even better, the authorities in Managua to look into this."

"Augusto, you know how business and politics works in Bluefields and throughout the Caribbean Coast. It's like the wild west out here, and it always has been. I don't want them in Managua snooping around in my affairs."

"Ok, Colin. I'll keep Managua away from you, but you need to give me the inside track."

"As a friend, I can tell you things, but you didn't hear them from me."

"Colin, you and I are local boys. The salt, sand and sea are in our blood. No one needs to explain the Miskito coast to us. You have my word; you will not be mentioned."

"I'm already concerned that people in my office know that I am meeting you."

"Tell them I was bitching about the harbour and all the construction material and crap you have left hanging around."

"That sounds like a real bitch."

"It is," smiled Augusto.

Colin told Augusto that twelve months ago he had won three construction projects at Puerto Kiabrata, Juticalpa Point and Aquila Creek. San Juan Structures SA awarded them to him. There wasn't really a tender process. Colin had to pass around some *small money into wet hands*, as he called it, and Martin Construction won the business. The three projects were worth a total $6m U.S. dollars.

"That is a great deal of money," said Augusto.

"The transportation and equipment costs are staggering."

"Even so, that's big business for Bluefields."

"There is no road access to these remote villages, we have to take everything in by barge. They have no electricity and no clean water. It's a planning nightmare."

"But worth it," smirked Augusto.

"Only if we can get paid the cost overruns. Hurricane Eta caused chaos."

"What do you call that? Act of God?"

"Force majeure."

"That's it. You have it watertight."

"Do you really think I will get any satisfaction from a Nicaraguan court?"

"What do you mean?"

"Regarding clauses in my contracts, that free my company from liabilities or obligations, due to an act of God?"

"I thought we were living in a catholic country?" said Augusto.

"It's more like a gangster's paradise." Colin frowned.

"So, Colin, who owns San Juan Structures SA?"

"Some people in San Juan de Nicaragua."

"Come on Colin, you must know whom they are. Who signed the contracts for San Juan Structures?"

"This is millions of dollars. I'm not saying anything else, take it up with them."

"I'll get to the bottom of this," said Augusto.

"You better be very careful, Augusto. There are some very large sharks in those waters, who wouldn't want you to reach the bottom, not alive anyway," said Colin.

CHAPTER 48

Pelican Island

Back on Pelican Island, all the guests were in the Stingray café, having breakfast. Jannie strode into the café.

"VIP guests, I'm pleased to announce that we will be offering a cultural trip into Pearl lagoon today. You will meet local people, visit a school, try your hand at fishing Caribbean style and then you will have lunch at the *King Marlin*, where the music will be blasting out."

"Do we have to go?" said Graham.

"No, of course not. You can sunbathe, relax, and enjoy the food and free drinks here on Pelican Island, no problem," said Jannie.

"It's not free, we have had to pay for it, all-inclusive is what we have paid for," said Graham.

Paul looked over at Charlotte and rolled his eyes.

"Who will be joining us today for the Pearl lagoon Cultural trip?" said Jannie.

"Paul and I will come along," said Charlotte.

"Yeah, Todd and I will also," said Becky.

"This holiday has cost me a great deal and I want to get my money's worth," said Graham. Bev nodded.

"That's fantastic. Six VIP guests. Please meet Ruben at 10.30am at the pier. Have a wonderful day."

"Do we have to take our passports?" said Paul.

"Yeah, because that crazy Sergeant is probably still around," said Graham.

Jannie said, "Yes, please take your passports. I have spoken to Lieutenant Commander Romero of the Nicaraguan Navy. He has promised me he will investigate this issue."

"Oh, we know Augusto," said Paul.

"How do *you* know him?" said Graham.

"We met him in Managua, he arranged a city tour for us," said Charlotte.

"He said that he'd noticed us in Mexico City, because of my Manchester City shirt," said Paul.

"I'm more of a rugby man myself, Leeds Rhinos," said Graham.

"Augusto said that he had lived in the UK," said Paul.

"Who is this amazing guy?" said Graham.

Jannie said "He is the top navy person in the region. He said he'll try to get over to Pelican Island today. He will sort out that Sergeant."

"He needs to do something. I'm a British subject. I will not accept being threatened by foreigners, with machine guns," said Graham.

Bev nodded in agreement.

Jannie wasn't quite sure why a British citizen got preferred treatment, however he decided to keep that to himself.

CHAPTER 49

Paul felt exhilarated, as the panga zipped across the waves. The holiday was everything he had imagined, and in fact, exceeding his expectations. He had formed the impression that the region was lawless, and that there was a real freedom here. Paul studied the mainland. There were palm trees and mangrove swamps dotted along the coastline, occasionally there would be a shipwreck, rusting in the sun. What was their history? How had they ended up here, of all places? What had the crew done once they reached land? The adrenalin surged through his body. This is the place he would think about when *his maker* asked, "What did you do with your life?"

He was having a real adventure, at last.

. . . .

Ruben beached the panga in a rural area of Pearl Lagoon. Local people came over to help drag the boat on to the beach. Paul suspected that it was to satisfy their curiosity. There weren't many boats full of Europeans turning up in this area, thought Paul.

"These are Miskito people," said Ruben. An elderly guy approached Paul.

"Greetings, where are you from?" said the elderly man.

"We are from the UK," said Paul. The man looked slightly confused.

"Britain. England?" said Paul.

"Oh, England," said the man.

"Yes, Great Britain," said Graham.

"We speak English here. We also speak Spanish," said the man

Pointing to Becky and himself, Todd said "We are from the United States."

"Yes, America." The man nodded and smiled.

Graham said, "I'm from Yorkshire," and then he walked away. The man seemed confused.

"Look over here," shouted Ruben, heading towards a group of palm trees, "These are breadfruit trees, *Fruta de Pan*."

"Oh yes, *Mutiny on the Bounty*," said Charlotte.

"Which movie? The Marlon Brando one or the Mel Gibson one?" said Graham.

"It was more than a movie, it was a real story and the root cause, if you excuse the pun, was the breadfruit plant," said Charlotte.

"I have no idea what you are rambling on about," said Graham.

"I'm a history lecturer, it is my solemn oath to educate you all," laughed Charlotte.

"Ruben already knows all about the breadfruit tree, so I am addressing you, yes you, Western heathens," said Charlotte. Ruben was smiling.

Charlotte explained "As most of you will know, in the eighteen century, William Bligh lost the captaincy of his ship, The Bounty. Fletcher Christian and his shipmates mutinied."

"Why did they mutiny?" said Paul.

"Because Captain Bligh wanted the crew to sail the Bounty from Tahiti back to England."

"They should have hung them all," said Graham.

Charlotte continued "The main purpose of the voyage was to collect breadfruit, and other useful plants, from the South Pacific and take them back to England. The expedition was to transport the breadfruit plants to the West Indies, then cultivate them as cheap food for slaves, who were working on the vast sugar plantations."

"Slavery, that's terrible," said Bev.

"It's just the way the world was back then," said Graham, "get over it."

Charlotte didn't want to take the time to explain the terrors of the slave trade, and Britain's leading role in that horror, to Graham.

She continued with the initial topic, "Bligh was dumped into a lifeboat with eighteen others and cast adrift. He managed to navigate the lifeboat for over 3,500 miles to the safety of the Dutch East Indies. It is regarded, as the greatest feat of navigation in a small boat, even today. Unfortunately for Bligh, the British admiralty sent him back to the South Pacific to get the breadfruit, which he finally did."

"It was a good movie," said Graham.

"What you are looking at today is botanical history," said Charlotte.

"I would have mutinied. Who wants to leave Tahiti and go back to the damp, cold and miserable UK?" said Todd.

"Nothing wrong with Yorkshire," said Graham.

"Now I know you are talking through your backside," said Paul.

. . . .

Ruben led the tourists to a local school. They were obviously a distraction for the pupils. One of the teachers came out and greeted the group. She welcomed everybody and fielded several questions from the tourists. Paul asked about job opportunities for the school leavers. The teacher state clearly that drugs were the biggest problem in Pearl Lagoon. Keeping the young people off drugs was the first challenge. The second was stopping them getting involved in the business of drugs. Paul was fascinated.

The teacher explained that "White Lobster has totally transformed society in Pearl Lagoon. When White Lobster is found in Nicaragua's largest coastal lagoon, this is seen by most residents as an opportunity to escape the poverty in the region."

Paul wanted to further discuss the topic of White Lobster. But the teacher was reluctant to provide more details. She said young people were attracted to the lifestyle of the drug dealers, and that the glorification of that type of living by the western media was a major problem.

Paul was fascinated by White Lobster and its impact upon the local people. He thought that although there were negative aspects to all this cocaine washing up on the beaches, surely it was also a gift from geography and the trade winds of the Caribbean. Paul concluded that it was an opportunity for the local people to build nice houses and live in comfort with their families. It didn't make them drug dealers, did it?

CHAPTER 50

The King Marlin, Pearl Lagoon

The group arrived at a popular entertainment venue, the *King Marlin*. It was a large seafood restaurant, built on wooden stilts leading into the sea. It consisted of the main restaurant, guest rooms and docks for fishing boats. It also had an infamous bar, with a raucous reputation.

All the VIP guests traipsed into the restaurant. It was basic, with red checked tablecloths and white plastic chairs. Cold beer and soft drinks were served liberally to the group. Courses of fresh seafood, rice, beans, and French fries covered the tables. Reggae music blasted away, as is typical of tourist bars in the Caribbean islands. The voice of Bob Marley is omnipotent.

The group gorged themselves, under the curious eyes of the locals. Once everyone's appetite was satisfied, the waiter brought the bill to the table.

"Are we supposed to pay in dollars or Nicaraguan Cordoba?" said Graham.

"Either will do" said Ruben, "but they prefer U.S. dollars."

"Then what is the point of Cordoba?" said Graham.

"Just pay in dollars, Graham," said Paul.

"What's that amount in British pounds?" said Graham.

Paul ignored him. "We're three couples, so, let's make it $50 dollars from each couple," said Paul.

"That's cool with me, it's a bargain," said Todd.

"Agreed" said Becky.

"100%," said Charlotte.

"I'm not sure," said Graham. Bev was silent.

"Graham, it's $50 per couple for drinks, fresh seafood and a tip. Just pay it," said Paul.

Bev's face flushed red. She was embarrassed

Graham reluctantly pulled out a handful of $10 dollar bills and said, "Hey look, *Hamilton*, I've seen that musical."

. . . .

They all shifted into the bar. Paul and Charlotte found themselves sat quite close to four local guys.

"Welcome to the *King Marlin*" said one of the guys.

"I have to apologise for the invasion of your bar," said Paul.

"That's no problem. We are used to happy people throwing their money around in the *King Marlin*," laughed the local guy.

"You mean other tourists?"

"No, when someone catches White Lobster everyone parties."

"Yeah, I heard about that. It's amazing."

"When the people who have caught White Lobster come to the bar, they buy everybody food and beers. They don't even care about the bill."

"It sounds amazing."

"Life is hard here in Pearl Lagoon, and across the Nicaraguan Caribbean coast. But when White Lobster is in season, everybody benefits in some way, even if it's just a free dinner and a few beers."

The music changed from reggae to country music.

"What's all this country music about?" said Paul.

"It was imported by the U.S. Marines."

"I find it fascinating here on the Caribbean coast," said Paul.

"Yes, it's like a Caribbean Island stuck onto the country of Nicaragua."

"Yes, not the first time I've heard that. The local English accent sounds more Jamaican than Spanish."

"We can all speak Spanish; it is the language of the schools in Nicaragua. But our roots are in the Caribbean, and if you go further back, in Africa."

"There is a such a diversity of people here." said Paul.

"It's so interesting," said Charlotte.

Paul and Charlotte could hear a loud debate across the bar, Graham was vigorously arguing with the bartender whether it was pronounced Cari-bee-an or Carib-e-an.

"Even in paradise Graham can cause an argument," said Paul.

They both started laughing.

CHAPTER 51

The group said goodbye to all their newfound friends at the *King Marlin* and walked to the Pearl Lagoon harbour. There were many small shops attached to people's houses.

"That's very entrepreneurial," said Paul.

"They are called *pulperias*, it is a way to make a living," said Ruben.

"Life here seems tough."

"Nicaragua is the poorest country in Central America. One in seven Nicaraguans live in extreme poverty."

"It's difficult to understand, because it's so beautiful and the people as very friendly."

"Pearl Lagoon is Nicaragua's largest coastal lagoon. But fishing is very seasonal, and there are many people trying to catch the fish, crabs, prawns, and shrimps," said Ruben.

Paul saw two young boys selling brightly coloured birds.

Paul asked Ruben "What's all this about with the birds?"

"A local person might want to take a bird home and put it in a cage or tie it to a perch. A tourist, or even a kind local, may want to buy the bird and let it free," said Ruben.

Charlotte and Becky wandered over to one of the young bird sellers, gave him $10 and then let two of the birds fly away.

"I've noticed quite a few vagrants and beggars," said Paul. "Most of them are crack addicts, you can tell by their glazed eyes and rotten teeth," said Ruben.

"Is this because of White Lobster?"

"The crack addicts, yes. There is no reason for the Colombians to create a market on the Caribbean Coast. We are poor and there's not enough people here, therefore no market. This is local business. The addicts know dealers who are involved with White Lobster."

"These local people took crack cocaine and then got addicted?"

"Probably, people started making crack cocaine because they saw it on TV, and thought it was a way to get rich."

"It's terrible to see," said Paul.

"White Lobster, the blessing and the curse," said Ruben.

CHAPTER 52

Pelican Island

The navy patrol vessel docked at the Pelican Island pier. Augusto had contacted Jannie from the navy satellite phone, which was called the *sat phone* by everybody. He was waiting on the pier with his broad smile. Augusto saw him and returned his smile.

Augusto didn't know what to make of Jannie. He was the first South African that he had ever met. Certainly, the first Afrikaner to which he had ever spoken. Augusto had trouble understanding his accent. He tried to tune into him and gather what he was saying.

"So *howsit*? happy to see you Augusto, come, grab a dop."

"Hi Jannie, assuming a dop is a beer, regrettably I'm on duty at the moment. But if you can get your staff to bring over soft drinks and juices for the crew, that would be appreciated."

"No problem at all, consider it done," said Jannie. "Why don't we go over to the Stingray café and have a soft drink?"

They seated themselves in the café and Jannie organised drinks for them.

"So, what's happening in paradise?" said Augusto.

Jannie went through a detailed account of the recent events at Maria Cay. Augusto was concerned that Sergeant Gamboa had pointed an AK47 into the face of one of Jannie's employees. He also didn't like the incident regarding the tourist and the U.S. passport. Augusto resigned himself to the fact that the Nicaraguan government had brainwashed the public, and the armed forces, into believing that the CIA was all around them.

"Augusto, we have six VIP guests on Pelican Island. Four British and two American. They have paid a great deal of *geld* to be here. Guests such as these sustain the employment of over fifteen full time jobs for local people, plus all the additional business in Bluefields. This type of enterprise is the future of Nicaraguan tourism. We must ensure our guests have a lekker time; however, the priority is their safety," said Jannie.

Augusto didn't like being lectured by a resort manager, especially a foreign one, with a strange accent. But, Jannie was correct. The tourists were important, and they both had a duty to ensure they were safe.

"Listen Jannie, I'm going over to Maria Cay and will arrest Sergeant Gamboa. He will be charged for previous offences, not related to this incident. That should solve your immediate problem."

Jannie thanked Augusto profusely. They continued to chat about the economy, the availability of essential and scarce goods in Bluefields and the lack of skilled labour around the region. They both agreed that the new Carretera from Managua to Pearl Lagoon would enhance the local economy.

As they were putting the world to rights, Augusto's eye was attracted to movement in the distance. A young woman was walking towards them. She was wearing a canary yellow blouse that appeared to shimmer in the sunlight. As she got closer, Augusto recognised her.

"Fiona Alston. Is that you?"

"Well, if it isn't the little sailor boy himself," said Fiona.

"You two obviously know each other," smiled Jannie.

"Oh yes, Fiona was top of the class at school. Head girl, Valedictorian, Miss Goody Two shoes."

"That was because all the boys in our school were only interested in baseball, video games and ultimately, you know what."

"I thought you were in Havana?"

"I was in medical school for three years, but I had to come back."

"Because of the passing of your father?"

Fiona was surprised that Augusto knew about the death of her father, "Yes, I had to stay in Bluefields to care for my mother."

"I was so sad to hear of his passing. I remember your father; He was a good man."

"Yes, God bless him. My mother also passed a year ago."

"I'm deeply sorry to hear that. Will you be going back to Havana to complete your studies?"

"No, not now."

'That's a real pity."

"Anyway, I am devoted to my career on Pelican Island and working for the magnificent Mr Jannie," laughed Fiona.

"Fiona, I'm not sure you are being kosher," said Jannie.

"Always," said Fiona, with a smile.

"Is there something I can help you with Fiona?" said Jannie.

"Yes, is it okay if I get Ruben or Kenner to buy sand flea and mosquito repellent? We also need hydrocortisone cream and antihistamines."

"Sure, go ahead. But isn't Kenner's daily spraying of the island controlling the sand fleas? He has that expensive spraying equipment in his maintenance shack."

"It's certainly reducing them, but you know, it's a constant war."

"Maybe it's a CIA plot," said Augusto.

"Very clever, sailor boy," said Fiona.

"Listen Augusto, why don't you come back to the island when you are free and stay over as our guest? All gourmet meals and drinks on the house," said Jannie.

"That's a generous invitation Jannie. I'll take you up on that. Just make sure Fiona doesn't get too close to the kitchen though, I don't want this Cuban-trained special agent to slip any strychnine into my dinner."

"Please. Casto-trained DGI agent, your death is unavoidable," said Fiona.

"Is that the current marketing campaign for the Cuban Tourist Board?" said Augusto, with a broad smile.

CHAPTER 53

Maria Cay

It had been a pleasant surprise to see Fiona, thought Augusto as his vessel departed Pelican Island. He'd had a crush on her since they were young. She'd always been highly intelligent and a bit aloof. He had managed to steal a few youthful kisses from her over the years. He recalled that when she was awarded the Cuban scholarship it had been in the local Bluefields paper. He also recollected that the story of three young Nicaraguans winning the scholarships had been in La Prensa, the biggest national newspaper. Her family, and the town of Bluefields, had been immensely proud of her. One of their own.

He had been happy for her, but sad to see her go to Havana. However, he had new adventures and challenges to face. Everyone had their own destiny to fulfil thought Augusto.

. . . .

The crew docked the navy patrol vessel at Maria Cay. They saw that rubbish was strewn across the beach. There were empty *Flor de Cana* bottles, plastic bags, and ripped pieces of clothing. The crew members called Augusto over and pointed at the signpost. Underneath the billboard, *Armada de Nicaragua 1er Batallon de Marina de Nicaragua*, there was a skinny, brown dog, it was dead. It had been shot multiple times. Augusto looked up at the sign. It had originally displayed *Orgullo, Partiotismo, Honesto,* it now read *Kill CIA*. One of the crew whispered that the message had been daubed in faeces.

The island fuel tanks were empty, and the drinking water tanks were contaminated with soil and rubbish. Bullet casings were found to be scattered everywhere. The crew discovered that the majority of the island's palm and coconut trees had been damaged, most likely by continuously throwing a large knife at the trees. The ablution block had been destroyed by an explosion. Augusto deduced that the damage had been caused by a grenade being thrown into the toilets.

The RIB was gone.

CHAPTER 54

Pelican Island

Fiona returned to the building to check up on Danny. She announced herself as she entered the building, but there was no response. When she saw Danny, she was stunned to see his face was pale grey. The sand flea bites on his arms had become infected. He was slumped on the old mattress. There was a half-eaten breakfast spilled on the floor. The gun was laying at his side. She kicked it out of reach and then tried to rouse him.

"Mr Danny, Mr Danny, hello, how are you? Mr Danny?" whispered Fiona.

He slowly opened his eyes. "Nurse Fiona, you …. must save me …. the vultures," said Danny.

"You are very pale, Mr Danny, are you thirsty?" said Fiona.

"Yes, thirsty and....tired. Is .... anybody looking .... for me?"

"No one knows you are here, Mr Danny. You're safe."

"They are looking .... for me! What is Ruben and .... Kenner doing? Are they bringing the .... police?"

"No, Mr Danny, they are on your side. You remember, Ruben brought you the medical supplies. Kenner tells me he has fixed your boat. You must get better and then you can sail off on your journey."

"I don't know where .... to go. I can't go home. I'm .... lost. Please help me."

Fiona tried to calm Danny, but he was paranoid. She knew it was common that gunshot victims could suffer from post-traumatic stress disorder. She was aware that some traumas could cause great physical injury, but the mental toll from gunshot wounds is sometimes deeper, for unknown reasons. Fiona was also concerned that the infection was triggering a type of delirium or panic. She pondered whether a sedative to reduce the tension and anxiety might help.

Fiona pulled on a new pair of disposable gloves and grabbed a fresh bottle of water. She quizzed Danny on whether he had been taking his antibiotics medication. He seemed confused. She counted the remaining capsules in the bottle. It seemed to tally. Fiona cleaned and redressed the wound. She decided that sedatives would help.

Fiona felt useless and incompetent. Danny was going to die, and it would be her fault.

CHAPTER 55

Augusto called Josue on the sat phone, "Hey Josue, what's happening?"

"Lieutenant Commander, glad you called. I wanted to remind you that it's the funeral of Seaman Centeno tomorrow," said Josue.

"Thanks for the reminder, I'm definitely attending," said Augusto.

" I will be there with you, Sir. How has it gone today, Sir?" said Josue.

"Not good, my friend. I'm aboard the patrol vessel, we are on our way back to Bluefields from Maria Cay."

"What's happened?"

Augusto outlined what they had discovered on Maria Cay. "What?" said Josue, "Where is that bastard?"

"That's the question. He has weapons, fuel, water, and food. He could head back to Bluefields, Pearl Lagoon or across to the Corn Islands."

"Sir, we need to find him and quickly."

"Send an alert to HQ in Managua. He might turn up in Masaya. You know that's his hometown, he still has family there."

"Yes Sir, I will. The police will look out for him at their Carretera roadblocks, on the route from Bluefields."

"Make sure you warn them that he is armed," said Augusto.

"Will do, Sir. Do you think he will cause more trouble with the tourists or even the local people?" said Josue.

"It's possible. I had planned to go back to Pelican Island this week."

"There are other Islands in the area where there's also tourists. We can't guard them all."

"The way to protect them is to locate and neutralise Sergeant Gamboa," said Augusto.

"With all due respect Sir, we need to terminate him," said Josue.

CHAPTER 56

Lady of the Rosary Cathedral , Bluefields

Augusto, Josue, and the crews of the Bluefields based navy vessels attended the funeral of Seaman Rafael Centeno. The service was held at the Cathedral of Our Lady of the Rosary, the Roman Catholic church in Bluefields.

Augusto was surprised by how many people attended the funeral. There was over one hundred people. Navy personnel wore their dress uniforms. Numerous mourners wore black, some with a black tie or headscarf. Augusto had a feeling of shame that Centeno had been killed whilst under his command.

Seaman Centeno's coffin was draped with the Nicaragua national flag. It was carried into the church by six of his navy colleagues. The coffin was placed at the front of the alter and the candles surrounding the coffin were lit. There was a smell of melting wax. Inside the church, all the pews were occupied, and many mourners were standing. Augusto saw that Mrs Centeno was sat at the front of the church. She was being comforted by an older woman that he assumed was her mother. Mrs Centeno appeared to be cradling a baby, whilst a small child huddled close to her.

The priest spoke for five minutes and then began a series of prayers. He then invited the congregation to sing one of the nominated hymns. Once the hymn had ended, the priest started the funeral mass.

As the mass was reaching its conclusion, the priest sprinkled holy water on the coffin. Navy crew members then carried the coffin to the graveside. A member of the navy crew folded the Nicaraguan flag into a compact triangle and passed it to Mrs Centeno. She began to cry. The priest delivered a final prayer, and the ceremony came to an end.

Augusto and Josue made their way over to Mrs Centeno. "Please can I offer my condolences, Mrs Centeno.

Rafael was a good man; he will be sorely missed. As I said previously, if you have any problems with pensions or the navy, please do not hesitate to contact me," said Augusto.

Mrs Centeno raised her face to Augusto. Her eyes were glazed with tears, her lips quivered, she looked many years older than her age.

"Lieutenant Commander, I will not repeat what I have said to you. You know my opinions. I doubt that you are aware that a journalist was shot dead in Puerto Cabezas yesterday. He was gathering information on drug trafficking, government involvement and police abuse. He was using his smartphone to stream the clashes between police and protestors. He was shot by an unknown gunman.

"I will investigate this incident," said Augusto.

"*None is so blind, as he that will not see,*" said Mrs Centeno.

"I'm sorry, I didn't know anything about the shooting."

"There is a great deal you don't know, Lieutenant Commander. Understanding can't be forced upon someone who decides to remain ignorant," said Mrs Centeno.

. . . .

Augusto and Josue walked back to their navy vehicle.

"Don't take it personally Augusto. It wasn't your fault the narco traffickers killed Seaman Centeno," said Josue.

"I am responsible. These men are my responsibility. I placed them in harm's way," said Augusto.

"Actually, you didn't, Sir. I did. It was my decision to engage the narco trafficker's go-fast boats."

"But I delegated you to be in charge whilst I was away."

"That's correct. I took a decision and you'd have taken the same decision."

"Yes, I would have engaged. But at the end of the day, what's the point of it all? Centeno lost his life and for what?"

"Sir, that was his job, it was his duty."

"Two boats got away, and they were probably the ones with the most cargo."

They both sat in the vehicle in silence. Josue's phone rang. He answered.

"You can't be serious?" said Josue.

"What? What is it?" said Augusto.

"There has been a break-in at the armoury. The bales have gone."

CHAPTER 57

Aguila Creek

As darkness descended, the headman was inspecting the construction site. He peered into the trenches. He looked closely at the building foundations. He nodded his approval at the window fittings. The villagers all agreed that he must be very experienced in these matters.

The Martin Construction team had just finished another challenging day and had no problem with the headman wandering around, but only if he didn't want to start changing things.

It was dark when the headman and his entourage finally became bored with inspecting. A small boy approached the headman.

"You told me not to bring anyone," said the boy.

"What you mean?" said the headman.

"The navy, here again."

"Where they?"

"At creek."

The headman walked through the gloom towards the creek. What did they want again? Not more questions about the houses and school? What's wrong with these *Chele* Spaniards anyway?

As he came out of the mangrove swamps, he could see one of them peering into the creek. He couldn't see his face. As the headman got closer, he instinctively slowed his pace.

What is this? thought the headman.

The navy person spun around; it was the Sergeant.

. . . .

"So, Indian, we meet again," said the Sergeant.

"Ah, Mr Sergeant, it is good to see you. I hope you enjoyed the fish," said the headman. He could see that the Sergeant was dishevelled. He had scratches on his face and smelt of alcohol.

"I don't care about the fish. All I know is that you attacked me," said the Sergeant.

"No Sir, you are mistaken," said the headman. He saw that the Sergeant was carrying a rifle at his side, the headman recognised that it was an AK-47.

"Some stupid officers will be coming to interrogate you. You will tell them that you hit me and that I didn't fire at the panga boats."

"They have already been here. Two men, one called Romero."

"Shit, what did you tell those bastards?"

"That you did not steal any fish, that we gave them to you and your men, as a gift."

"What else?"

"Mr Sergeant, I did say that the boats got damaged, but it was an accident."

"What about the child, and me hitting you?"

"I said it was a misunderstanding and that we will not be pressing charges."

"Pressing charges?" laughed the Sergeant. "Where do you think you are? Managua? You are a barbarian, an uncivilised native."

The headman said, "Everything will be ok, we can carry on as though this never happened."

The Sergeant turned and shot the headman in the face.

CHAPTER 58

The Armoury, El Bluff Navy base, Bluefields

Augusto and Josue arrived at the armoury. They saw that the two heavy padlocks on the door of the armoury had been cut off using an oxy-fuel gas cutting or welding torch.

"Have any weapons been taken?" said Augusto.

"Sir, we have an inventory in progress." said one of the navy seamen.

"So why wasn't the armoury guarded?" said Augusto.

"Sir, that's down to me, Lieutenant Commander," said Josue.

"You left the armoury unguarded?"

"Both crews went to the funeral, they all wanted to show their respects."

"So, there was no one here? No one at all?"

"No Sir. I apologise."

"I should put you on a charge."

"Yes, Lieutenant Commander. I accept full responsibility."

"So, no one saw a vehicle approach or depart the armoury?"

"We will make enquiries Sir. I'm sorry, Sir."

"Nobody heard the robbery in progress?"

"Sir, we are making enquiries, but it doesn't look good."

"Seaman Centeno's death was even more pointless now," said Augusto.

"We can alert the police, Sir, hopefully they can identify the vehicle transporting the bales."

"The thieves knew about the funeral, and that we would all be at the church," said Augusto.

Augusto was dreading it, but he had to contact Navy HQ in Managua. He went to his office and dialled the direct number for Captain Colindres. The phone was answered immediately.

"Pablo Colindres, Captain of the Navy," said Colindres.

"Sir, this is Lieutenant Commander Romero, in Bluefields, Sir," said Augusto.

"Oh yes, I suppose you are going to tell me about a villager being killed in Aguila Creek," said Colindres.

"Sir? No. Sorry, what's that about Aquila Creek Sir?" said Augusto.

"A villager at Aquila Creek was shot dead last night. Do I have to tell you what is going on in your region, Lieutenant Commander?"

"Sorry Sir, no report has reached Bluefields on that matter, Sir."

"Yet it has reached Managua, and I know about it."

"Sorry Sir. I will investigate the matter on an urgent basis."

"I am sure you will. So, why are you calling me, Lieutenant Commander?"

"Sir, the three bales of narcotics, that we seized in the recent contact with the go-fast boats, Sir."

"What about them, Lieutenant Commander?"

"Sir, they have been stolen from our armoury," said Augusto.

The telephone line was silent. Then Colindres spoke,

"We have an altercation with narco traffickers, one of your men is killed, two go-fast boats escape north, probably with significant narcotics. You only seize three bales of cocaine from the other go-fast boats, and now they have been stolen from you."

"That is a correct summary of the situation, Sir."

"Now villagers are being murdered in your region and you don't know anything about it."

"Sir, I will investigate that matter on an urgent basis."

"Lieutenant Commander, as I have asked before, who's side are you are on, or are you just incompetent?"

CHAPTER 59

Old Cotton Tree district, Bluefields

Augusto drove back home to the Old Cotton Tree district. He slumped down at the dinner table. He poured a large *Flor de Cana* into a heavy crystal tumbler and gulped the rum. The weight of the tumbler felt good in his hand. His throat warmed from the alcohol. Augusto's head was buzzing.

There was an armed and psychotic Sergeant sailing around his region. The armoury had been looted, and the bales stolen. There were these mysterious construction projects, exactly where Madison claimed the narco centres were based. Now a villager had been murdered at Aguilla Creek.

Augusto was positive these events were interconnected. They weren't random acts, somebody was behind all this, moving the chess pieces.

. . . .

Augusto woke with a dull throb behind his eyes. Through his bleared vision he checked his phone. A couple of missed calls from Josue and one from Pedro Zamora, Nicaraguan Police Chief in Bluefields.

Augusto called Pedro.

"Pedro, it's Augusto, how's it going?"

"Hi Augusto, I'm well. How are you on this fine morning?" said Pedro.

"I'm surviving, Pedro. I saw a missed call from you," said Augusto.

"Yes, I wanted to update you. The navy is having a few problems, I hear."

"You could say that. If you could assist us, it would be appreciated."

"Not sure we can be of any help. Anyway, I'll give you a rundown. The roadblocks we have on the Carretera to Managua, they've had no success regarding the stolen bales."

"No surprise there."

"Now regarding the navy Sergeant, called Gamboa?"

"Yes, Sergeant Luis Gamboa."

"He hasn't been seen at any of the roadblocks."

"All good news then," said Augusto.

"At least you still have your sense of humour, Augusto," said Pedro.

"Anything else, Pedro?"

"The murder at Aquila Creek."

"Another problem," said Augusto.

"The villagers have informed us that the killer was a navy marine, dressed in a blue camouflage uniform. They said that he was the same one who shot up their boats a week ago."

"It's Gamboa! He must have sailed down to Aquila Creek."

"I thought it might be the same guy you were looking for."

"Thanks for the information, even if it's bad news."

"But why did he kill the headman?"

"The headman?" said Augusto.

"That's what the villagers said. The navy marine shot the headman in the face."

"This is a nightmare," said Augusto.

"What's going on?"

"It's a long story, but he assaulted the villagers and damaged their property during a search last week. I was about to charge him with those offences when he disappeared."

"It sounds as though Gamboa has seen too many Vietnam War movies, going into villages, search and destroy.

Certainly not winning the hearts and minds of the locals." said Pedro.

"We now have someone in the region, who is armed, mobile and has no problem murdering people," said Augusto.

"Okay, we can add him to the list with all the others," said Pedro.

. . . .

Following the call with Pedro, Augusto rang Josue.

"Lieutenant Commander, thank you for calling me back," said Josue.

Augusto said, "I have just spoken to Chief Pedro Zamora; he has updated me regarding the roadblocks and the killing at Aguila Creek."

"So have they found the bales?"

"No. But the killing at Aquilla Creek, it was Gamboa. He went back to the village and killed the headman."

"Why? Why would he do that?"

"It's obvious that the guy is crazy." said Augusto "You should have seen the mess at Maria Cay."

"What's the plan for locating him, Sir?" said Josue.

"We need to protect the coastline and the tourist islands. Let's start regular patrols with the sole purpose of apprehending Gamboa."

"Sir, as you know, it's a large area, but we should be able to spot the Sergeant if he's headed back north. I'll give orders to the crews at once," said Josue.

"If Gamboa tries to land at Pearl Lagoon, or any of the other populated places, then he will be spotted," said Augusto. "I doubt he has many friends within the local community."

"Sir, what about the tourist islands?" said Josue.

"Contact them all. Arrange that an armed marine stays overnight on each of the islands for the next seven days or until we locate Gambo."

"Consider it done, Sir," said Josue.

"Heaven forbid that one of the overseas tourists gets harmed," said Augusto, "Managua will go *ape-shit*."

"Yes, Managua would be super-pissed if that should happen, Sir," said Josue.

"Agreed. I'll contact Jannie at Pelican Island. I'll stay overnight on the island for the next couple of days."

"Sir, that sounds like the best approach."

"This is a nightmare; we have a murderer roaming the coast."

CHAPTER 60

CIA Headquarters, Langley, Virginia USA

She drove her red Mustang across the Francis Scott Key Bridge with the Potomac River flowing below. She darted along the George Washington Memorial Parkway, took the slip road and headed towards the *George H.W. Bush Center for Intelligence*, CIA Headquarters.

Her identification and credentials were needed at the first armed checkpoint. She submitted to the obligatory car search and then drove down to the main entrance. After successfully passing through further personal security checks, she presented her credentials again. She was issued the appropriate badge and invited to sit down, in an uncomfortable seat in the reception area.

"Ms Walker? Hi, I'm Agent Bob Logan."

"Yes, hello, nice to meet you," said Madison, as she stood and shook Bob's hand.

"Thanks for taking the time to visit us," said Logan.

"Always a pleasure," said Madison.

"I'm sure it is, please follow me."

They entered the New Headquarters Building, and then used an elevator in one of the tower buildings. Logan led Madison to a corner office on the fifth floor. A woman was seated at a small meeting table. She had long brown hair, was smartly dressed and, Madison estimated, aged around forty.

"Ms Perez, may I introduce you to Madison Walker, DEA," said Logan.

"Madison, "I'm Gloria Perez, thank you for accepting my invitation," said the woman. Madison noted that she had a distinctive East Harlem accent. A cool Westside Story vibe thought Madison.

"Hopefully, I can be of assistance," said Madison.

"Bob, please grab us a few refreshments. Madison, coffee? iced tea? We have a Starbucks in-house, iced latte?" said Gloria.

"I'm okay with a bottle of water, thanks," said Madison.

Bob scuttled out. Madison wasn't positive whether Agent Logan was the gofer in this team, but it sure looked that way.

"So, let's get down to business. I was impressed with your OCD-ETF report on Nicaragua," said Gloria.

"I didn't know the CIA was a member of the OCD-ETF," said Madison.

"We're not. But we're copied into all relevant correspondence," said Gloria.

"I shouldn't be surprised."

"The CIA is always interested in the machinations of rogue states."

"Is Nicaragua now classified as rogue state?"

"It's not first tier rogue. It isn't Iran or North Korea status. It's way down the list. We've got Syria and Yemen as high priorities these days. Other interesting places are Pakistan, Somalia and even Belarus. And always Cuba, yes always Cuba." Madison smiled.

"Not sure that poor little Nicaragua can have much impact upon the great U.S. of A these days."

"The illegal narcotics entering our country are a major threat to our democracy and our economy."

"I agree. That's why we at the DEA are working, within the framework of the OCD-ETF, to reduce the flow of illegal narcotics into our country," said Madison.

"That's where Nicaragua comes onto the radar," said Gloria.

"Come on, surely Venezuela, Columbia, Peru and Bolivia, as manufacturers and major traffickers of the global cocaine product, are more important to the CIA."

"Okay, Okay, you got me."

"So, what are you really interested in?"

Gloria paused. Just before she spoke, Logan entered the office with the refreshments. Logan distributed the drinks and then left the office. After a brief period, Gloria got back to business.

"I'm sure you are aware of *Wikileaks*," said Gloria.

Madison nodded. She knew that *Wikileaks* was an organisation that had issued sensitive and classified information on-line. They were the archetypal whistle-blower.

"*Wikileaks* released documentation that alleged that President Daniel Ortega and his FSLN Sandinista party received campaign contributions from the narco cartels, in lieu of freeing jailed drug traffickers," said Gloria.

"Anything is possible in Nicaragua," said Madison.

"Further *Wikileaks* documentation alleged that Nicaraguan senior government officials returned from meetings in Venezuela, with their suitcases full of cash."

"Again, very possible."

"In your professional opinion, do you believe that the Nicaraguan Government participates in the transportation of illegal narcotics, across their country and through their territorial waters?"

"Very good question. You've read my report. It states clearly that the DEA understands that senior Nicaraguan government officials, in partnership with others, are facilitating the shipment of cocaine from the northern coast of Colombia, though the Caribbean to Honduras."

"Yes, but is the Nicaraguan Consulate official in Mexico City, and the senior Captain of the Navy in Managua, facilitating on behalf of their government, or for themselves?"

"There is no evidence, at this stage, to enable me to give you an unequivocal answer to that question. Why is that of prime important to the CIA?"

"The FSLN government in Managua has faced many issues during recent years. We have trustworthy reports that the FSLN are deeply unpopular with the Nicaraguan masses. The violent repression of the public protests in Granada, Leon and Managua were the final straw. It's just a matter of time before the whole edifice collapses."

"You consider that the FSLN government engaging in narcotics trafficking, as another crack in the edifice?"

"Yes, that's a concise point of view. My current remit is Central America. My team gather accurate intelligence from the southern border of Mexico to the northern border of Colombia."

"So, Nicaragua is of great interest to your department?"

"Nicaragua is the largest country in Central America. The FSLN - Ortega government in Nicaragua is struggling. There is an inner circle of FSLN people who rule the country. The military, police and legal infrastructure are all controlled by the FSLN. Nicaragua is not a democracy."

"That's not news to anybody. My report is interesting to you because of what it *may* indicate?"

"Most countries have an internal Security Services division. In Nicaragua, the internal Security Services division has a country," said Gloria.

"That's clever, but that's big picture stuff. The DEA is focused on stopping narcotics reaching our borders, not regime change."

"If Nicaragua is teetering on the edge of an uprising or significant political change, I need to know."

"As stated in my report, we have identified two known individuals and one unknown individual who are behind this local initiative," said Madison. "We don't know whether they are acting on behalf of their government, or for themselves."

"What about these logistics centres?"

"As the report explains, the three centres are refuelling and rest areas, for the go-fast boats that are attempting to reach Honduras," said Madison.

"The CIA have utilised satellite facilities to assess these three centres in detail. As you are aware, major construction is taking place at all three locations. This costs money and requires local authority for these projects to proceed."

"Money from the narco cartels and authority from the Nicaraguan government?" said Madison.

"Exactly," said Gloria, "What about..." She looked at her notes, "Lieutenant Commander Augusto Romero, based in Bluefields? Is he involved in this?"

"He comes from a lengthy line of revolutionaries, Sandinistas. His loyalty is to his country and his people."

"Wow. He sounds like a real *Che Guevara*. I didn't know there were any left in the world. He's obviously an idealist."

"The Nicaraguan people were treated like indentured labourers during the previous regimes, they had a hard time. I'm not surprised that thousands rebelled against their governments," said Madison.

"So, he's another revolutionary?" said Gloria.

" Augusto's grandfather was by Sandino's side in the civil war. Sandino failed to liberate the people and was assassinated for his efforts." said Madison.

"The U.S. has always supported the legitimate Nicaragua government," said Gloria.

"As you are aware, there was a civil war," said Madison, "Daniel Ortega's Sandinistas fought, and ultimately prevailed against the Somoza regime."

"This is Central America 101. It was just another communist coup," said Gloria.

"Augusto's father was by Ortega's side in the civil war."

"A true revolutionary family, maybe we should buy them all black berets and red neckerchiefs."

"His father also successfully fought against the CIA funded Contras."

Gloria ignored Madison's barbed comment.

"So, he's a communist?"

"Do they still exist?"

"Fascist, socialist, communist, I'm not sure I can tell the difference anymore," said Gloria, with a sneer.

"What is your question again?"

"Is Lieutenant Commander Augusto Romero involved in narco trafficking?" said Gloria.

"No, he isn't, said Madison.

. . . .

When they had finished their discussion, Gloria escorted Madison out of the building. She thanked Madison for coming to Langley and being forthright in her opinions.

"I've seen your file," said Gloria.

"I'm not surprised. That's what the CIA does," said Madison.

"When you left the Marines, why didn't you apply for the Agency?" said Gloria.

"It did cross my mind, but I was concerned that I might have ended up behind a desk, here in Langley," said Madison. She grinned.

"Yeah, I understand," said Gloria, with a frown.

Madison said, "I'm a Baton Rouge, Louisiana girl. I need wide rivers, mangrove swamps, the occasional alligator, and real action now and then. Central America suits me fine."

"I hear that. You could apply for operations in the Agency."

"It's something to think about," said Madison.

"In fact, you should apply, and I will support your application," said Gloria.

CHAPTER 61

The navy RIB surfed across the Caribbean waves. The late afternoon sun glowed a shade of burnt orange. Pelicans bobbled on the sea. A boy and his boat, that's all he had ever wanted to be.

Augusto throttled back reducing the engine speeds of the RIB. As he approached Pelican Island, he saw numerous small islands in the distance, Little Pelican Cay, Compass, Pear Reef, Diamond, and Maria Cay. It's a needle in a haystack, for sure, he thought.

Jannie was on the pier to greet him. "Augusto, it's lekker to see you, come grab a dop before it's time to eat," said Jannie. Augusto tied up the RIB and wandered over to the pool bar with Jannie, whilst trying to comprehend Jannie's accent.

There were a few guests sat around the pool bar. A bartender was diligently keeping all their drinks refreshed. Jannie introduced Augusto to the guests. There were two Americans, Todd and Becky and the two Brits he had met before, Paul and Charlotte.

"Ruben, please serve the Lieutenant Commander a cold dop," said Jannie. "My VIP guests, the cavalry has arrived."

"A slight exaggeration," said Augusto.

"Hopefully, you're not General Custer," said Paul.

"Maybe I'm Sitting Bull," said Augusto.

"Maybe the Sergeant is Crazy Horse," said Todd.

"That's very smart. Someone knows their history," said Augusto.

Becky said, "I'm a 12th grade teacher, in Atlanta, Georgia, so I try to make sure Todd doesn't embarrass me too much," said Becky.

"I've Irish blood, so I'm programmed to embarrass my wife," said Todd.

"I call him Plastic Paddy, because he's a pretend Irishman," said Becky.

"I'm also in education," said Charlotte. "I'm a history lecturer at Manchester Metropolitan University in the UK."

"Interesting, which branch of history do you teach?" said Augusto.

"I specialise in The British Empire and Colonialism," said Charlotte, "and you studied American History and Politics at Manchester."

"You have a good memory, I'm impressed," said Augusto.

"It's not every day that you meet a Manchester City supporter, who's an American history and Politics graduate, in a Managua shopping centre," said Charlotte.

. . . .

Jannie led Augusto towards the visitor's lodge. This was specific accommodation for third party visitors such as police, tourist boards and special contractors. However, compared to Old Cotton Tree, it was luxurious thought Augusto.

"So, what's happening with that terrorist?" said Jannie.

"We have two navy vessels patrolling the coastline. I have navy personnel on all the tourist islands. He has nowhere to go. We will catch him very soon."

"I'm concerned about allowing my VIP guests to go to the mainland. You need to bliksem this guy." Augusto didn't bother to ask what bliksem was.

Jannie left to supervise the dinner preparation. Augusto emptied his overnight bag on the bed. He placed the sat phone on the side table and carefully inspected his handgun. It was an *Israeli Jericho 941F* semi-automatic pistol. Satisfied that the weapon was clean and fully functional, he placed it into his side holster.

There was a knock on the lodge door. Augusto placed his hand on the weapon and opened the door.

"It's the little sailor boy himself," said Fiona. She smiled.

"Well, if it isn't Bluefields answer to Fidel Casto," said Augusto. "Would you like to enter my lair?"

"No thank you, sailor boy. I just wanted to say hello and hoped that we could catch up later, after your dinner."

"You're not joining us?"

"The hired help doesn't eat with the VIP guests; we know our place."

"Oh no, big trouble in our socialist utopia."

"Enjoy your dinner, capitalist-imperialist running dog."

She smiled, turned, and sauntered away across the sand. The moonlight framed her body. She had become quite a woman thought Augusto.

CHAPTER 62

Fiona made her way over to the building. She wanted to check on Danny. As she entered the building, she heard voices. She stopped and listened. It was Kenner talking to Danny, boring him to death, thought Fiona. She turned and faced them at the back of the building.

"Ah, Nurse Fiona, my guardian angel," said Danny.

Kenner said "I was just telling Mr Danny that his boat is repaired and is now seaworthy. I used my tools from the maintenance shack." He had a wide grin on his face.

"You seem to have made an amazing recovery, Mr Danny," said Fiona.

"Yes, thanks to you Nurse Fiona, I'm feeling a great deal better."

"No, Mr Danny, it's thanks to Alexander Fleming and his colleagues formulating penicillin, the first antibiotic."

"Nurse Fiona, you are way too smart to be working on this island," said Danny.

"I am too," said Kenner.

It was the first time that Fiona had seen Danny laugh out loud. She couldn't help herself and she began giggling.

Fiona inspected Danny's wound. She checked his temperature, examined his eyes and peered into his mouth and throat using a small LED penlight. "You appear to have made an amazing recovery. Even your sand flea bites have responded well to the hydrocortisone cream and antihistamines."

"I'm feeling much better, I should be making plans to sail off into the ocean blue."

"Give it another 48 hours, Mr Danny. If everything is progressing satisfactorily, you should be okay to leave."

"What about the navy guy?" said Kenner.

"What navy guy?" said Danny.

"A big-cheese navy guy is on the island, Lieutenant Commander Romero, didn't you know?" said Kenner.

"How would I know? Why is he here?" said Danny.

"Mr Danny, please don't concern yourself. It's not good for your health. There is a navy Sergeant in the region who has been causing trouble with tourists. Augusto is here to make sure we're all safe," said Fiona.

"Augusto? You know this guy?" said Danny.

"They were sweethearts," said Kenner.

"Give me a break. We know each other from school in Bluefields. He was only at the school for one year. We were just kids," said Fiona.

"Fiona and Augusto sitting in a tree, K-I-S-S-I-N-G, first comes love, then comes marriage, then comes baby, in a baby carriage," sang Kenner. "You really need to grow up," said Fiona. Danny started laughing again.

White Lobster

CHAPTER 63

Augusto was preparing to leave the visitor's lodge, when his sat phone rang.

"Lieutenant Commander Romero," said Augusto.

"It's Karl Marx, himself."

"How did you get this number, Mustang?"

"It's what we do, Karl Marx," said Madison.

"What mind-bending information are you going to provide this time?"

"Come on, you know you enjoy our chats."

"Like a stone in the shoe."

"If you don't want to know what's happening on your coastline, I'll hang up."

"Yeah, yeah. Come on, what's happening Mustang?"

"Today we tracked two go-fast boats departing from Puerto Lempira in Honduras. They headed south into Nicaraguan territorial waters and then docked at Juticalpa Point, on your turf."

"For refuelling, and also preparing for the long journey, across the Caribbean to Cartagena," said Augusto.

"Correct. We tracked them and when they entered international waters, we pounced."

"I'm not sure what you were hoping to find. The narcotics would have already been delivered," said Augusto.

"We wanted to get eyes on these guys, who they were, where they were from, and are they known to us?" said Madison. "One of our coastguard cutters intercepted them, about 50 nautical miles east of Bluefields, close to the Corn Islands."

"Sounds interesting," said Augusto.

"The go-fast boats rapidly turned around and headed back into your territorial waters."

"Smart guys."

"Yeah, but they weren't that smart. They made it into your waters, but then crashed into each other."

"Smart guys, but not good sailors."

"We observed them from a distance with our satellite imaging system. The narco traffickers began throwing bales into the sea. We were surprised. One go-fast boat then sank. Once the seaworthy boat discharged its cargo, they retrieved their colleagues from the sea and then headed inland."

"Have the Nicaraguan authorities been informed?"

"We contacted your people through the necessary diplomatic channels. They said that they will deal with it, whatever that means."

"I will expect a phone call," said Augusto, "I'll try to sound surprised."

"I bet that they won't even contact you."

"Yeah, your probably right. This is all screwed up. It doesn't make sense. Why were they bringing narco bales south?"

"Why don't you find out, Karl Marx? you're the man on the ground."

"I will Mustang, I will."

He thanked her for the information, blew her a kiss and hung up.

Augusto placed the sat phone on the side cupboard and holstered his Jericho pistol. Deep in thought, he wandered off to dinner.

CHAPTER 64

All the guests had gathered at the Astral Bar and Grill for dinner. Jannie was fussing over them, and Augusto could see that he was making a nuisance of himself. The only people he didn't recognise was an overweight, red faced, balding guy and a small skinny woman, who had obviously undergone breast augmentation. Augusto made a mental note to avoid being seated next to them.

Paul approached Augusto, "Hi, we meet again. This is becoming a habit."

"Are you enjoying your Nicaraguan vacation?" said Augusto.

"It's fantastic. It's so exciting and unpredictable."

"You could call it that. I would say chaotic."

"Nicaragua seems so dynamic. Things are happening all the time. It's as though people are really alive here."

"Interesting. When I was in the UK, I was impressed by how most things were orderly and everything seemed to work."

"What do you mean?"

"After I passed the driving test, my UK driving licence just arrived, no hassle."

"You seemed to be impressed by the most boring, mundane things."

"Boring to you because you know it will just happen, you take it for granted."

"I prefer this life. You never know what's around the corner. Every day is an adventure, here you are living in the moment."

"The Nicaraguan Caribbean Coast is a dangerous place. Someone recently said it was like the wild west. People make their own rules. It's a Caribbean Island stuck onto the Nicaraguan landmass," said Augusto.

"I keep hearing that description. But it's exhilarating, random, dynamic."

"That's what travel does to people; it gives them a different viewpoint, however distorted."

"I love the unpredictability and the undercurrent of anarchy."

"Please! You're wrapped in cotton wool here on Pelican Island. You're not exposed to the daily struggles that people face here on the Caribbean Coast."

Paul shuffled his feet, "You have a valid point. What do I know? Sorry," said Paul.

"No, I'm that one who should be sorry. We are very happy that you chose Nicaragua for a vacation. Please enjoy your time here, that's all that matters to us," said Augusto.

"I will, no doubt about that. Are you joining us for dinner?"

"Yes. I heard there was no such thing as a free lunch, but there is such a thing as a free dinner."

"I suppose it all depends on what Jannie wants from you," said Paul.

"Don't worry about me, I wouldn't understand what Jannie was asking for anyway."

They both started laughing.

. . . .

At dinner, Augusto was relieved to find himself sat next to Paul on his left and the American woman, Becky, to his right. The overweight English guy, and the small skinny woman, were seated away from him. He later discovered this was Graham and Bev. Jannie was sat to the side of the group, fussing about the service of drinks and the specific dinner courses.

Augusto was obviously the centre of attention. He noted that he was the only dinner guest who was Nicaraguan. The questions came thick and fast.

"Is it called soccer or football in Nicaragua," said Paul.

"It's football. But our national sport is baseball," said Augusto.

"Baseball? How did that happen?" said Todd.

"Your Marine Corps spent so long in Nicaragua that we practically became the 51st state. Today we play baseball and listen to country music," said Augusto.

"Who cares about baseball, in fact who cares about country music? Nobody. It's all bollocks, if you ask me," said Graham.

Augusto laughed; he hadn't heard that British expression for years.

As the dinner ended, the guests moved towards the Astral bar. Jannie had obviously taken advantage of the free-flowing alcohol. He began jabbering away in a South African patois, "ag man, my china, I'm jags. I'm going to have a babelaas tomorrow." Paul winked at Augusto, they both laughed.

. . . .

Augusto peered through the darkness at the distant islands of lights. Even at night the coast was beautiful. Fiona appeared in front of him, "hey, sailor boy, how was dinner?"

"It was very nice, but I would have been pleased with *Baho* or *Rondon*," said Augusto.

"Now you're trying to get down with the peasants," said Fiona.

"Yeah, yeah. One day people are going to rise up and take their share," said Augusto.

"Isn't that a *Tracy Chapman* song?" said Fiona.

"I think so. What's that old saying? the Devil has all the best tunes."

"You are becoming a cynic, sailor boy."

"Oh yeah? And what did you see in Cuba that kept you on the straight and narrow, comrade?"

"I've seen things you wouldn't believe. Attack ships on fire, off the shoulder of Orion. I've watched C-beams glitter in the dark, near the Tannhauser Gate. All those moments will be lost in time, like tears in the rain."

"Hang on, isn't that from *Blade Runner*?" said Augusto.

"Yeah, still better than your *Tracy Chapman* lyrics."

CHAPTER 65

Little Pelican Cay

The panga boat slipped silently away from Pelican Island and headed towards Little Pelican Cay. They had brought along bottles of red wine, snacks, and a beach blanket. Kenner had collected the fishing gear from the maintenance shack. The stars were conspicuous and smeared across the cloudless sky. A light, cool breeze wafted across their faces.

After around twenty minutes, Kenner beached the panga on Little Pelican Cay. Ruben jumped out onto the sand and scouted for a nice spot for their evening picnic. He laid out the beach blanket and open one of the bottles of wine. Kenner walked over with a bag of snacks and the fishing gear. Their eyes began adjusting to the darkness.

"Should we at least try to catch something?" said Kenner.

"Okay, but let's drink the wine first," said Ruben.

They settled down on the blanket, sipped the red wine and munched the snacks.

"What are you going to do with your thousand dollars?" said Ruben.

"I'm not sure. I might buy a moped or a motorbike."

"They're death traps."

"No, they're great. I'll keep it in Awas, at my sister's place. Whenever I go home, I'll be mobile and I can get around."

"But you'll you have the maintenance costs, and it might get stolen and ………."

There was a noise behind them, a crunch of foliage.

"Surprise! well if it isn't the creole gay boys from Pelican Island."

Ruben was stunned to see the Sergeant, emerging from the darkness.

"What's happening here then? Gay disco? You really are the *Village People*, aren't you?" said the Sergeant.

Ruban gathered his thoughts then said "Hi Sergeant, nice to see you again. We're just having a midnight picnic."

"Yes," said Kenner, "Getting away from work for a couple of hours."

Ruben couldn't see clearly in the darkness, but he recognised the outline of an AK47, in the Sergeant's hands.

"Tell me what's happening on Pelican Island," said the Sergeant.

"Just the usual, tourists coming and going, it's boring really," said Kenner.

The Sergeant shot Kenner three times in the chest. The noise was deafening. He collapsed, falling backwards onto the ground. Ruben screamed.

Blood oozed into the sand.

"No! Oh my God. What have you done?" shouted Ruben.

"Piece of shit," said the Sergeant.

"Kenner, Kenner, Kenner," cried Ruben.

The sand around his body was black, a mixture of his blood and red wine. Kenner struggled to breath, then stopped.

"Now you will tell me what is happening on Pelican Island," said the Sergeant.

The three bullets had gone straight through Kenner's chest and resulted in a catastrophe on the beach. Ruben was sobbing and pulled Kenner's dead body towards him. He was drenched in Kenner's blood.

"So gay boy, what is the CIA doing on Pelican Island?" said the Sergeant.

"Why? Why did you do this?" said Ruben.

"Listen gay boy, tell me what's going on over there or I'll shoot you as well."

"Nothing's going on," Ruben was crying as he tried to pull Kenner towards him.

"Okay, say goodbye to your dead boyfriend." The Sergeant pointed the muzzle of the AK47 towards Ruben's face.

"Wait, it's not CIA," said Ruben, through his tears.

"That's better. What is it?"

"There is a narco trafficker hiding on the island. His go-fast boat is loaded with bales of cocaine. He's wounded."

"Now that is interesting. Where is he hiding?"

"Why did you kill Kenner, you bastard?"

"Where is the narco guy hiding?"

"In the building at the north of the island."

"Who else knows about the narco trafficker?"

"Only Fiona. This is a nightmare, I can't believe Kenner is dead."

"Who's Fiona?"

"She's the person on the island who has medical experience. She's treating him."

"The nurse. So that's why you bought medical supplies."

"Yes. We also bought marine parts because the boat had been damaged by gunfire. Why? Why did you do this?"

"Is he armed?"

"Kenner, Kenner, no, oh my God."

"Is he armed, Gay boy?"

"Yes, he has a handgun, hopefully he will use it on you, bastard."

The Sergeant digested this information. He would seize all the bales of cocaine and the go-fast boat. He would deal with this narco trafficker and that Fiona. He would pin the headman's killing on the narco trafficker. He would be a hero.

"There is also a senior navy guy on the island, you are going to have to explain what you have done to Kenner," said Ruben.

"Who? Who is the senior navy guy?" said the Sergeant.

"Lieutenant Commander Romero from Bluefields."

"Why is that bastard Romero on the island?"

"He was invited by Jannie, my boss. You are going to have some explaining to do, murderer," said Ruben.

"Romero, I hate that half-breed traitor," said the Sergeant.

"Isn't he your boss?" said Ruben, with a scowl.

The Sergeant shifted and faced Ruben, and then shot him through the throat, at point blank range. Blood and flesh splattered across the sand.

Ruben slumped to the ground, clawing at his throat. His body shook briefly and then he died.

Ruben and Kenner's bodies lay in the surf, as the rising tide began to engulf them.

CHAPTER 66

Pelican Island

Fiona and Augusto left the Astral Bar and strolled into the darkness together. They wandered along the east coast of the island. The sound of waves lapping on to the beach were occasionally interrupted by the guttural call of a pelican.

"Do you miss Cuba?" said Augusto.

"No, but I miss my studies. I was so close and now it's all come to nothing," said Fiona.

"Can't you study in Managua or go back to Cuba?"

"Easier said than done. I don't have the fees for the American University in Managua to study medicine."

"And Cuba?"

"No chance to return. It was a full scholarship, a one-off opportunity."

"What happens now?"

"I'm stuck in Bluefields and Pearl Lagoon for the rest of my life. A victim of circumstance. What about you?"

"I enjoyed studying in the UK. But I returned home and joined the navy for the love for my country and my passion for the sea."

"So, it's all worked out for you?"

" Mostly, I've done quite well; Lieutenant Commander is not a bad rank," said Augusto.

"So, what's troubling you?"

"It's all the politics and the underhand manoeuvring."

"You mean the FSLN?"

"Yeah, I'm not seeing the big picture and it's obvious that I'm being manipulated."

"Augusto, you know we're the forgotten people here on the Caribbean Coast. You aren't going to change that."

"But it's becoming a crisis. Narco trafficking is impacting the people of the region and the independence of Nicaragua."

"Augusto, you can't carry the worries of Nicaragua on your shoulders." Fiona pulled him close and kissed him. He returned the kiss.

"I'm feeling better already," said Augusto. They walked along the beach, holding hands.

There was a sudden loud noise. Augusto said, "that's an automatic weapon."

"Where did it come from?" said Fiona.

He pointed towards Little Pelican Cay. "In that direction, who's over there?"

"Nobody. There's nothing to see."

"Someone is there now."

Another shot rang out.

"It's an AK47, I'd recognise that anywhere. I'm going to have to call this in. I need to get back to the visitor's lodge and call Josue on the sat phone," said Augusto.

"I'll come with you."

"I should have brought the sat phone with me, damn," said Augusto.

As they turned around to head back to the visitor's lodge, Augusto noticed something move out of the corner of his eye.

"What's that?" said Augusto.

"What? Where?"

"There, floating in the sea."

There was a flotilla of bales drifting towards the beach.

"I can't believe it. White Lobster," said Fiona.

Augusto plunged into the sea and dragged the first bale onto the beach. He worked steadily, until there were nine bales aligned on the sand.

"I'm definitely going to have to call this in," said Augusto.

"Stop," said Fiona "I need to tell you something."

Augusto looked at her. "I'm worried about what you're going to say."

"Okay, here goes, please don't get angry," said Fiona.

"That depends," said Augusto.

CHAPTER 67

Fiona told Augusto everything, the building, Mr Danny, the go-fast boat, the gunshot wound, the medical treatment, Ruben and Kenner and the boat repairs.

"What have you gotten yourself into?" said Augusto.

"I was just trying to help; Mr Danny would have died."

"Now you face ten years in prison, minimum."

She started to cry. He paused for a moment, then pulled her towards him.

"We can figure this out," said Augusto. Truthfully, He wasn't that sure.

Augusto stared at the nine bales resting on the sand. He needed to hide them somewhere, until he could decide what to do.

"What's that small building over there?" said Augusto.

"It's Kenner's maintenance shack," said Fiona.

"Who's Kenner? Tell me again."

"He's the groundsman. He keeps all his tools and equipment in the shack, but it's never locked."

"Where is Kenner right now?"

"Not sure, probably with Ruben somewhere."

"Okay, let's do this."

Augusto dragged each bale across the beach towards the maintenance shack. Fiona switched the shack lights on. The place was full of equipment, tools and a large lawnmower. Once all the bales were inside, Augusto closed the doors. He pulled out a Swiss Army knife and began cutting open one of the bales.

"What are you doing?" said Fiona.

"Call it natural curiosity," said Augusto.

"Curiosity killed the cat."

"Cats are the last thing I'm worried about, Sharks maybe."

Augusto managed to cut a sizeable hole into the side of the bale. He forced his hand inside through the opening. He grabbed some of the contents and pulled it out through the hole.

He held a block of U.S. currency in his hand, sealed together by shrink-wrap. It consisted of hundred-dollar notes.

"Nice to see you again Mr Franklin," said Augusto.

"Where has this come from?" said Fiona.

Augusto looked at Fiona. "I know what this is."

He told Fiona about the call he had received earlier from Madison. "I don't understand. Why would a DEA agent call you?" said Fiona.

"It's a long story. I met her in Mexico City, and we agreed to keep each other informed."

"Her?" said Fiona.

"I told you it's a long story."

"Doesn't this make you some kind of collaborator?"

"Oh, come on, it's not like that."

"Are you sure that she isn't CIA?"

"I told you; she is DEA. These bales were tossed into the sea by the narco traffickers."

"Let's rewind for a moment. These bales are from the go-fast boats that the U.S. Coastguard tried to intercept today?" said Fiona.

"Yes. The go-fast boats moving north are transporting the narcotics. I think the go-fast boats moving south are moving U.S. dollars."

"How much do you think there is here?"

"I don't know, but definitely millions. It depends upon the denominations of the notes," said Augusto, "but it looks as though they are mostly one-hundred-dollar notes. "Whatever the total amount, it's a great deal of money," said Fiona.

"Life changing," said Augusto. He pulled Fiona towards him and kissed her. She wrapped her arms around him.

CHAPTER 68

The Building, Pelican Island

Danny had been asleep on the old mattress. He was woken by noise in the building. He wasn't too concerned. Everything had gone according to plan. Kenner had fixed the boat, and the guys had provided him with a regular supply of food and drinks. Nurse Fiona had fixed him up and he was feeling the best he had since Aquila Creek.

"Kenner, is that you?"

"Nurse Fiona? Don't be shy, I'm ready for a full examination," said Danny.

A man in a blue camouflage uniform, stepped out in front of Danny. He was pointing an AK47 at him. He spoke in Spanish.

"Who are you? Why are you here?" said the Sergeant.

"Hi, I'm Danny. I'm a fisherman. I've been sick and I had trouble with my boat. I've just had it repaired and I'll be leaving in the morning."

"Who fixed your boat? The gay boys?"

"Oh, you must be Lieutenant Commander Romero. The friend of Nurse Fiona. Nice to meet you."

"I'm not that bastard Romero," and he spat on the floor.

"Oh, sorry for my mistake, who are you, Sir?"

I'm Sergeant Primo Luis Gamboa, Nicaraguan Navy."

"Nice to meet you, Sir. I'm Danny McCoy from Pearl Lagoon. Are you a local, Sergeant?"

"I am from the city of Masaya. The city of flowers, a city of culture, not like this backwater of a place, full of blacks and Indians." The Sergeant spat on the ground again.

Danny slowly reached out for his Glock.

"Don't even think about it, Creole."

The AK47 was pointed directly at Danny's chest. The Sergeant stooped down and picked up the Glock, without losing eye contact with Danny.

"I'm just a fisherman. The handgun is for protection."

"This go-fast boat over here, you say this is your fishing boat?"

"Yes, it's more that I need. But useful for fishing trips out as far as the Corn Islands.

"Move over to your boat, now."

Danny hobbled over to the go-fast boat. He was dismayed to see that the bales could be seen.

"Open one of the bales," said the Sergeant.

"These are not mine. Someone must have put them in the boat while I was sick."

"Open a bale now or I will shoot you. Just like I shot your creole gay boyfriends."

"What? Kenner and Ruben? They've been shot?" said Danny.

"Correct, for resisting arrest and assaulting a navy Sergeant Primo."

"Are they okay?"

"Unlikely. They're probably crab food by now."

"Oh my God."

"God cannot help you. Just open the bale, African boy, or whatever you are," said the Sergeant.

Danny struggled with the bale, but eventually managed to get the corner open.

"Now tip the bale on its side."

Danny turned the bale over, brown soil split over the floor of the building.

"What's that? Step back," said the Sergeant. He bent down and grabbed a handful of the soil.

Danny thought that this might be his moment, but he hesitated. He would wait for a better opportunity.

"It's sand, beach sand," said the Sergeant.

Danny peered at the sand. It didn't make sense. Had he risked his life to just bring sand from Cartagena?

"Someone is trying to make a fool out of me. The CIA. Yes, it's them. They are behind this," said the Sergeant.

"I don't know anything about the sand or the CIA. I'm just a fisherman," said Danny. He then realised why the Miskito villagers had begun shooting at him at Aguila Creek.

"Yes, the gay boys, the Americans, the CIA, even Romero, you are all wrapped up in this."

Without another word, the Sergeant shot Danny in the chest.

Danny screamed in pain as he fell backwards.

The Sergeant shot him another five times.

Blood, tissue and body fluid oozed across the building floor.

CHAPTER 69

The Maintenance Shack

Shots rang out across Pelican Island.

"That's very close," said Augusto, "I'm certain it's an AK47". He gripped his Jericho pistol.

"What should we do?" said Fiona.

"I have to get back to the visitor's lodge. I need to call Josue. We need back up," said Augusto.

There was a loud explosion and the lights in the shack went off.

"What's going on? It's as though the island is being invaded," said Fiona.

There was another loud explosion.

"Grenades, someone is tossing grenades."

"Who is it?"

"It's got to be Sergeant Gamboa. The AK47. The grenades. He's as crazy as a starving shark."

"What should we do?"

"You need to stay here. I'm going outside and see if I can locate him."

"Don't leave me," said Fiona.

"This is the safest place for you. If I locate him and we exchange fire, then you'll be in danger," said Augusto.

"And if he comes here, to the maintenance shack?"

"Why would he come here?"

"For millions of dollars?"

Augusto thought for a moment.

"Okay, you come with me. But if I tell you to hit the ground, you do it, right?"

"Yes Sir." She gave him a long kiss, "Be careful. I've just found you again. Don't be getting shot," said Fiona.

"I have no intention of being shot," said Augusto, he kissed her forehead.

They stepped outside the maintenance shack, into the darkness, and into the danger.

CHAPTER 70

Suite 3

The gunshots and explosions had stirred him.

Was he imaging this? Was he dreaming?

Charlotte was also waking up. The pair of them had drank too much. Paul felt as though he was still drunk. He could still feel the alcohol in his bloodstream.

"Is it fireworks?" said Charlotte.

"It sounds like a war movie," said Paul.

"What should we do?"

"I'm going to see what's happening outside."

"Please be careful."

Paul left the suite and walked up the sandy path towards the Astral bar. As he approached the bar he could see two figures in the darkness, they were walking towards him.

"Hey, what's going on?" he shouted.

"Be quiet, keep your voice down," Paul was relieved to see it was Augusto and one of the island employees, Fiona. The three of them stood close to the Astral bar.

"What's happening?" said Paul.

"Not good news, I think that Sergeant Gamboa has arrived on the island," said Augusto

"No, you can't be serious?"

"It is the only logical explanation for what's happening." Augusto didn't bring up the murder of the headman, he didn't want to frighten them.

"But why would he be firing a gun and causing explosions?" said Paul.

"He could be suffering from a psychotic disturbance," said Fiona.

"Yes," said Augusto, "it's called starving shark syndrome."

"You mean he's insane or deranged?" said Paul.

"Now's not the time to assess the mental health of Sergeant Gamboa," said Augusto, "Paul, where's your wife?"

"Charlotte is in Suite 3, just down there," said Paul, pointing to the hut nearby.

"Fiona, go and grab Charlotte, you should both hide underneath the suite," said Augusto.

"Augusto, please be careful." She kissed Augusto and ran towards Suite 3.

Even during the current chaos, Paul was surprised to see that Augusto and Fiona were in a relationship.

"Paul, you and I are going to call for back up and then locate the Sergeant. Sound okay with you?"

"Definitely. I'm your man," said Paul.

"Excellent. Have you ever fired a handgun?" said Augusto.

"No."

"Ever fired any weapon?"

"No."

"Great."

"Sorry," said Paul.

"No problem. Last question, are you still enjoying the excitement and unpredictability of the Nicaraguan Caribbean Coast?"

. . . .

Paul and Augusto made their way towards the visitor's lodge on the west coast of the island. They hadn't walk for more than five minutes when further gunfire shattered the silence. They crouched behind a cluster of coconut trees.

"What was that? It sounded different," said Paul.

"That's a pistol. We could be dealing with more than one adversary. Then again, maybe he has two or more weapons," said Augusto.

"Two guns and some grenades?" said Paul, with a grimace on his face.

"Yes. Let's make our way through the trees and see if we can spot him or them," said Augusto.

They moved hesitantly towards a residential building.

Paul said "This is Jannie's house. I had a drink with him one afternoon on the veranda. He calls it a *stoop*". They approached the door of the house. Augusto could taste the acrid bite of gunpowder. He also smelt death.

Augusto entered the house first, with his Jericho pistol at the ready. Jannie was lying spread-eagled on the living room floor. He has been shot more than once. Blood pooled beneath his body.

Paul began to sob. "He was such a nice guy. He didn't deserve this."

Augusto checked for a pulse. Nothing. "Let's get out of here. We need to get hold of that sat phone."

Through his tears, Paul said "I've been trying my mobile phone, but no reception at all, not even that local service *Movistar*."

"Gamboa took out the power and cut the communications. Standard practice," said Augusto.

"I suppose that's why we heard two explosions."

"Exactly. Come on, let's grab that sat phone," said Augusto.

"It's a tragedy what's happened to Jannie," said Paul. "This feels unreal. It's as though I'm in a very frightening movie."

"It's no movie, it's real life in Nicaragua. Click your heels three times…… you're not in Kansas anymore, Toto."

CHAPTER 71

They moved through a cluster of palm trees. After five minutes they made it to the visitor's lodge. The sat phone was on the side table. Augusto grasped the phone and rang Josue.

"Lieutenant Amander" said a sleepy Josue.

"Josue, this is Augusto."

"Sir, this must be an emergency," said Josue, as he shook off the last vestiges of sleep.

"We have an Active Shooter on Pelican Island. I think it's Sergeant Gamboa., maybe with others. Earlier, I heard AK47 rounds from Little Pelican Cay, but now I'm hearing them on the island. I also identified a pistol shot. There were two grenade explosions. I have one confirmed fatality, Jannie van Rensburg, the manager of Pelican Island," said Augusto.

"Jesus Christ. Are you armed?" said Josue.

"Only with a Jericho pistol," said Augusto.

"Okay Sir, keep your head down, we are on our way. We'll use one of the navy RIBs; ETA + ninety minutes," said Josue.

"Thanks Buddy."

"Keep safe, and if you have a chance Sir, shoot that bastard."

Augusto made another call.

"Uncle Dereck, is that you?"

"*Naksa* nephew, it's the middle of the night, what do you want?"

"Uncle, can you arrange your Miskito friends to come to Pelican Island? They need to arrive in one of their go-fast boats."

"Can I ask you why, nephew?

"That bastard Sergeant Gamboa and also Narco Traffickers."

"When do the villagers need to be there, nephew?"

"In one hour, latest."

"That's tough. They could leave from Net Point, which would take fifteen minutes travelling time. But they are all asleep now."

"You can do it. If they can't locate me when they arrive, then they should find a local woman called Fiona."

"This is very worrying, nephew."

"And tell them to come fully armed and prepared for confrontation."

CHAPTER 72

Augusto and Paul headed back towards the guest accommodation. Augusto gripped the Jericho in one hand and the sat phone in the other. They quickened their pace and headed in the direction of the suites.

In the moonlight, they saw a large figure running along the path towards them. "Help me, Help," shouted the person.

"It's Graham," said Paul.

Graham approached Augusto and Paul, and then stopped and bent over gasping for air. "It's that Sergeant, I saw him. He went into the American's suite and there was all kind of noise and screaming, you've got to help me."

"Where's Bev?"

"I'm not sure, I couldn't see her in the dark, I think she's hiding in a wardrobe."

"You left her alone in the suite?" said Augusto.

"What was I supposed to do? It's me he's after. Successful British businessman, someone who won't take his nonsense."

"Graham, you stay right here. Paul and I will go to the suites," said Augusto.

"Where shall I hide?"

"If you go and lay down in those bushes over there, no one will see you in the dark."

"There might be snakes."

"Just go into the bushes, for Christ's sake," said Paul.

Augusto and Paul ran towards the suites. Paul looked back and saw Graham stepping cautiously towards the bushes.

. . . .

Augusto and Paul approached Suite 2.

"Who's staying here?" said Augusto

"The Americans, Todd and Becky," said Paul.

Augusto knocked on the door. No reply.

"Todd, Becky, are you there?" said Paul.

Silence.

Augusto tried the handle. The door opened; Paul switched on the lights.

There were a pair of binoculars and a damaged telescope on the floor, hundreds of U.S. dollars were scattered across the room. The bed was drenched in a dark red liquid. At the back of the room two bodies lay on the floor, their hands tied behind their backs. It was carnage, blood was everywhere. Augusto saw that their throats had been cut.

"Oh my God," said Paul. He vomited.

Written in blood, on the white painted wall, were three letters: CIA.

CHAPTER 73

Fiona and Charlotte squeezed underneath Suite 3.

Charlotte grimaced.

"Better to face numerous creepy crawlies under the suite than some madman with a gun." said Fiona.

The recent gunfire and explosions had shaken them. They were lying underneath the suite whispering to each other when they heard footsteps.

Someone knocked on the door of the suite above and tried the handle, "Hello, this Sergeant Gamboa. I check for intruders, open door."

After a brief period of silence, "You must open door. CIA are on island. Is important that you are safe, and you not prisoner of CIA."

In the darkness, Fiona and Charlotte looked at each other.

"Ok, I'm coming. Not my fault if you get injured," said the Sergeant. He opened the door.

Fiona and Charlotte could hear the Sergeant stomping around above them. There were crashes and loud noises. They could hear him talking to himself in Spanish. The Sergeant then exited the suite.

The Sergeant saw two men walking in his direction. One was wearing a navy uniform. The Sergeant raised his AK47 and switched to rapid fire mode.

. . . .

Paul was hit first and fell backwards. A bullet smashed into Augusto's left shoulder knocking him over. Augusto felt a burning sensation in his foot and suddenly became overwhelmed with weariness. His foot seemed to be on fire, as he drifted into oblivion.

CHAPTER 74

The two men were sprawled across the ground. Paul had been floored by a bullet that had skirted across his cheek, searing his right ear. He turned his head and glanced over at Augusto. He looked dead.

The Sergeant strode towards the two men, preparing to deliver the *coup de grace*. He would enjoy this moment, CIA bastards. They had been terrorising Nicaragua for over two hundred years. The man from Masaya was fighting back.

There was a noise behind him. He spun around. A woman was climbing out from beneath the suite. She spoke in Spanish,

"Heaven help us, what have you done?" said the woman.

"Who you? identify yourself," said the Sergeant pointing his AK47.

"I am Fiona Alston; I work here on the island."

"Oh, the famous Fiona. The creole woman who gives medical treatment to narco traffickers."

"This is not the time for your stories, I need to help Augusto and Paul."

"Augusto? You mean that bastard Romero. He is CIA spy."

"Let me past, he is bleeding to death."

"Better than he deserves, he ------."

Three shots rang out. The Sergeant shrieked and then collapsed to the ground.

Paul lowered the Jericho.

Fiona stepped towards the Sergeant. He was face down in the sand. Blood seeped from a large wound in his back. She kicked away the AK47 and grabbed the Glock handgun which was laying by his side. Fiona handed the Glock to Paul and then hurried to Augusto.

"Augusto, Augusto, can you hear me?" said Fiona. There was dark blood oozing from his left shoulder. "Get me some material, anything, quickly" she said.

Charlotte arrived with towels and a shirt. She handed them to Fiona and then rushed over to Paul.

"Paul, are you ok?" said Charlotte. She hugged him.

"Don't worry about me. A bullet glanced off my head, I think my ear is bleeding," said Paul.

Charlotte looked at Paul's right ear, half of it had gone. He had a deep wound across his right cheek, but it wasn't bleeding much. She kissed him.

"You'll live, Scarface. It looks as though you have just gone three rounds with Mike Tyson," said Charlotte.

She turned and looked over to Fiona "How's Augusto, will he be ok?"

"He's lost a lot of blood. If the bullet has hit the brachial artery, he's in big trouble."

"Can we help?" said Paul, he was frightened that Augusto would die.

Fiona said, "Charlotte, help me apply direct pressure to the wound. He also has an exit wound. He's been shot in the foot, but that isn't bleeding too much. Where is Ruben or Kenner? I need my medical bag from the staff quarters."

The Sergeant was laying on the ground in a pool of blood, however he had turned his face towards Fiona and Augusto.

"Hey Fiona, I killed narco guy, you wasted time fixing him."

"You Bastardo."

I shot creole gay boys, Little Pelican," rasped the Sergeant.

"You are a murderer."

"And I killed CIA spies. They are all dead. I save Nicaragua. You save me now."

"I'm not saving you. You are a devil."

"Si, El Diablo de Masaya," said the Sergeant.

"Will somebody shut that *Chele bastardo* the fuck up," said Fiona, in English.

Paul walked over to where the Sergeant was motionless on the ground.

The Sergeant smiled at him, a smirk, exposing his twisted and blood smeared teeth.

Paul pointed the Glock at the Sergeant's head and shot him. Brain, bone and blood dispersed across the ground.

Charlotte's scream echoed across the beach.

CHAPTER 75

Paul was relieved to see that Augusto was conscious. Fiona managed to stem the bleeding from his shoulder and the exit wound. As she was about to inspect Augusto's foot wound, a group of men appeared from within a cluster of palm trees.

Paul gripped the Glock.

"Miss Fiona? Is that you?" said one of the men.

She saw that they were Miskito villagers, and that they were armed.

"Yes, *Naksa*, who are you?"

"*Naksa*, Miss Fiona, Boss Dereck told us to come here," said one of the men.

"We are from Net Point," said another of the Miskito villagers.

"Yeah, Augusto called an Uncle Dereck on the sat phone and asked him to send these guys," said Paul.

"Okay, I know what this is about. Charlotte, please keep the pressure on Augusto's shoulder wound, front and back."

"Will do," said Charlotte.

Fiona looked directly into Augusto's eyes "I won't be more than ten minutes, darling, you are going to be ok." She kissed him on the lips and tasted blood.

He grunted, "come back safely."

"Paul, go to the staff quarters quickly and ask someone to pass you my medical bag, it's next to the bed."

"I'm on it."

Fiona beckoned the Miskito villagers," You guys, please come with me."

. . . .

When Fiona had left with the villagers, Augusto said "Charlotte, please…. please pass me ….the sat phone that's lying on the ground."

"Come on Augusto, Fiona will kick my ass if she sees I'm letting you make a call."

"It's very …. important. Please pass it to me…. right now," said Augusto.

She passed him the sat phone.

He struggled to make the call with his one useful hand.

The phone rang five times and then she picked it up.

"Hey Mustang. Glad to hear your voice. It's now my turn …… to give you the ……inside track."

CHAPTER 76

El Bluff, Bluefields

Josue made a call and discussed the incident with Colindres in Managua. He then issued an urgent report to navy headquarters, as requested by Colindres. The report clarified the events on Pelican Island and surrounding small islands.

A Nicaraguan registered go-fast boat became unseaworthy and beached at Pelican Island.

The go-fast boat was being used by narco traffickers in the illegal trafficking of narcotics.

A confrontation arose between the Nicaraguan navy and the narco traffickers.

There have been seven fatalities and two seriously wounded.

These are as follows:

- Kenner Bufo, a Nicaraguan citizen employed at Pelican Island as a groundsman, was shot and killed on Little Pelican Cay.
- Ruben Downs, a Nicaraguan citizen, employed at Pelican Island as a bar tender, was shot and killed on Little Pelican Cay.
- An unidentified narco trafficker was shot and killed on Pelican Island.
- Jannie van Rensburg, a South African citizen who was the manager at Pelican Island, was shot and killed on Pelican Island.
- Todd Cavanagh, a US citizen who was a guest on Pelican Island, was stabbed and killed on Pelican Island
- Becky Cavanagh, a US citizen who was a guest on Pelican Island, was stabbed and killed on Pelican Island.

- Sergeant Luis Gamboa, Sergeant Primo, Nicaraguan Navy, from Masaya and based in Bluefields, was shot and killed on Pelican Island.

- Paul Taylor, A UK citizen who was a guest at Pelican Island, was shot and wounded on Pelican Island. He has minor facial lacerations, and the lower part of his right ear has been lacerated.

- Lieutenant Commander Augusto Romero, Nicaraguan Navy, Caribbean Coast Region was severely wounded on Pelican Island. He has bullet wounds in the left shoulder and left foot. His life was saved by the prompt actions of the Pelican Island staff.

No seizures of illegal narcotics were made.

In the report there was no mention of the go-fast boat's cargo of sand. There was no mention of the role of Sergeant Gamboa in the incident. There was no mention of Aguila Creek or the murder of the headman.

. . . .

The Nicaraguan Minister of Foreign Affairs made the obligatory phone calls to the U.S. ambassador in Managua, the South African ambassador in Mexico City and the British ambassador-designate to Nicaragua, based in San Jose, Costa Rica.

He personally informed them of the tragic incident. He stated that the confrontation was related to narco traffickers, most likely operating from South America, and that the Nicaraguan Navy had engaged the narco traffickers.

The Minister offered his condolences on behalf of the Republic of Nicaragua. He reassured them that they would give the incident their highest priority. He said that the Republic of Nicaragua would assist the citizens of their respective countries, and their families.

Within hours, the incident had gone viral on social media and was front-page news around the globe.

CHAPTER 77

Washington DC

The OCD-ETF scheduled an urgent meeting in their headquarters on 441 G Street, Washington DC. Participants that could not attend in person used secure video conferencing applications to join the meeting.

The Director of the executive office of the OCD-ETF opened the meeting. He clarified that all representatives of the OCD-ETF were present, DEA, FBI, U.S. Coast Guard plus delegates from the CIA. He thanked everyone for attending this important meeting at such short notice, whether in person or via video conferencing.

The Director informed all meeting participants that he had been contacted by the Attorney General. A report had been demanded by the AG, which detailed the Pelican Island incident. Two U.S. citizens had been killed. The Department of Justice, and the President, wanted to know exactly what had happened.

Throughout the meeting, participants offered their perspectives. After fifteen minutes discussion it was clear to all involved that the meeting was going nowhere.

Gloria Perez of the CIA spoke, "I believe it would be beneficial if we allow Madison Walker of the DEA to speak."

The Director thanked Gloria for her intervention and asked Madison for her opinion regarding the incident.

Madison paused to steel herself, then spoke, "Narco traffickers are increasing utilising the Caribbean route from the Northern Columbian coast to Honduras. Three narco trafficker logistics centres have been established on the Nicaraguan Caribbean coast. These are utilized to refuel vessels and further assist said narco traffickers on their journeys," said Madison.

"Hi, Madison, do we have proof that the narco cartels are behind the establishment of these logistics centres?" said Carl Weber, U.S. Coast Guard, via video conferencing.

"Hi Carl, nice to hear your voice again. The source of the funding for these logistics centres has not been confirmed at this stage. However, the narco cartels have the cash. The Nicaraguan government is bankrupt. They needed a loan from the Central American Bank to buy vaccines," said Madison.

"What a way to run a country," said Gloria Perez.

Madison continued, "Very recently, a convoy of narco traffickers, utilising five go-fast boats, attempted to make use of this Caribbean route to reach Honduras. They were engaged by the Nicaraguan Navy, south of Bluefields. Two go-fast boats escaped north, and three others were sunk."

"It sounds as though the Nicaraguans are trying to stop the narco traffickers," said Carl Weber.

"Please continue Madison," said the Director.

"A sixth go-fast boat arrived late to that confrontation, and evaded capture. The vessel that is the centre of the recent incident on Pelican Island, is probably that sixth go-fast boat." said Madison.

"What happened to it?" said a representative from the FBI.

"It seems that it developed engine trouble and ultimately ended up on Pelican Island, unbeknown to the resort manager at the island."

"The Nicaraguan Navy should have spotted it," said Carl Weber.

"Our intelligence has subsequently confirmed that the go-fast boat, hidden on Pelican Island, was revealed to have been carrying a cargo of beach sand, and not cocaine."

"What are we supposed to deduce from this?" said Gloria Perez.

"We at the DEA have concluded that this go-fast boat was a decoy, utilized to enable two go-fast boats, loaded with cocaine, to proceed north to Honduras."

"That's rather devious," said the FBI representative.

"And clever," said the Director.

"The Nicaraguan Navy managed to only seize three bales from the intercepted go-fast boats. So, we can assume that at least two of those sunken go-fast boats were also decoys."

"Three bales? Yes, that seems a low quantity for the number of go-fast boats intercepted," said Carl Weber.

"The three bales of cocaine seized have subsequently been stolen from the Nicaraguan Navy Armoury in Bluefields, by parties unknown," said Madison.

"It sounds like Nicaragua is out of control," said the Director.

"It's certainly lacking law and order on the Caribbean Coast," said Madison.

"And overall governance across the country," said Gloria Perez.

"The Pelican Island incident has a further dimension," said Madison. "It appears that a serving seaman in the

Nicaraguan Navy, a certain Sergeant Gamboa turned *Active Shooter*."

"My God, Nicaragua is in chaos," said the FBI representative.

"We believe that the Sergeant was responsible for the deaths of seven people, including Todd and Becky Cavanagh, of Atlanta, Georgia and a village headman at one of the logistics centres."

"So, what happened to this piece of shit," said the Director.

"The Sergeant was shot dead by a UK citizen, Paul Taylor," said Madison.

"Not all bad news then," said the FBI representative.

"Paul Taylor? Is he British SAS or other special forces?" said the Director.

"We don't know," said Madison.

"We at the CIA will find out who he is," said Gloria Perez.

White Lobster

CHAPTER 78

The *United States Department of State* issued an urgent diplomatic communication to the Embassy of Nicaragua, New Hampshire Avenue, Washington D.C.

The diplomatic communication was addressed for the immediate attention of the Ambassador.

The key points of the communication were:

- The Government of the Republic of Nicaragua is to immediately clarify the situation regarding the murder of two U.S. citizens by a serving member of the Nicaraguan Navy.

- The Government of the Republic of Nicaragua is to immediately clarify the situation regarding three narco-logistics centres at Puerto Kiabrata, Juticalpa Point and Aquila Creek on the Nicaraguan Caribbean Coast, including the source of the funding to construct said narco-logistics centres.

- The Government of the Republic of Nicaragua is to immediately clarify the situation regarding narco traffickers using *decoy* go-fast vessels to further obstruct U.S. federal agencies, and Central American national security services, in their duties to apprehend and seize illegal narcotics.

The communication was copied to the *United Nations Office on Drugs and Crime*, the *Organisation of American States*, and *INTERPOL*.

CHAPTER 79

Masaya Volcano

It was late evening and the Masaya Volcano National Park had closed for the day. However, the flash of a government identity card ensured that the park guard raised the entrance barrier.

As Espinoza drove into the car park, he saw the red glow emanating from the mouth of the volcano. He could also see Colindres crouched in the driving seat of his black BMW, the radiance of the volcano illuminating his face. Nobody else was around. Espinoza parked up and strode over to his colleague's car. He tapped on the driver's window.

"Are you staying in there all night? Come out and smell the rotten eggs," said Espinoza.

Colindres got out of his car. "Why are you in such a good mood? We have a crisis to deal with," said Colindres.

"Crisis? It will soon be forgotten, and then we can get back to business."

"You live in Mexico City. Here in Managua, all hell is breaking loose."

"So, some people get killed by a crazed navy Sergeant, what's the big deal?"

"This could impact us."

What's this got to do with our operations?"

"Some of those people were Americans, tourists. That's not playing well here in Managua."

"The narco traffickers weren't responsible for these killings. In fact, one of their guys got killed."

"There are questions being asked about our villages. Managua wants to know who sanctioned their construction and where the money came from."

"That's your job. You need to run interference. It will all blow over, I guarantee you."

"And what all this about beach sand and decoys?" said Colindres.

Espinoza grinned.

"The guys in Colombia recruit decoys, or patsies, whatever you want to call them. The Colombians pay these decoys a small amount to pilot go-fast boats from Cartagena, Colombia. They are paid to transit through Nicaraguan territorial waters and onto Honduras."

"They're aware that they're carrying beach sand?"

"No, they think they are transporting cocaine, keeps them on their toes."

"I'm still confused."

Espinoza was becoming exasperated, "the decoy route and timing coincide with the journey of the actual narco traffickers. The Nicaraguan Navy sink the decoy boats, and the valuable cargo progresses onward to Honduras."

"I don't see the advantage," said Colindres.

"You can be really stupid sometimes. The DEA is happy, Managua is happy, everybody is happy, except for the decoy," snickered Espinoza.

"But why would the navy only sink the decoy boats? How can they tell the difference?"

"A personal deal."

"What do you mean?"

"I have an inside man in the navy," said Espinoza.

"Who?" said Colindres.

A vehicle entered the car park.

CHAPTER 80

Espinoza and Colindres both peered at the white Toyota HiAce Minivan, as it arrived in the Masaya Volcano visitor car park.

Four muscular men got out of the minivan and walked over to them.

"Senor Colindres? Senor Espinoza?" said one of the men.

"Admiral Antonio Espinoza and Captain of the Navy, Pablo Colindres" said Espinoza".

"Perfect." The four men seized Espinoza and Colindres.

"What are you doing? This is outrageous," said Colindres.

"We are members of the government," said Espinoza.

The men tied the hands of Colindres behind this back, with large plastic cable-ties. Two of the men lifted him above their heads and then threw him over the rim of the volcano. He screamed. Colindres plunged into the lava lake below. The screaming stopped.

"No, no, there must be a misunderstanding," said Espinoza, "I am the Minister Plenipotentiary, First Class at the Nicaraguan Consulate in Mexico City. I am a senior member of the government of the Republic of Nicaragua."

"It's looking as though your days in government have finally come to an end," said one of the men.

They bound Espinoza's hands, behind his back.

"Hold on, stop, I know you," said Espinoza, speaking to one the assailants.

"Well, it's been nice knowing you," said the man.

"No, you are one of the Presidential bodyguards."

"Not relevant. We have a job to do, and that job is you."

"Stop, there must be a big misunderstanding. We can make a personal deal."

"I understand that making deals is what got you into this situation."

The men carried Espinoza to the crater rim, whilst he struggled and continued to protest. They flung him into the volcano.

Espinoza rolled down into the crater, then his body became entangled with a cluster of broken rocks. He was teetering on the edge of the abyss. Espinoza could barely breath, the noxious gases were choking him and stinging his eyes. The sharp rocks were stabbing him in his side. Through the smoke, he could see one of the men edging towards him.

"I have money. I will give you everything I have," pleaded Espinoza.

Through the choking smoke, the man said, "Sure, this is stupid. Let's make a personal deal." He grabbed Espinoza and helped him to stand up.

Espinoza said, "Oh my God, thank you, thank you. I can get the money today. I will -----."

The man thrust Espinoza over the broken rocks and into the fiery lake below. A brief scream echoed around the volcano crater.

Espinoza's days of making personal deals came to an end.

CHAPTER 81

Greytown, San Juan del Norte

The grey-haired baseball fan sat by the café window and scanned his phone. He hadn't received a call from Espinoza in over 48 hours, not even a text or social media message. He'd phoned and messaged Espinoza, but there had been no response.

Since the killing at Aguila Creek, and the massacre at Pelican Island, the communication between them had gradually increased. Now it had abruptly stopped. It was as though Espinoza no longer existed.

As he was studying his phone, he heard a familiar voice.

"You're looking well."

His son bent down and kissed his father on both cheeks.

"It's wonderful to see you, Son. How is Bluefields these days?" said his father.

"Chaos as usual," said Josue, he sat down at the table.

"I have to congratulate you on the recovery of the three bales from the Bluefields armoury" said his father, "Great piece of work."

"It wasn't easy. Augusto was angry at me, but I don't think he was suspicious."

"Augusto was shot in that Pelican Island situation, what a nightmare."

"Nightmare? It was a bloodbath. When I arrived on the island and I saw the bodies, I couldn't believe it. Gamboa was insane."

"When he killed the headman at Aquila Creek, it did us no favours."

"Augusto was going to bust him because of his initial actions at Aquila Creek."

"How is Augusto?" said his father.

"He was shot twice, but he's now out of danger. The wound in his shoulder was the worst. He may lose the use of his left arm," said Josue.

"When the alpha male lion weakens, the next fittest dominant male takes over the pride."

"I should see this as an opportunity?"

"Definitely Son, you would be the Nicaraguan Navy's top man on the Caribbean Coast. That'll be very convenient for us."

"You're right, as usual, Father. You can continue to supply me with all the information from our friends in Managua and Cartagena."

"On that subject, I haven't heard anything from Espinoza for a few days, hopefully he isn't a political casualty of this Pelican Island incident."

"Espinoza is a wily old seadog, he knows how to weather the storm. If he gets replaced, then we will just have to deal with Colindres," said Josue.

"Yeah, Espinoza and his personal deals."

"I don't see what could go wrong."

"Yes, we have a fool-proof system, regardless of whether Espinoza, Colindres or anyone else has the required authority."

"The decoy go-fast boats get intercepted and sunk. The genuine narco trafficker boats then head north and rest and refuel at any one of our three villages," said Josue.

"They can then zip through to Honduras, when the coast is clear, so to speak."

"And the DEA, the U.S. Coastguard, and the United Nations, can see that the Republic of Nicaragua is continuing to fulfil their international responsibilities."

"Nicaragua are making great strides in their efforts to stop narco traffickers in their territorial waters," said his father, with a smirk.

CHAPTER 82

As Josue and his father sipped their coffee and congratulated themselves, they were being observed.

Four muscular men had arrived that morning on a private flight from Managua to Greytown Airport. The men were now sat in a Hyundai H1 people-carrier parked across from the cafe. They watched and waited.

Josue's father paid the bill, and they left the café together. The two were still talking when the Hyundai people-carrier pulled up beside them.

The sliding passenger door opened, and the targets were bundled inside the vehicle. They were gagged and black hoods thrown over their heads. Their hands were tied behind their backs with large plastic cable-ties. The Hyundai people-carrier then drove away.

Nobody on the street paid any attention.

. . . .

Three weeks later, a group of Canadians were led around the Greytown colonial graveyard by a local tourist guide. The guide gave a professional and concise explanation of the history of the graveyard and how it was divided into specific sections. The Canadians tourists found it fascinating.

The guide enquired whether the group had any questions. A tourist from Ontario asked whether the graveyard was still utilized for burials. The guide said that it wasn't used anymore, as there was a modern cemetery in New Greytown. The tourist said that she had asked the question because she'd spotted two freshly dug graves in the Catholic section of the cemetery.

The guide could not explain the two new graves. He did not raise the tourist's observations with the local police station.

CHAPTER 83

Managua International Airport

The Pelican Island guests disembarked from the twelve-seater prop plane. They were met at arrivals by the Honorary British Consul to Nicaragua, Dr Jose Martinez.

"Welcome back to the safety of Managua," said the Doctor.

"I suppose that's a phrase you don't use very often," said Graham.

"I am here to ensure you return safely back to the UK.

"It's about time someone from the British Embassy turned up," said Graham.

Paul noticed that Bev was stood apart from Graham and not speaking to him.

"We have a mini-bus arranged to take you to the Intercontinental Hotel. I will explain everything to you all, once we arrive at the hotel," said Dr Martinez.

The journey took about fifteen minutes. Paul looked out of the minibus window. Managua didn't look threatening any more, thought Paul.

When they arrived at the hotel, a familiar face greeted them in the hotel lobby. Tico hugged Charlotte and Paul. He inspected Paul's face and the injuries to his ear, "My friend, what has Nicaragua done to you? The bastardos," said Tico.

"We're ok, we survived" said Paul, "have you heard anything about Augusto?"

"He's in the police hospital. I understand he is out of danger, but his arm is a mess," said Tico. I've been sending him food and soft drinks, but they won't let me visit."

"He was shot twice. Fiona saved his life," said Charlotte.

"Thank God she was there," said Tico.

"I wouldn't be stood here right now, if it wasn't for her bravery," said Paul.

Dr Martinez strode over to them, "Thanks to the efficiency of Mr Tico and his team, we have day-rooms organised for you all. You can freshen up and then if you could meet me in the Jacaranda meeting room in one hour, I will debrief you," said Dr Martinez.

Tico said "Yes, please collect your keys at the reception. Go ahead and take anything you want from the mini bar, it's the least we can do."

"Anything we want?" said Graham.

"Sure, eat as much Toblerone as you want, go wild," said Tico, with a smile.

"What's all this about a debriefing?" said Graham.

"Mr Graham, please be in the Jacaranda meeting room in one hour, we will explain everything then," said Dr Martinez.

"Is the British embassy flying us home?" said Graham.

"One hour in the Jacaranda meeting room," said Dr Martinez.

CHAPTER 84

Jacaranda room, Intercontinental Hotel

After freshening up, Paul and Charlotte located the Jacaranda meeting room. They knocked on the door and entered. Dr Martinez greeted them both and invited them to take a seat. Graham and Bev were already sat at the meeting table. As they were all making themselves comfortable, two people entered the meeting room. Dr Martinez introduced them.

"Paul, Charlotte, Graham, Beverly, this is Robert from the British Secret Intelligence Service, and this is Madison from the United States Drug Enforcement Administration, DEA," said Dr Martinez. "They would like to ask you a few questions regarding the incident, if you have no objection."

" British Secret Intelligence Service, MI6? Like James Bond?" said Graham.

"Not exactly," said Robert.

Charlotte was surprised that Paul didn't speak. He had lost his enthusiasm for 007.

"Wow. I didn't realise we were so important," said Graham.

"All UK citizens in Nicaragua are important to us," said Dr Martinez.

Robert said "We already have a detailed overview of what has occurred on Pelican Island. However, we would like to understand your perspective of the incident."

"No problem," said Graham, "Where should I start?"

Madison said "Actually, I would like Paul to provide us with his recollection of the incident."

"So, nobody's interested in what I have to say. I was going to be murdered," said Graham.

"You weren't a hero, were you? Running off like a coward in the night and leaving me all alone," said Bev.

"The Sergeant was after me, not you, that's for sure," said Graham

"Why would the Sergeant have been interested in you, I'm not," said Bev.

"I'm just saying I was the target," said Graham.

"Once Paul has provided his account, if you have anything further to add, we can discuss this, okay Graham?" said Madison.

"You aren't even British. Who put you in charge?" said Graham.

"As a representative of the United States DEA, Madison is an invited participant to this meeting. This is sanctioned by the Secret Intelligence Service, and therefore the UK Government," said Robert.

Graham was silent.

"Paul, please, go ahead," said Madison.

He supplied a detailed description of the incident. Paul began with the stop and search by the Sergeant at Maria Cay. He then gave an account of the night on Pelican Island and the discovery of the bodies of Jannie, Todd, and Becky.

Charlotte began to cry. Dr Marinez offered his condolences.

. . . .

Paul explained the circumstances that led to Augusto and himself being shot and the ultimate death of the Sergeant. He omitted Fiona's *Chele bastardo* comment.

You shot at the Sergeant three times with the Jericho and once with the Glock?" said Madison.

"Yes" said Paul

"Why change weapons?" said Madison.

"I did it without thinking," said Paul.

The Jericho handgun was Lieutenant Commander Romero's officially issued weapon?"

"I think so, he dropped it when he was shot."

"How did you get possession of the Glock?"

"I took it from the Sergeant's waistband when he was slumped on the ground."

"Even though, according to your account, he was lying face down on the sand?"

"Watch it Paul, these guys are tricky," said Graham.

"His body was twisted to one side; I could see his face," said Paul.

"After you had shot him with the Jericho?"

"Yes. I don't think all three shots from the first pistol hit him, but he did go down."

"According to our intelligence, one shot struck him in the back, severing his spine. This disabled him," said Robert.

"One out of three" said Graham, "not very accurate."

"If he was disabled, then why shoot him again, with his own pistol?" said Madison.

"A fatal head shot," said Robert.

There was a period of silence.

"I don't think you understand," said Paul.

"We don't, help us to understand," said Madison.

"Careful Paul, I would say no comment," said Graham.

"This isn't a court of law. We are just trying to understand what happened," said Madison.

There was another period of silence and then Paul spoke.

"He had killed people, good people, people who were our friends," said Paul.

Charlotte and Bev were crying.

"We can leave that for the moment," said Robert.

Paul described the arrival of the Miskito villagers.

"The Miskito villagers, what purpose did they serve?" said Madison.

"Augusto requested their assistance, you'll need to ask him."

"Why do you think Lieutenant Commander Romero requested their assistance?"

"My impression was that Augusto had wanted them for back-up."

"Back-up?"

"In case the Nicaraguan Navy took their time to arrive. He told the villagers to come to the island armed, he was expecting a confrontation."

"But there was no confrontation that involved the villagers."

"No. When they arrived, the Sergeant was already dead. Augusto had been seriously wounded. He didn't speak to them."

"So, who spoke to them?"

Paul hesitated.

"When the Miskito villagers saw that the hostilities were over, they left," said Paul.

"Did you see the villagers take anything away from the island?"

"No" said Paul.

"Which village had they come from?

"I don't know."

"Did you see any bales on the island or floating in the sea?"

"You mean White Lobster?" said Paul.

Madison smiled, "I'm surprised you're aware of the colloquialism; did you see any?"

"No."

"Did any of you? Bales containing cocaine or sand?"

"Sand?" said Graham.

"Did you see any bales that contained white powder or sand."

They all said no.

"Did you see any of the Nicaraguan Navy or employees of Pelican Island with a bale or possible contents of a bale?"

They all said no.

"You will not be in any trouble; we will not share this information with the authorities in Nicaragua. You have my word, on behalf of the British government, that you will still be able to leave Nicaragua today and you will face no charges," said Robert.

However, we need the truth," said Madison, "Lieutenant Commander Romero? Fiona Alston? The victims, Ruben and Kenner, Jannie van Rensburg? The U.S. Citizens, Todd and Becky Cavanagh? Did you see any of them with bales or packets of white powder or even sand?"

Again, they all said no.

The Jacaranda meeting room became silent.

Madison eventually spoke, "Why do you think the Sergeant became an active shooter and started killing innocent people?"

"That question has a simple answer," said Paul.

"Then give me the simple answer," said Madison.

"Because He was *The Devil*," said Paul.

CHAPTER 85

Bogota, Colombia

El Dorado International Airport in Bogota is modern, efficient, and clean. Colombians are proud of their premier international airport. Compared to the mess of Lima and Mexico City, it is a dream.

As El Jefe entered the passenger arrivals hall, he was met by three men. Brief nods were exchanged, and his case was carried for him. He followed them in silence to a black Cadillac Escalade, which was parked directly outside the terminal, in a prohibited zone.

El Dorado airport was less than 10 miles from Bogota city centre, so El Jefe relaxed, sipped chilled mineral water, and prodded at his phone. Again, no one spoke.

After around twenty minutes, the Cadillac came to a stop on Avenida Circunvalar, at the entrance to the Monserrate Mountain cable car.

"What's this? Am I going on a tourist trip?" said El Jefe, "Are you going to taking me to La Candelaria next, so I can buy a t-shirt?"

"Senor Garcia is waiting for you in the Basilica, at the top of Monserrate," said one of the men. El Jefe entered the first available cable car. Two of the men followed him inside and they rode to the top of Monserrate.

Senor Garcia was sat down inside the empty church.

"Senor Garcia, it is so wonderful to see you again, I hope you haven't been waiting long," said El Jefe.

"I enjoy sitting in this elegant church and contemplating," said Senor Garcia.

"Yes, yes I can understand that."

"There are also panoramic views across Bogota City from Monserrate. It makes me realise how insignificant we all are."

"Yes, yes it's very beautiful up here."

"So, let's get down to business," said Senor Garcia, with a smile.

"Happy to discuss everything with you, Senor Garcia."

"We need to talk about this disaster in Nicaragua," said Senor Garcia.

"Senor Garcia, it is far from a disaster, I can manage the situation."

"Really? The wasted funds on these logistics centres? Losing $8m in cash? Shoot-outs on remote islands? Clashes with the Nicaraguan navy, tourists being killed. The U.S. Department of State issuing urgent diplomatic communications to the Nicaragua Embassy in Washington D.C. and raising the scenario to INTERPOL and the United Nations?"

"If you don't mind me saying, it sounds bad when you describe it like that Senor Garcia."

"The golden rule is to stay low profile; you have achieved the exact opposite."

"I know, I know, but I can rectify it all."

"How?"

"I will kick Espinoza's butt and get him to tighten up the whole process."

"He's dead."

Oh shit, then I'll give Colindres a kicking."

"Dead."

"Amander in Greytown then."

"Dead."

His son, Josue?"

"Also, dead."

"Oh my God."

"Yes, there certainly appears to be a macabre pattern developing here."

"Then I will find more contacts in Nicaragua."

"No, you must stop now, your strategy hasn't worked. Recruiting people in Cartagena, the dummy loads of sand, the logistics centres, smuggling cash back through the

Caribbean. The co-operation with the Nicaraguan navy must cease, now. Even the route itself, across the Caribbean, skirting the Nicaraguan coastline, it must stop immediately.

"Senor Garcia, I can get this back on track, I promise you."

"You have failed, miserably."

"Please, I can sort this out. Senor Garcia, I am begging you."

"Yes, my name is Garcia, the name means *rule of the spear*, and that is how I rule."

. . . .

The Bogota Post, a Columbian English language newspaper, had a brief article outlining that a man had fallen to his death from the Monserrate cable car. The cable car had been closed to visitors until safety checks could be completed. Police were investigating.

There was no mention in the article that the man's hands were tied behind his back, before he fell to his death.

White Lobster

------- Part Three -------

CHAPTER 86

Manchester, England U.K.

Following a transatlantic flight from Miami, Paul and Charlotte arrived at the Lowry International Airport in Manchester. They used the airport biometric passport scanners and eased through immigration. They gathered their bags from the luggage carousels and pushed their baggage trolly through the exit door, into the passenger arrivals terminal. They were finally home.

Cameras flashed, strangers started shouting and pushing towards them. There were at least fifty people waiting for Paul and Charlotte in the terminal.

"*BBC*. Could you provide us with a comment, Paul?"

"Paul, *The Times,* are you available for an interview?"

Sky News, how are your injuries, Paul? Will you be having cosmetic surgery?"

Charlotte, *The Daily Mail,* what happened on Pelican Island?"

"*The Sun newspaper,* Paul, did you take out the gunman?"

. . . .

The following hours were chaotic for Paul and Charlotte. A semblance of order was established when a specialist media consultant contacted Paul. Jonathan Adamson from *Blackbird Sholver Associates* spoke to Paul on the phone.

"We deal with the media on behalf of individuals, such as yourself. You'll find it stressful and worrying, however we'll guide you along the most beneficial route," said Adamson. "You just refer all the media and paparazzi directly to us."

Paul needed someone to face the media. The turmoil was upsetting Charlotte and also causing him a great deal of stress. He agreed to hire Blackbird Sholver Associates on a percentage of fees contract.

"We will arrange brief interviews with the most generous TV channels and UK newspapers. There will be interest from the majors in the U.S., Canada, and Australia, possibly from Japan, South Africa and Mexico. However, syndication should deal with that," said Adamson.

. . . .

Paul appeared on the *BBC* and *Sky* news channels the next morning. Excerpts from the interviews ran on multiple national radio channels including *BBC Radio 4*, *BBC Five Live* and *Times radio*. Paul also spoke to *ABC* and *CNN* in the United States. Paul's scarred face and his bandaged ear played well with global TV audiences.

All the major British newspapers ran articles and stories focused upon *The Pelican Island Massacre* that week. The majority were fabricated and contained numerous errors. Paul gave extensive interviews to *The Times* and *The Sun* newspapers, both owned by *News Corp UK*. The *New York Post* interviewed Paul via Zoom.

Graham was featured in a *Daily Mail* newspaper article and appeared on a morning TV programme, *Good Morning Britain*. *The Mail on Sunday* newspaper had a double page spread with pre-incident photos of Graham and Bev on Pelican Island. Graham's actions and bravery were central to both newspaper articles and the TV appearance.

The U.K. public lost interest in the Pelican Island Massacre after a week.

CHAPTER 87

Grand Cayman, British Overseas territory

Fiona drove out of the St. Matthew's University Campus into Lime Tree Avenue. She turned left into the Esterley Tibbetts Highway and drove south towards the Owen Roberts International Airport.

Fiona manoeuvred her way around all the roundabouts, or *rotaries*, as the Americans from Boston called them. She had started to enjoy driving her Yaris Hatchback, with the funny steering wheel.

She had struggled to cope with driving on the *British* side of the road. She initially drove a car with the familiar left-hand steering wheel. But driving on the left-hand side of the road in that car just blew her mind. She was a traffic accident waiting to happen.

After three months, she eventually conceded. She had driving lessons in a right-hand steering wheel vehicle. She passed the driving test and secured herself an official Cayman Islands driving Licence. Legal at last.

The other surprising side of living in the Cayman Islands for Fiona, was the language. The islands were a British Overseas territory; therefore, the official language was English. Fiona thought she spoke quite good English; she was to be disappointed.

The local people spoke a dialect called Cayman Creole; some people called it Bay Islands English. It differed from the English creole that was spoken in Bluefields and along the Nicaragua Caribbean Coast. However, the Cayman Creole sounded like Jamaican Patois, but also included words that were indecipherable to Fiona.

As Fiona physically resembled a Caymanian, she was continually addressed in the local patois. Typically, local guys tried speaking to her. She wished that she had a dollar for every time she had said, "Sorry, I'm not Caymanian, I'm from Havana."

. . . .

Fiona weaved her way through the rush hour traffic and passed the airport. She edged through the Bodden Town district and passed the Lighthouse landmark.

Fiona then pulled into the *Blue Shark Bar and Grill* car park. She spotted her friend Aayisha.

"Hey, Aayisha, your looking good, girl."

"What's happening *bobo*? you goin' home *ah wah*?" said Aayisha.

She smiled at Aayisha's usage of Cayman creole slang. "It's all good. I've come in to pick up four pieces of your blueberry cheesecake," said Fiona.

"No surprise. If your man knows you passed my place without collecting his favourite, you'd be in big trouble, especially if he's charged up." They both laughed.

Aayisha returned with the cheesecake in a large container. "Here you go *bobo,* everything the master demands."

"Thanks. What do I owe you?"

"Don't give me no *stoopidness*, just take it, you're *breddren*."

"You embarrass me. Thank you, Aayisha, see you in a couple of days."

They kissed and hugged. Fiona then started her final leg of the journey home.

Fiona kept a watchful eye out for iguanas. On the Cayman Islands, iguanas had the right of way. She thought that would never be law in Nicaragua or Cuba. She enjoyed driving on the Seaview Road, it gave her a beautiful view of the Caribbean Sea. She imagined that she could see Nicaragua, and her mother and father, on the horizon.

Eventually, Fiona saw the frigate birds circling above the *Tukka restaurant*. She was home at last.

CHAPTER 88

Colliers Bay Resort, Grand Cayman

Fiona drove her Yaris Hatchback into the car park of the Colliers Bay Resort.

"Hola, Doctor Fiona, great to see you," said Tico.

"Hi Tico, what's happening?" said Fiona.

"Busy, busy. Full occupancy. No rest for the wicked."

"You must be the only person in the whole of the East Side of Grand Cayman that is stressed."

"I get no help from your husband, he's either in his office or sailing one of his boats."

"That sounds right. He's probably in his office now looking at boats for sale on his computer."

"He's always faking being disabled and helpless," said Tico, with a smile.

"Don't stress, we will be closed in August for three months, you'll be begging to come back in November."

Tico shrugged and then rushed off to berate the restaurant staff.

Fiona walked through the resort to the office block at the rear of the property. She opened his office door. Augusto was leaning across his desk and peering at the computer screen.

"I bet you're looking at boats, sailor boy," said Fiona.

"Well, if it isn't the love of my life, Florence Nightingale herself," said Augusto.

"More like Sister Theresa, having to cope with you, sailor boy," she kissed him on the forehead, "How's your arm today?"

"Not too bad, still struggling to move my fingers, but managing to type."

"And your foot?"

"Still feels like Frankenstein's boot."

"Your war wounds don't stop you sailing those boats around to Spotter Bay though, do they?"

"I've become one of the characters in Hemmingway's *Old Man and the Sea*," said Augusto.

"Yeah, you look nothing like when we met on Pelican Island. With that beard, the expanding waistline and your greying long hair, you're starting to look like Hemmingway himself," laughed Fiona.

. . . .

Once Tico's staff had served dinner to the guests, the bar staff and waiters began to serve after-dinner drinks and digestifs to the early diners. Augusto, Fiona, and Tico then gathered to have a late dinner together.

"How is it progressing at medical school, Fiona?" said Tico.

"It's going well. Now that I have managed to master *medical English*, which unfortunately contains a great deal of Latin."

"I'm a good Catholic boy, Latin is no problem for me."

"It's just us protestant heathens from the Moravian Church that have to suffer, is it?"

"Absolutely. Burn in hell, unbelievers."

"We've already been through hell and survived," said Augusto.

"I'll drink to that," said Fiona.

. . . .

Tico outlined the schedule for the next few days. The number of guests, the occupancy, the staffing levels, and the planned excursions.

"So Boss, are you and one of the guys going to take those guests around to Spotter Bay tomorrow? said Tico.

"Yeah, no problem. I'm looking forward to it."

"There's two Americans, female. One of them is quite beautiful."

"I thought you would be tagging along and stalking them," said Fiona.

"No. They're a couple. In fact, I think they're married, because I heard one of them mention to the barman that her wife would have an *El Presidente* digestif," said Tico.

"I bet you were disappointed," said Augusto.

"Yeah, but there are many more fish in the sea," said Tico.

"At least I won't have to be worried about my husband running off with two American women to Miami," said Fiona.

"Stranger things have happened," said Tico.

"Oh, shut up, you bloody Costa Rican Car'e picha," said Fiona.

"Calling your General Manager, a Costa Rican dick face, is not good manners," said Tico.

They all began laughing.

CHAPTER 89

In the morning, Augusto meandered over to the pier. His only crew for the day was Henry, who dealt with all the diving related issues. He was a qualified PADI instructor and had been with Augusto since he had officially opened the resort twelve months ago.

Henry saw Augusto approaching with his characteristic limp.

"Morning Boss," said Henry.

"Hi Henry, how's it hanging?" said Augusto.

"Always poised for action, Boss."

"Just two guests today, Henry?"

"Yes, Boss. Two Americans. I've already spoken to them and inspected their PADI certification, they're ready to go."

"Do they understand that they shouldn't fly tomorrow, if they've dived today?"

"Yes, they know. They seem to be experienced, especially the one who was a U.S. Marine."

"U.S. Marine? A woman?"

"Yes, I was impressed too. She's fine as well, Boss."

"What does she look like?"

"Slim, short black hair, very hot. She has a southern U.S. accent."

"Is she from New Orleans?" said Augusto.

"No, definitely not New Orleans, I would have remembered that."

"Oh, that's okay then. I thought it was someone I'd met before."

"No, she said she was from Baton Rouge, Louisiana.

Augusto was stunned, surely it couldn't be Madison. What would she be doing on Grand Cayman? But it was too much of a coincidence and Augusto didn't like coincidences.

He was deep in thought when Henry spoke.

"Here they are, Boss."

Two women were walking towards the pier, carrying their diving bags. Augusto adjusted his sunglasses and pulled down the peak on his Boston Red Sox baseball cap.

"Morning Ladies, are you ready for the dive of your life?" said Henry.

"We most certainly are," said Madison.

"Please can I introduce you to Boss; he will be piloting the boat today," said Henry.

"Good morning, ladies," said Augusto and shook their hands, whilst keeping his head low. He now valued his beard, long grey hair, and extended waistline.

"Hi, I'm Madison and this is my wife, Emma," said Madison.

"Sorry Boss, what your name?" said Emma.

"Everyone calls me Boss."

"Where are you from, Boss?" said Madison.

"Costa Rica. Shall we get on board?" said Augusto.

Madison noted that Boss had an incapacitated left arm.

Everyone clambered on board the boat. Henry conducted a few final checks on the diving equipment, and then Augusto eased the boat away from the pier.

Augusto piloted the boat around the east coast of the island into Spotter Bay. Henry was advising the women as Augusto prepared to drop anchor.

Henry said, "I will be diving with you, please keep me in your vision at all times."

"Is it dangerous?" said Emma.

"No, not at this time of year. The weather is very calm, perfect conditions for diving Spotter Bay."

"Are there any wrecks here?" said Emma.

"The closest wreck is *The Glamis*. But that's for the more experienced divers," said Augusto.

"*Club Hole* and *Barrel Sponge Wall* are shallow dives and should be ideal. *Turtle Pass* and *Cabana* are amazing wall dives, but we will give them a miss today, until we are all confident with your dive experience," said Henry.

"Safety first?" said Emma.

"Absolutely" said Henry.

"You're not diving Boss?" said Madison.

"No, I've retired from diving."

"Because of your injury?"

"Something like that."

She was staring at him.

"Come on ladies, let's do this," said Henry.

They put their fins on, secured their mask and regulators, and then after being given the okay by Augusto, the three of them conducted perfect backward rolls into the sea.

White Lobster

CHAPTER 90

Augusto slumped in his seat. He couldn't believe this. It had been close to three years since he had spoken to Madison. On that fatal night, he'd given her all the background to the Pelican Island incident over the sat phone, even whilst he was on the verge of dying. That was the last time they had spoken. No WhatsApp messages, texts, email, nothing. Now she was here, on Grand Cayman, at his resort.

What did she want? Was she investigating him? Had she tracked him down?

He hadn't committed a crime, not one that people knew about. The Miskito villagers had taken the nine bales of U.S. currency to Net Point. Uncle Dereck had managed the situation locally. A new harbour, four berths and a small, refrigerated seafood warehouse were built at Net Point, by *Martin Construction of Bluefields*.

The families of Jannie van Rensburg, Ruben Downs, Kenner Bufo and Todd & Becky Cavanagh each received $200,000 U.S. dollars, from an anonymous benefactor. Another $200,000 U.S. dollars was given to the family of the Miskito headman villagers living at Aquila Creek. It was not possible to reliably locate the immediate family of Danny McCoy.

$4.035 million dollars was transferred into a Cayman Islands bank account. The business account was in the name of Cotton Bank Limited, registered in the Cayman Islands. The identity of the owners or executives of Cotton Bank Limited were not fully transparent. Several shell companies and a trust were utilised to create the holding company.

Augusto sat in the boat and considered what to do next.

. . . .

He was surprised when he saw that Henry had surfaced.

"Boss! Emergency! One of the women is drowning," said Henry.

All three divers were then visible on the surface. One of the women was not moving. With help from Henry, Augusto dragged her onto the deck of the boat. He was very conscious of his left arm.

Emma said "It's my fault. I was struggling with my mask. Madison swam over to help me. I panicked and ripped her mask and mouthpiece off. It was an accident. What have I done?"

Henry held Emma back.

"Madison, Madison, can you hear me?" said Augusto, He shook her shoulders.

Madison was unresponsive. She wasn't breathing. Augusto pushed her head back and gave Madison five initial rescue-breaths. He then started chest compressions. Augusto gave CPR for two minutes, two breathes, thirty compressions. He struggled with this arm.

"Oh my God, she's dead," said Henry.

Emma screamed.

Augusto continued with the attempted resuscitation.

To Henry, it looked a lost cause.

Suddenly Madison started coughing and then vomited sea water.

Augusto and Henry quickly rolled her onto her side. She continued coughing. Augusto ensured her breathing pathway was clear.

"Madison, Madison, I'm so sorry," said Emma.

CHAPTER 91

Fiona knocked on the villa door. Emma peered through the opening.

"Hi, I'm Fiona, one of the owners of the resort. Can I come in?" She was carrying her medical bag.

Madison was laying in the bed. Emma was sitting next to Madison holding her hand.

Fiona spoke to Madison, "How are you feeling?"

"As though I've just come back from the dead," said Madison.

"You have," said Emma.

"I was concerned when I heard that my husband had been kissing a beautiful American woman."

"If it was only that simple," said Madison.

"We've contacted a doctor and he is coming over from Health City, here on Grand Cayman."

"I'm not sure I need a doctor; I just feel tired," said Madison.

"The Boss saved her life. He was amazing," said Emma.

"My husband has been called many things, amazing doesn't arise that often."

"He is a God-send," said Emma.

"He told me that as he was following the resuscitation procedure, and carrying out the chest compressions, he was singing to himself *Stayin Alive by The Bee Gees*" said Fiona, "He said it helped him get his rhythm right."

"That's very funny, in a ghoulish way," said Madison.

Emma noticed the medical bag that Fiona had with her, "Are you a doctor?"

"The doctor is on the way. However, I would like to have a quick look at you if you give me permission."

"Do you know first aid?" said Emma.

"Full declaration; I'm currently on the medical programme at St Matthews University, here on Grand Cayman. I'm not a qualified doctor, yet."

"Go ahead Fiona. Emma can always call the staff, if you start murdering me for kissing your husband," said Madison.

Fiona took Madison's temperature, peered into her eyes using an LED penlight and then listened to her breathing with a stethoscope, "are you struggling to breath at all?"

"No, as I said I just feel tired," said Madison.

"That's normal in this situation. Everything seems fine. But the doctor from Health City will need to see you."

"That's ok. I'd like to thank your husband in person, is he around?" said Madison.

"No, he's gone to Cayman Brac to look at some boats for sale. He won't be back for three days."

"Oh, that's unfortunate. We'll be going back to the States in two days," said Emma.

"Then you won't see him again."

"Please Fiona, give him my sincere thanks, especially for saving my life. He's my hero," said Madison.

"I will. He's my hero, every single day."

"I'm sure he is, Fiona," said Emma.

"Where are you originally from, if you don't mind me asking?" said Madison.

"Cuba."

"And your husband, where is he from?"

"Costa Rica."

"What's his actual name? It's not Boss," said Madison.

"Alfredo."

"It's lovely place you have here," said Emma.

"Thank you. It's demanding work," said Fiona. "I spend a great deal of time at St. Matthews University and my husband is partially disabled."

"Yes, I noticed he had a problem with his arm. Was he involved in an accident?" said Madison.

"Yes, a car accident in Costa Rica."

"So, it must be challenging to run the place."

"Tico is our general manager, He's the beating heart of the resort. Well, that's what he keeps telling us." They all laughed.

"Tico is Costa Rican, isn't he?"

"Yes, he is. How did you know that?"

"I think I know Tico from the Intercontinental in Managua, Nicaragua. Wasn't he the manager there?"

"I'm not sure, he's worked at many places. He has a great deal of experience in the region."

"How long have you been running this place?"

"It took us a year to build it and get operational. We opened to guests about twelve months ago."

"It's a beautiful resort, on a picturesque and peaceful island. It's certainly a great business," said Madison, "and you can study to be an MD."

"Thank you very much. Yes, we are truly blessed," said Fiona.

CHAPTER 92

Manchester, England U.K.

Blackbird Sholver Associates contacted Paul and informed him that he was being considered for a *Heroes of Britain* award.

He declined the nomination.

They subsequently informed Paul that he would be invited onto a Channel 5 TV programme presented by an ex-member of the SAS. The presenter travelled the world to dangerous hotspots and assessed the hazards and perils that awaited the naive tourist. Typical holiday locations on the programme were South Africa, Jamaica, and Mexico.

Paul expressed his disinterest in participation in the programme.

The agent of a renowned author contacted Paul. The celebrated writer had received an advance from Puffin-Longfellow publishing house in London to write a semi-fiction book, with the working title *The Pelican Island Massacre*. The agent enquired whether Paul would be willing to cooperate with the author.

Paul refused the invitation.

Jonathan Adamson from Blackbird Sholver Associates contacted Paul. "Paul, if you keep declining these great opportunities then you will never make any money, and neither will we."

"We're not interested in the money. We just want to return to our normal lives."

"Paul, it's time to wake up, you will never have a normal life again," said Adamson. "You're the guy that was there at the *Pelican Island Massacre*, you're the guy who shot dead a mass murderer. You're famous."

White Lobster

CHAPTER 93

Colliers Bay Resort, Grand Cayman

The Caribbean Sea glittered in the sun. To Augusto, the view appeared more stunning than ever. Fiona told him that the two women had already departed, so the coast was clear.

"They just left and that was that?" said Augusto.

"The doctor gave her the green light to fly back to the States, so they left."

"What do you think?"

"She asked a lot of questions. Your name, where did we used to live? how did you get injured? how long we had been here? She was also enquiring about Tico. She is very suspicious of us."

"She could dig deeper, when she gets back to the U.S."

"It would be unfair for her to expose us, when you've just saved her life."

"She was a U.S. Marine, now she's DEA, and maybe even CIA. She's might not look it from appearances, but she's hard core," said Augusto.

"Nicaragua comes back to haunt us," said Fiona.

CHAPTER 94

Augusto limped around the resort, with no specific destination in mind. He decided to head towards the pier. He spotted Henry and called to him.

"Hi Henry, how's it hanging today?"

"I'm cool as a fool, Boss."

"Any dive guests planned for the next few days?"

"No, all quiet. Good for me, bad for you."

"I suppose a day without any dramas is what we need," said Augusto.

"For sure. I'm glad to see Boss. I was looking for you earlier. "Miss Fiona said that you had gone over to Brac."

"Yes, I was looking for some potential additions to our armada."

"That's sounds good. Anyway, I wanted to speak to you, Boss."

"Yeah, what's happening?"

"You know those two American women?"

"Will I ever forget them?"

"No, probably not. Anyway, the beautiful one who nearly drowned, the hot one-----."

"Madison?"

"Yeah, she came looking for me before they left, she gave me $500 dollars."

"Wow, that's impressive. Did she say why?"

Nope. In fact, I was surprised, as she nearly drowned on my watch."

"It wasn't your fault. It was an accident."

"Yeah, well, she gave me the money and then she handed me something for you."

Henry leaned into the boat, retrieved a bottle, and passed it to Augusto.

"It seems I get $500 dollars and you only get a bottle," said Henry, with a smirk.

"That doesn't seem fair," said Augusto.

"She said to give the bottle to you, and only you."

Augusto looked at the label on the bottle.

Mezcales de Leyenda

Someone had scribbled on the label with a sharpie:

Karl Marx, Thanks for saving my life

Semper Fidelis, Mustang x

"Whose Karl Marx?" said Henry.

THE END

8.0